WINDS OF CHANGE

THE WITCHES OF WHEELER PARK: BOOK 3

CHRISTINE POPE

WINDS OF CHANGE

Copyright © 2020 by Christine Pope

ISBN: 978-1-946435-35-4

Published by Dark Valentine Press

Cover design by Lou Harper

Book formatting by Indie Author Services

1

HIS PHONE WAS RINGING. JAKE WILCOX rolled over in bed and cracked an eyelid, noting how his bedroom was still quite dark, with only a faint dim glow beyond the wooden blinds telling him that morning was on its way, that it wasn't still the middle of the night.

He rolled over and grabbed the phone so he could look at the screen and see what time it was. Six-twenty, which felt about right, based on the amount of low light filtering into the room. He'd set his alarm for six-thirty, wanting to get on the road as soon as he could. Now that he had his parents' blessing—well, more or less…they weren't exactly happy about his decision to move to Wyoming with Addie Grant, the woman who had stolen his heart, but neither had they tried to stop him—and now that he had his cousin Molly to watch the house until he decided whether to sell it or rent it, he didn't have any reason to linger in Flagstaff.

But then his brain locked on the uncomfortable realization that no one called at six-something in the morning unless it was an emergency or something was terribly wrong.

The number on the phone wasn't familiar.

"Jake Wilcox," he said, hoping he sounded calm and assured, not like someone who'd just been awakened from a deep sleep by a call he hadn't been expecting.

A man's voice, one he knew he'd never heard before. It was deep and slow and deliberate, something in its timbre indicating that the person speaking was at least several decades older than he. "Jake, this is Carson Archuleta."

At once, Jake sat up in bed, the unease that had already been nagging at him morphing into a flash of sharp-edged anxiety. "What's wrong?"

Because he couldn't think why the head of the Northern Arapahoe tribe would call him at such an ungodly hour of the morning…unless something awful had happened.

"Addie," Carson replied, his voice heavy with worry. "She's been taken."

"'Taken'?" Jake repeated. At first, the simple word didn't want to penetrate his sleep-fogged brain. Almost at once, though, realization dawned, bright and terrible as the lightning bolts Addie commanded with her weather-working powers. "By Randall Lenz?"

"I believe so…unless she had someone else trying to track her down."

God, Jake hoped not. Agent Lenz on his own was quite enough for them to deal with. Scrubbing his hair again in the vain hope that doing so might help to wake him up more quickly, Jake asked, "What happened?"

"He must have brought a team with him," Carson said. "That's the only explanation, because I had three men guarding Addie's house in your absence. She was feeling worried about being alone."

With good cause, apparently. Right then, Jake cursed himself for leaving her in Riverton by herself. She'd assured him that she would be fine, and they'd both honestly thought she was safer in Wyoming than she would have been if she'd come with him to Flagstaff, but it seemed they'd both been mistaken.

Horribly mistaken.

And he also cursed the miles that separated him from Riverton now, even though he didn't know what the hell difference being there would make.

Addie was gone.

"My men were overpowered," Carson went

on. "They didn't see their attackers, which tells me they were skilled and stealthy."

"Are your people okay?" Jake asked. Even though worry for the woman he loved knotted his gut and sent adrenaline surging through his tired limbs, he had to hope that Carson's men hadn't paid the ultimate price for the protection they'd offered.

"They were knocked out, but they'll be all right in a day or so," the older man replied. "I have a feeling Lenz's team wanted to make sure they didn't suffer any life-threatening injuries. Even on tribal lands, that sort of thing would have opened up all sorts of inquiries by the authorities."

Although he guessed the question was probably futile, Jake decided he needed to ask it anyway. "Any idea where they took her?"

A pause, and then Carson said, "I have a feeling you probably know the answer to that better than I do."

"Maybe," Jake allowed. Carson had been nothing but an ally in this mess, but at the same time, Jake didn't feel comfortable telling him that yes, he actually had a damn good idea where Lenz had taken Allie, thanks to his younger brother Jeremy's superior computer-hacking skills.

Archuleta didn't seem put off by the equivocation, and went on, "I have reports that a private jet landed at the airport outside Riverton a little before dusk and then took off around ten-thirty last night. I assume the jet belonged to Agent Lenz."

"Probably." A pause as Jake rubbed his forehead, all the while wishing he could snap his fingers and make a mug of coffee appear magically in his hand. However, while his telekinetic gift sometimes came in useful, it didn't allow him to bend time and space quite that much. "But how did he even know to look for her in Riverton? She did a damn good job of covering her tracks."

"You found her," Carson said, his tone so mild that the words couldn't really be construed as a rebuke.

"Yeah, but…." The words trailed off there as Jake realized he probably shouldn't explain his brother's magical gift with computers to someone who was next thing to a stranger, even if the other man did happen to know there was a hell of a lot more to Addie than met the eye. "She told me she would be careful," he added, knowing even as he spoke how inadequate those words sounded.

A sigh rustled its way through the phone's speaker. "No doubt that was her intention. Unfortunately, the universe decided otherwise."

"I don't understand."

"There was a fire. A prairie fire, threatening the casino. She didn't want the tribe, the town, to lose something that supported so many people in the community. So…."

Carson went silent then, but he didn't need to finish the sentence. Jake understood all too well what must have happened. A fire that no ordinary methods could put out, but one that Addie, with her vast weather-working gifts, could extinguish easily. She brought the rain, and saved the casino.

And doomed herself at the same time.

Amazing how steady his voice sounded as he said, "Thanks, Carson. I need to talk to my cousin, figure out what to do next."

Most people probably would have asked what Jake's cousin could possibly do in such a situation. However, the tribal leader didn't question his words, whether because he knew something of how witch clans were structured, or simply because he didn't think it was his place to probe too deeply. Instead, he responded, "Is there anything you need me to do?"

Not unless you've got a team of people there on the reservation who know something about breaking into secure government facilities, Jake thought, although he didn't bother to say those words aloud. As much as he would have liked the help, he had a feeling the Wilcox clan was on its own with this one.

"Can you keep an eye on Addie's house?" he asked instead. "And maybe come up with some sort of cover story as to why she won't be in to work for a while?"

"Consider it done," Carson replied. "It's the least I can do, when there's a very good chance the casino wouldn't still be standing if it weren't for her intervention."

"I appreciate it," Jake said, and left it at that. There was no point in telling Carson that he didn't think the casino was a fair exchange for the life of the woman he loved. Obviously, Addie had believed it was worth the risk. She'd known that Randall Lenz had tracked her to Kanab because of the storm she'd caused there, and so she must have known there was a very good chance he'd be able to find her in Riverton if she used her powers in such an obvious way. Those worries hadn't been enough to stop her from doing what she knew was right, though.

And that was why Jake loved her…or at least, it was just another in a long list of reasons why she'd stolen his heart. Addie Grant was not the sort of person to shy away from making the hard choices, even when she understood all too well what those choices might cost her.

"I'm sorry," Carson said again. "All my well wishes—and those of my tribe—go with you."

"Thanks," Jake replied.

Right then, he wasn't sure whether well wishes would be enough.

Adara Grant lay on the bed in the suite that had been prepared for her, the monitors at her bedside showing the slow, strong beat of her heart, her steady respiration, blood pressure holding at an optimal one-twenty over eighty. Randall Lenz sat at her bedside, watching her, even though he knew it would be several more hours before the drug released its hold on her and she swam back up to consciousness.

He'd expected to feel triumphant at the real-ization that she was finally here, that her amazing talents would soon be put through a battery of tests to determine their limits and strengths. All the other participants in the program had gone through similar testing, although those tests had each been tailored for their individual talents.

In that moment, however, he felt more exhausted than anything else. Too much running from place to place, he supposed; too many time zones and not enough sleep.

And perhaps the after-effects of the lightning bolt he suspected she'd zapped him with nearly two weeks earlier. Although he still didn't know for sure what had really happened to him, whatever it was, it had definitely caused some lasting damage. No, his headaches weren't quite as bad as they'd once been, and he hadn't experienced any further nosebleeds after the first one, but Lenz guessed his body still hadn't completely recovered from the shock—no pun intended—it had experienced.

What would Adara do when she awoke? Would she know immediately what had happened, and attempt to use her powers to defend herself?

Very possibly, but the effects of such an attack probably wouldn't be what she'd intended. There were no windows in the rooms where she would be living at the secret government facility just outside Alexandria, no way for the weather to affect him or anyone else inside what was, to all intents and purposes, an underground bunker. The suite had been furnished to look like a well-appointed vacation condo…except for a complete lack of windows, along with state-of-the-art biometric locks on the doors. Those locks wouldn't open for anyone except Lenz himself and a few others, like Dr. Richards and her team, and those whose job it was to bring the subjects their meals and make sure they weren't lacking for anything.

Well, anything except their freedom.

At any rate, it would be difficult to use lightning as a weapon when there weren't any windows to give it access, and where the facility's electrical system had been shielded to protect it from any unusual surges.

That thought comforted him somewhat, as did his memory of the raid on Adara's rented home in Riverton, Wyoming. Really, the operation had been pretty much textbook. Just the slightest bit of a surprise when he and Ives and Tolliver discovered that her house was being guarded by three tough-looking Native American men, but they'd been able to regroup and re-strategize, and the guards had been dispatched easily enough. Quite possibly they were good to have around during a barroom brawl, but they were no match for a group that included a former Air Force pilot, an ex-SEAL, and an agent who'd trained in hand-to-hand combat for more than fifteen years.

The street where Adara's house in Riverton was located was a quiet one, and no one had taken any notice of Lenz's group driving her away in a dark SUV. The men they'd knocked out would wake in the morning with a set of nasty headaches, but they would be fine in a day or two. And because he and his commandos had made sure to wear masks during the raid, there was no way those guards could identify their attackers. No one should have any idea who had taken Adara Grant, or why.

Except possibly the mysterious Jake, the man

who'd come to her rescue in Kanab. Lenz still couldn't quite figure out what the connection was between the two of them.

But he had Adara now, and soon enough, she would tell him what he needed to know, including who Jake really was, and why he'd been able to find her in Kanab. Once he was in possession of those particular facts, Lenz had a feeling a great many things would be explained.

He couldn't wait for her to wake up.

2

MY HEAD POUNDED. I LIFTED A HAND TO touch my temple, thinking I might find a bump on my forehead, something to explain the throbbing ache I was experiencing, but my searching fingers couldn't find anything out of the ordinary. And I felt strange all over, too, oddly limp and weak, as if I'd been in bed with a fever for days.

But my skin didn't feel hot. If anything, it was almost too cool to the touch, as though the room where I lay was overly air-conditioned. I realized I wasn't dressed for a warm summer night, though —I wore a loose dark sleep shirt with long sleeves and what felt like some kind of lightweight knit pants that hit mid-calf. Maybe I'd turned up the air conditioning in my rented house because the only nightclothes I had were too warm for a June night.

Problem was, I couldn't remember turning on the A/C. It had been a pleasantly cool night in Riverton, with a gentle breeze wafting in through the open windows. I couldn't even smell the remnants of the fire that had threatened the Wind River Casino, a fire I'd put out by summoning a tremendous thunderstorm to quench the flames.

A storm….

Memory hit with the force of a gale wind, and the weakness I'd just experienced fled. I sat bolt upright in bed—only to realize I wasn't in the house I'd rented only a few days earlier, but a nicely furnished yet somehow anonymous room I'd never seen before, with dark oak furniture and autumn landscapes on the walls, which had been painted a warm tan shade. Next to my bed was a hard-backed chair that looked as if it had been brought in from another room, and sitting in that chair was Randall Lenz.

A squeak of fright escaped my lips before I could hold it back. At once, his ice-blue eyes met mine, and his rather thin lips lifted in a smile.

"Awake?" he asked—quite unnecessarily, since it was pretty obvious that I'd finally shaken off the effects of whatever drug had been in the needle he'd poked me with.

I didn't bother to dignify his question with a reply. No, I pressed my hands down flat against the mattress and blinked, willing the room to stop spinning. Obviously, sitting up that quickly after I'd been out of it for God knows how many hours hadn't been a very good idea.

"Where am I?"

He didn't blink. "In a secure facility."

"The one where you're holding all the other people like me?"

Still no blink, but I saw the way his eyes flared in surprise for less than a second before his expression grew shuttered once again. As I watched him, I noticed that he was only in his shirtsleeves, the tie and jacket he seemed to always be wearing nowhere in evidence. And he looked tired, with shadows under his eyes, much more shadowed than the eyes of a man around forty should have been. Had those shadows been there before I hit him with that lightning bolt? I couldn't remember. Frankly, when he'd confronted me at the cottage in Flagstaff, I'd been so shocked to see him that I hadn't taken in many details of his appearance. His mere presence had been enough to throw me completely off balance.

Lenz's voice was even as he responded, "What other people?"

"Like I said, the ones like me. The ones with…powers."

Maybe the slightest compression of his lips.

He was pretty good at hiding whatever might be going through his mind, but I'd been watching closely for his reaction. I already knew the truth; I wanted to see whether he'd keep trying to cover it up.

He crossed his hands in his lap. For the first time, I noticed he wasn't wearing any rings. No big surprise, I supposed—I couldn't really imagine someone like him having a normal life with a wife and family.

"How do you know about that?" he asked after a lengthy pause.

As victories went, it was probably a minor one, and yet I still allowed myself to experience a slight surge of satisfaction. I certainly wasn't going to tell him the truth, but that didn't mean I wouldn't mess with him if given the opportunity.

The bastard deserved it.

I shrugged and ventured, "Maybe I just… know things."

Once again, his mouth tightened, possibly in a slightly more pronounced manner this time, since I noted the way the lines that bracketed his lips grew slightly deeper. However, the cool, neutral timbre of his voice never changed. "That's not your talent, though. We've been observing you for some time, Ms. Grant, and you've never shown the slightest hint of psychic abilities. Your talent for interacting with meteorological phenomena is well-documented, but it seems that's the only arena where your particular gifts lie."

"That you know of," I returned.

"Perhaps," he said, his tone still mild. "If you're psychic, then go ahead and tell me what I'm thinking."

Damn. Well, he had me there, because I wasn't any more psychic than the next person, despite being one of the Wilcox clan's witches. That wasn't how our talents worked. I hadn't gotten the chance to ask Jake if there were any actual mind-readers in my newly discovered family, but I knew I sure as hell wasn't one.

Still, I thought I might as well try to bluff my way out of this and see what happened. Maybe I'd get really, really lucky and guess correctly. "You're wondering why, if I can control the weather, I haven't zapped you with some lightning to get myself out of here."

An eyebrow lifted a fraction of an inch, but that was his only reaction. "Close. Or rather, I considered that possibility a while ago, when you were still sleeping, even if it's not what I'm thinking now. However, I suppose I should let you know that you won't be able to use those gifts here."

"Why not?"

His head tilted to one side, but he didn't smile. "Why don't you tell me?"

No need to close my eyes, not when I could simply let my gift awaken and reach out to the world. Or rather, while I could vaguely sense that somewhere far above me was a sky with clouds and possibly—just possibly—a bit of rain some place off in the distance, I couldn't really do anything with those clouds. The room where I lay felt as though it must be hundreds of feet below the surface, which meant I was dangerously disconnected from the weather far above. Maybe if I sweated and strained, I could reach out to those clouds and coax the lightning from within them, but that lightning would only hit a building I guessed was shielded against electrical surges. It wouldn't do a damn thing.

Panic wanted to swell within me, but I told it to take a hike. I couldn't lose my control now, not with Randall Lenz watching me with something close to amusement in his glacier-hued eyes. He knew he had the upper hand.

For now, I told myself. *You know Jake will find out what happened to you, and then he'll do whatever he has to in order to get you the hell out of here. I'd like to see what Mr. Smug over there will do when he's face to face with a bunch of pissed-off Wilcox witches and warlocks.*

That mental image helped to steady me. Voice calm, I said, "This room is a hundred feet underground, so I can't use my weather powers effectively."

"Very good." He leaned forward slightly, although his hands remained clasped on his knee. "So, you can still sense the sky, even when you can't see it?"

If I answered him, I'd only be giving him something he wanted—namely, more information about me, about how I used my gift. Maybe I was already fighting a losing battle, but I resolved right then not to give the bastard anything he could work with.

I said, "Is there any water? I'm thirsty."

For a second, he didn't respond, only continued to observe me in silence. Then his shoulders lifted, and he rose from his chair. As I watched, he left the bedroom and went out somewhere—to another room, I supposed, since I got the feeling that my prison cell was some kind of suite, maybe designed to look like an upscale condo so I wouldn't feel so out of place.

Of course, the joke was that I couldn't think of many spots where I'd feel more out of place than in an upscale condo.

He returned, a glass of water—an ordinary tumbler like you'd find in a regular house—in one hand. Still without speaking, he handed the water to me.

There wasn't much I could do except take it. Actually, I hadn't been lying—I really was thirsty. So, I lifted the glass to my lips and swallowed some water, which was sweet and cold, welcome against my dry throat.

Finally, he said, "Maybe now you can take another guess at what I was thinking."

He wasn't going to let it go, was he? Then again, if I'd learned anything about Randall Lenz, it was that he'd proved to be the most tenacious person I'd ever met.

Well, except for Jake Wilcox.

"That grabbing me will get you a nice raise?" I ventured, even though I had a feeling that whatever the reason for Agent Lenz's pursuit of people with special powers, it had very little to do with filthy lucre.

Maybe just the faintest twitch at one corner of his mouth. "I'm afraid not. I had my last evaluation only three months ago, so it'll be a while before I'm due for another raise. But no fear—the government pays me well for what I do."

Why was I not surprised? He probably got six figures for traveling around the country and wreaking havoc in people's lives, while those who actually did some good in the world—nurses and teachers and firemen—made a hell of a lot less than that.

"No," he continued, not giving me a chance to reply, "I was actually thinking about your friend Jake. Why don't you tell me about him?"

Suddenly, my mouth felt dry, despite the water I'd just swallowed. Trying to hide my racing thoughts, I lifted the glass to my lips and took another sip before saying, "There's not much to tell."

"Oh, I think there is." Lenz leaned back in his seat, expression so bland that I knew I wouldn't be able to detect a single thing about what was passing through his mind right then. "Obviously, he's someone you're close with. Or are you in the habit of going off with complete strangers when the mood takes you?"

That question made me smile, despite my lingering dizziness and a very real fear about what Lenz and his team planned to do with me. As far as I could tell, Angela and Connor's amnesia spell —for lack of a better way to explain the magic they'd used on him—appeared to be holding. If Randall Lenz had actually been able to recall what had gone down in the interval between the day when he'd tried to collect me at my house in Kanab and the evening when he'd confronted me in Flagstaff, then he probably would have known I'd been in Jake's company the whole time.

And actually, since Connor had found Lenz's Ford Taurus parked down the street from the cottage, that meant he'd most likely been surveilling me the entire evening, waiting for a chance to swoop in. I remembered how I'd walked with Jake to the front porch, how we'd drawn close for a lingering kiss.

If I'd known the entire encounter had been happening under Randall Lenz's pale, watchful gaze, I might not have been quite so abandoned in that embrace. At the moment, I could only be glad that he clearly didn't remember a single second of it.

"Well," I said, "you nearly convinced me to leave with you, and it wasn't as though we were exactly besties."

Not even a blink. "True. Still, it seems you were in Jake's company for several days. If his only motivation had been to get you out of my clutches, one would think he would have left you to your own devices once he'd determined you were safe."

About all I could do was shrug. Because obviously, Jake's primary goal had been my safety, but besides that, he'd wanted to make sure he got me to Flagstaff so I could meet my family...the family I hadn't even known existed.

No way could I tell Randall Lenz any of that. Bad enough that he was holding more than a dozen witches and warlocks in the same facility where I was currently imprisoned; there wasn't a snowball's chance in hell that I would ever let him know his "subjects" weren't flukes or genetic anomalies or freaks of nature, but witches and warlocks with the bad luck to have grown up outside a clan's protection. Because they hadn't known who—or what—they were, they hadn't understood the importance of keeping their magical gifts hidden. Being a member of a witch clan was all about keeping things on the down-low. But if you hadn't been schooled on that very important fact, then you wouldn't realize how much danger you might be in if you weren't discreet about using your powers.

However, just because I had no intention of telling Randall Lenz about witch clans didn't mean I couldn't do my best to mess with him a little. My mother had told me more than once that I had an overactive imagination; this seemed like the perfect opportunity to put it to use.

I lifted an eyebrow and leaned against the pillows. The water I'd drunk seemed to be help-ing, or maybe it was only that I'd been awake long enough for the effects of the knockout drug Lenz had given me to wear off. Either way, the dizziness had subsided, and right then I realized how hungry I was. Very likely, I'd been unconscious for hours and hours. I had no way of knowing what time it was, not with the room where I sat located far underground, hiding me away from the sun and the sky. No clocks, either; I was pretty sure that omission hadn't been an oversight.

"What makes you think you're the only agency interested in someone with my abilities?" I inquired, then sipped some more water.

His eyes narrowed for a second. Because he had thick lashes a few shades darker than his mid-brown hair, the icy glint of those eyes was obscured briefly. But then he tilted his head to one side, and even smiled.

"Who's he working for?"

"He wouldn't tell me," I replied. "But I heard him talking on the phone once, and he wasn't speaking English. I think it might have been Russian."

No mistaking the frown that creased Randall Lenz's brow at that revelation, and I had to hold myself still so I wouldn't let out a chuckle that gave the game away. It seemed I'd hit a nerve with my little lie.

However, his tone was still calm as he said, "You're sure it was Russian?"

"No," I said, figuring it was probably a good idea not to sound too emphatic. "I mean, it's not like I speak Russian or anything. That's just my best guess based on what I've seen in the movies or on TV. I suppose it could have been another language that sounds similar to Russian."

"Did he ever tell you his last name?"

"No," I replied. "Honestly, I'm not even sure 'Jake' is his real name. I mean, if he's a Russian spy or something, then he would have given me an alias, right?"

"Most likely." A pause as Lenz appeared to consider what I'd just told him, and then he said, "What happened after he took you from Kanab?"

"We went to Las Vegas." I figured it was safe enough to tell Lenz that, since Jeremy had already said that the agent had tracked Jake and me to Vegas. Maybe Randall Lenz didn't remember anything about that part of his pursuit, but even if his memories came back, it wasn't as though I was giving away state secrets. However, it had been two weeks since he'd appeared on my doorstep in Kanab—well, unless I'd been knocked out for more than twelve hours, in which case I had no idea what day it was—and so I knew I'd better think fast to come up with a plausible story that would explain the passage of so much time. "We were there for a few days—we kept moving to different hotels."

"And after Las Vegas?" Lenz inquired. If he thought it strange that a Russian operative had taken me to Sin City and then kept me hopping from hotel to hotel while we were there, he didn't give any indication of it.

"I'm not sure where we went," I lied, then added quickly as he began to frown, "I mean, I think it might've been somewhere up near Lake Tahoe. There were a lot of trees, and the weather was cooler. But he took me there in the middle of the night, and I was asleep most of the way. Actually," I said, hoping I'd injected the right amount of wounded surprise into my tone, "now I wonder if he drugged me or something to make sure I didn't see where I was going."

"That's entirely plausible," Randall Lenz said, expression smoothing itself once again. "So, you were up in the woods near Lake Tahoe."

"If that's even where we were. I've never been there, so I don't really know what it's supposed to look like."

Did he buy my expression of—I hoped— puzzled innocence? Impossible to tell for sure, because his features remained as impassive as ever when he spoke. "For now, let's assume it was Lake Tahoe. How did you end up in Riverton, Wyoming?"

"He thought it would be safe for me to lie low there for a few days," I replied, which actually wasn't all that far from the truth. "I don't know exactly what was going on—I kind of got the impression that he was working on smuggling me out of the country, but it wasn't going well."

"And so he just left you alone in Wyoming while he went to work on his plans?"

Lenz's aspect was still so flat, I honestly couldn't begin to guess what he was thinking. But since I'd already embarked on selling him this pack of lies, there wasn't much I could do except continue and hope that he'd buy my story.

In a way, it was a lot less fantastic than the truth.

"Well," I hedged, brain working furiously to come up with yet another plausible lie. "I'm not sure I was really *alone,* alone. I mean, I got the feeling that he had people watching me."

"Which people?"

"I think they might have been members of the local tribe." Actually, I was kind of proud of myself for coming up with that reply, since it would explain why there had been some Arapahoe men watching the house when Randall Lenz and his team—that is, I assumed he'd worked with a team to kidnap me, since Jeremy had made a comment about a team when I was back in Flagstaff—slipped me out of Riverton with no one apparently the wiser.

"Why would a Russian operative be working with a group of Native Americans?"

I widened my eyes in what I prayed was a look

of bewildered innocence. "Maybe they didn't know who he was. Maybe they were just glad to make a little money under the table."

This theory seemed to meet with some measure of approval; at least, Randall Lenz gave the faintest nod, as if allowing the possibility. "Did he say where he was going?"

"No," I replied at once. "He just told me to keep going in to work and that he'd be back in a few days."

"About your work," Lenz said. "Why did you go to work at the Wind River Casino if you were planning to leave the country?"

"Because Jake thought a job like that would provide good cover. People come and go at places like that all the time, so no one would probably have thought too much about it when I left suddenly."

"Perhaps. Why didn't you ask for help from someone at the casino? I'd think that once you were left on your own, you would have reached out to someone for assistance."

Well, maybe. I had to admit he had me there, and I hesitated, trying to think of a believable reason why a woman taken someplace against her will wouldn't have immediately gone to the authorities or at least told the tribal management what was really going on with her. Fear of retaliation against a family member made sense—or it would have, if I had any family members to threaten. As far as Randall Lenz knew, I was all alone in the world, now that my mother was gone. He had no idea that I was pretty much the opposite of alone, thanks to my position as the daughter of a Wilcox *primus*.

Still, even though I supposedly didn't have a family to protect, that didn't mean I'd want to drag innocent bystanders into my mess.

"I thought about it," I said, hoping my brief hesitation hadn't set off any alarm bells in him, "but then I decided it was too risky. Anyone who helped me would be in danger. I didn't want that on my conscience."

"Very noble of you."

Once again, his tone was so flat that I couldn't be sure whether he was being sarcastic or whether he was only making a simple observation. I shrugged, saying, "I don't know about 'noble.' Besides, if I'd told anyone about what was really going on, they would have wanted to know what was so important about me that I'd get dragged across state lines by a Russian agent. I couldn't very well tell them about my ability to control the weather, could I?"

"You could," he responded. "Whether or not they would have believed you is, of course, an entirely separate matter." His phone beeped from inside his pants pocket, and he paused so he could get it out and look down at the screen. Because of the angle, I couldn't see anything of what might be displayed there, but apparently, it was something important; his lips thinned for a second, and then he put the phone back in his pocket and stood up. "I'm afraid I need to go. We can continue this interview at a later date."

"How much later?" I returned, glad that my voice sounded steady. "I mean, how long are you planning on keeping me here?"

"As long as it takes," he said, which did nothing to reassure me. After all, I'd seen the dossiers of the other test subjects held at the facility, and so I knew that some of those people had been held there for years.

I couldn't be in that place for years. I'd go crazy.

Since I didn't trust myself to make a measured response, I said nothing, only clenched my fingers in the thin blanket that covered me and prayed my rescue would come much sooner than that.

Randall Lenz paused at the door to my room. His wintry blue gaze held mine, and I tried not to shiver.

"Oh, and Ms. Grant—"

"Yes?" I asked, willing my face to be as blank as his. The last thing I wanted was for him to see my fear.

"Next time we speak, try telling me the truth. Things will go much better for you if you do."

After delivering that parting shot, he exited the room. A few seconds later, the door to the suite closed, a soft *thud* that contained a terrible note of finality.

I had to get out of there.

3

JAKE KNEW AN IMPORTANT CONVERSATION like this needed to happen face to face. After taking probably the world's fastest shower and making sure his dog had gotten her breakfast and a perfunctory walk down the block so she could take care of business, he'd texted Connor.

I need to come talk to you.

Luckily, Connor hadn't told him it was way too early for that sort of thing—seven o'clock had come and gone—but instead responded, *Let me come to your house. Angela's kind of got her hands full with the kids.*

Right. The twins had just finished first grade, but they were now out of school for the summer, and of course, Miranda was still too young for anything except a few hours of pre-K each day. And this was definitely not the kind of conversation he wanted to have with a bunch of little kids rampaging through the house.

Sure, he texted back. *Come on over. I'm going to tell Jeremy to come, too.*

It's bad, isn't it?

Yes, Jake replied, but didn't add anything else.

On my way.

They ended the convo there, but Jake didn't put down the phone. Instead, he sent off another text—*meeting w/Connor at my house in 15*—and then went to brew another batch of coffee. He had a feeling they would need it.

His phone buzzed, and he glanced down as the coffee began to brew.

Coming over.

Jake allowed himself an inner sigh of relief. His brother could be annoying sometimes, but he also had very good instincts about when it was okay to give his sibling a hard time and when it wasn't. It was pretty obvious that Jeremy had been able to tell immediately that something major must have gone down...if for no other reason than Jake wouldn't have texted him so early in the morning over anything that wasn't extremely urgent.

About ten minutes later—ten minutes during which he had to force himself not to pace the floor in impatience, since he felt as if he needed to be doing something, even though he was damned if he knew what—there was a quick knock at the door, followed by Jeremy calling out, "Hey, I'm here!"

"In the kitchen," Jake replied. It made sense that his brother had been the first to arrive, since his place was closer than Connor's house in Forest Highlands.

Jeremy entered the room. His hair was damp-combed back from his face and even more scruff than usual covered his chin, making it obvious that he'd only done the bare minimum to get himself out the door. "Coffee?"

"Help yourself."

A nod, and he went over to pour himself a cup. He didn't say anything, as if he understood that whatever Jake wanted to discuss, it needed to wait until Connor got there.

Jeremy had just taken his first sip of coffee when the doorbell rang. Since Jake knew the *primus* wouldn't just let himself in the way his brother had, he hurried to the front door. As he'd expected, Connor stood there, a little more put together than Jeremy…probably because having three young children had gotten him in the habit of being up and ready for the day at an early hour.

"What's up?" he asked.

"Get some coffee, and then we can go in the family room so we can sit down and talk."

For a second, Connor didn't say anything,

only gave Jake a quick, piercing glance, as if wondering why their business couldn't be handled informally in the kitchen, although he merely nodded without comment. Once again, the similarity between his gray-green eyes and Addie's was so sharp, Jake could only be reminded of how she'd been stolen from him, the pain of her loss like a physical blow.

This wasn't supposed to be happening. About all he could do now was pray that Connor would think of some way to fix the situation.

They went into the kitchen, where Jeremy nodded at Connor and waited as the other two men got their own mugs of coffee. All fortified with caffeine, they headed into the family room and sat down, Jeremy and Connor on the sofa, Jake perched on an arm of the chair next to the couch, since he knew he was too full of nervous energy to actually take a seat.

"Lenz got Addie last night," he said without preamble, and Jeremy blinked while Connor stared at him in shock.

"He *what?*" the *primus* asked, tone incredulous. "I thought you said Riverton was safe."

"I thought it was," Jake replied, once again inwardly berating himself for leaving Addie alone. He should have known they were taking too large a risk, even though they'd both believed bringing her to Flagstaff would have been far more dangerous.

"How'd he find her?" Jeremy demanded. Something in his voice sounded almost offended, as if Randall Lenz had violated some agreed-upon law of nature by getting a jump on them all. "I mean, I scrubbed everything. All the traffic cams, all the security footage…gone. There was no way he could have tracked her to Wyoming."

If the universe was at all just, then there shouldn't have been any way for Lenz to find her. But she'd been forced into an impossible situation and had clearly decided that her own safety wasn't worth risking the livelihood of hundreds of people. Jake tightened his fingers on the knees of his jeans and said, "No…except she had to use her powers to save the casino. Obviously, Lenz was still keeping an eye out for any unusual weather activity, because he was on it within a few hours. Carson Archuleta—he's the head of the local tribe —says he thinks she was taken sometime before midnight."

"She had to save the casino from what?" Connor asked.

"Prairie fire," Jake said briefly. No need to go into lengthy explanations—judging by the way the *primus* nodded, he understood right away.

"So, Addie pretty much sent up a flare, and

Lenz jumped on it," Jeremy said. "Wasn't anyone watching her?"

"Archuleta had some guys guarding the house. They're all nursing concussions this morning, sounds like." Jake couldn't help experiencing a stab of guilt at the injuries those men had suffered, even though he assumed they'd walked into the situation with their eyes open, had understood the risks they were taking. Still, he hated the idea of people getting hurt just because they were trying to do the right thing.

Jeremy passed a hand through his damp hair, making it stick out this way and that. At another time, Jake might have grinned at the goofy image his brother presented, but he couldn't find anything particularly amusing about it at the moment. "That stinks."

Yes, it did. "Carson says they're going to be okay," Jake replied, and left it at that. It sounded as though Carson was on top of the situation, and none of them could do much to help out from a thousand miles away. "Now, though, we need to figure out how to get Addie back."

Connor began to frown, but Jeremy only shifted toward the edge of the couch cushion, leaning forward in eagerness as he pondered the problem. "Well, I know where the Special Enforcement Division facility is located—it's near Davison Army Airfield just outside Alexandria,

Virginia. But even though I've been poking around in their systems, I haven't been able to get into their security cameras yet. So, I don't have a very good idea of what's going on inside."

Damn. Even though Jake knew with his brother, it was always a matter of when he'd be able to crack a system and not if, he didn't want to think about hours and days passing with Addie in Randall Lenz's clutches while Jeremy hammered at a system that had probably been set up by some of the best cybersecurity brains in the U.S. government.

Unfortunately, they didn't have any other options at the moment. "Well, keep hacking at it. We need to figure out exactly where she's being held before we can get in there and take her away."

"Whoa, whoa," Connor put in, holding up his hands. "What, you think we're going to stage some sort of commando raid on a government installation? We're a bunch of witches and warlocks, Jake, not Seal Team Six or something."

"I know that," Jake replied. "But I also know that we have a hell of a lot of special talents at our disposal."

The *primus* didn't look particularly convinced by that argument. "Maybe we do, but we're still not exactly Special Forces. Besides, if we bring the fight to Lenz, we're practically asking to be discovered for what we really are. Do you really want to risk exposing the truth about the witch clans to the federal government?"

No, he didn't. However, Jake told himself there had to be some way to rescue Addie without tipping their hand. Forcing his tone to remain level, he responded, "Do you want to take the risk of having Addie tell the truth about us? We don't know what Lenz has planned for her. He could torture her to get that information. I wouldn't put it past him."

He had to stop himself there, because the mere thought of Addie being subjected to that kind of questioning made his blood want to turn to ice in his veins. But maybe Lenz wouldn't go that far—at least, not at first. If nothing else, she was valuable to him because of the powers she possessed. As far as any of them knew, he had no idea she was anything except a regular human with some extraordinary gifts. There was no reason to believe he knew anything about the existence of the witch clans.

Problem was, the longer Lenz had Addie in his custody, the greater the chance that he'd stumble across the truth. Unlike the other subjects being held in the facility outside Alexandria, she knew she wasn't a freak or a genetic anomaly, but a member of a magically gifted family, only one out of thousands like her.

They simply couldn't risk that truth getting out.

"Not at first," Jeremy said. His tone was musing, as if he was working through possible scenarios as he spoke. "He likes to run his test subjects through their paces, see what they're capable of. I have a feeling he'll be occupied with that for a while. But he'll also want to know about you, Jake—I was able to scrub a lot of data, but he saw you with his own eyes, saw you take Addie away from her house in Kanab, so he knows you're connected to her somehow, even if he can't figure out how or why, thanks to Connor and Angela wiping his memories. And I have a feeling he's going to hit her pretty hard on that once he gets past some basic measurements of her abilities."

"Which is why we can't just sit back and do nothing," Jake said. A nightmarish vision of Addie hooked up to all sorts of machines while immobilized in a hospital bed passed through his mind, and he did his best to push it away. Why the hell was his cousin being so damn stubborn about the situation?

"I didn't say we would do *nothing*," Connor protested. "I'm just saying that we can't go off half-cocked. You think I'm okay with leaving my sister to get poked and prodded by the federal government?"

The worry and outrage on Connor's features

was clear enough, so Jake didn't see the point in continuing that particular argument. Some of the tension that had knotted his gut eased just the slightest bit as he realized Connor was on his side in this, even if they didn't completely agree on how to accomplish their shared goal of getting Addie the hell away from Randall Lenz.

"I know you're not okay with it," Jake said. "And I'm not talking about some kind of commando raid. For one thing, until we know exactly where she's being held, there's no point in making a rescue attempt. At the same time, it doesn't hurt to start making plans."

"So, what do you propose?" Connor asked.

For a moment or two, Jake didn't respond, only sat on the arm of the chair and allowed his brain to churn as he considered one possibility after the other, only to reject all of them as too dangerous. While the Wilcox clan had members who possessed certain offensive capabilities, like throwing fireballs or his own telekinetic talent, he still didn't know whether any of those supernatural gifts would be enough to ensure victory in a straight-up firefight with trained government agents.

No, it seemed clear enough to him that whatever they did, it would be much more safely accomplished via stealth. Somehow, they needed to get in and out of the facility without anyone even knowing they'd been there at all.

Too bad none of the Wilcoxes knew how to make themselves invisible. That would have been a handy talent, something they definitely could have used to work their way through this current predicament.

But even invisibility on its own wouldn't be enough. They still had to infiltrate a building that had state-of-the-art security in place, the kind of facility where probably every door was guarded with the sort of measures even Jeremy would have a hard time hacking, especially if it was something that needed to be done on the fly. His brother was insanely talented, but he needed to do things at his own pace. There was no way to be certain he could even hack something fast enough for it to make a difference.

No, what they really needed was a way to drop in and get out before anyone in charge even realized they'd been there. Which sounded downright impossible.

Except....

Despite the tension that knotted his shoulders, Jake grinned suddenly. Both Connor and Jeremy stared at him, their expressions seeming to show that they both thought he'd taken leave of his senses.

"Want to let us in on the joke?" Connor inquired, his tone sour.

"No joke," Jake replied. "It's just that I think I figured out how to get into that facility and steal Addie right out from under their noses."

Jeremy crossed his arms and leaned against the back of the sofa. One eyebrow lifted, but otherwise, he didn't appear terribly convinced that his brother's solution might be practicable. "How?"

Honestly, Jake didn't know why he hadn't thought of the solution right away. When the *primus* and his *prima* wife worked together, they could accomplish feats that no ordinary witch or warlock could ever manage on their own. "Connor and Angela will teleport in with me and grab her."

"We'll what?" Connor said, looking startled.

"You teleported when you were fighting Joaquin Escobar, didn't you?"

"Well, yeah, but we knew where we were going."

Jake tilted his head slightly to acknowledge that slight impediment, but he also knew it wasn't an insurmountable one…especially with Jeremy on the case. "Which is why we need Jeremy to get into the facility's surveillance system. Once we're in, we'll know exactly where to go. Then it should be pretty simple, right?"

"I don't know about 'simple,'" Connor said.

The words came out slowly, as if he was analyzing each one before he allowed it to escape his lips. Clearly, he wasn't particularly thrilled with the idea.

On the other hand, he hadn't said no, either.

"But doable?" Jake persisted.

A long pause. Connor scratched the stubble on his chin, eyes narrowed. At last, he shrugged. "Maybe. I mean, if Angela and I have a good visual for where we're going, we can get in and get out pretty quickly. Even if they caught a glimpse of us on their security cameras, I doubt they'd be able to react fast enough to prevent us from getting away."

"If I'm in the system, I can shut down the cameras in Addie's room," Jeremy said then. His dark eyes had a glint in them that told Jake he was even more motivated to hack the security system now than he'd been a few minutes earlier. "They won't be able to see anything."

"Do you know how long it'll take you to get into their system?"

Jeremy ruffled the hair at the back of his neck, eyes narrowed. "Not sure. I mean, I've been messing around with it a bit, but getting in wasn't my top priority. I was focused on making sure there was absolutely no electronic trail Lenz could follow in order to locate Addie. But since she went ahead and gave up her position, there's not much point in me working on that anymore. Still, it's hard to say for sure. Maybe a day…maybe two."

Which was two days more than Jake was willing to wait. However, he knew his own impatience wouldn't make a bit of difference when it came to hacking the facility's security system. Jeremy would get in when he got in, and not a moment sooner.

"Okay," Jake said. "Do your best. And Connor—will Angela be all right with this?"

He'd forced himself to ask the question, just because he knew that no matter how strong his cousin and his wife were, they'd still be taking a huge risk. They couldn't think about just Addie, but also their children and the two clans who relied on them for guidance. Maybe Angela would decide that it simply wasn't worth putting themselves in jeopardy for just one person when so many lives could be impacted if something went wrong.

"I'll have to talk to her, of course," Connor replied. "But I have a feeling she'll be on board. She's not the type of person to sit back if a member of her clan is in danger."

While Jake wouldn't allow himself to be completely relieved—after all, Connor was just offering an opinion, and didn't know for sure how Angela would react to the situation—he couldn't help but experience a slight easing of the tension in his body. After all, if the *primus* was willing to go along with this plan, then that was half the battle right there.

"Thanks," Jake said…all he said, but he had a feeling that Connor understood.

Jeremy let out a breath and got up from the couch. "Well, looks like I need to get to work. I'll have Laurel keep an eye on the scanning algorithms so I can focus on hacking the SED's security systems. She's definitely up for that—although I kind of hope we won't locate any more 'orphans' until this mess with Addie is handled. We've got enough on our plate as it is."

While Jake tended to agree with his brother on that point, he knew they wouldn't ignore another possible clan-less witch or warlock if one happened to pop up on their radar. Still, sufficient to the day and all that.

"We'll just see how it goes," he said easily. "But yeah, I'd prefer not to split our focus if possible."

Connor rose from the sofa as well. "I'll go talk to Angela. Keep me posted if anything changes."

Jake nodded, and walked his brother and cousin to the door, with Jeremy promising once again to get to work as soon as he returned to their HQ across the street from Wheeler Park. Once the two men were gone, though, Jake leaned against the wall and let out a breath.

All he could do now was wait for Jeremy to infiltrate the facility's security system…and pray that it would take a lot less time than two days.

Hang on, Addie, he thought.

We're coming for you.

4

My jail was a pretty nice one, as those things went. After Randall Lenz departed—those ominous last words of his about telling the truth still buzzing in my ears—I waited for a few minutes, just to make sure he wasn't coming right back to torment me some more. However, as time crawled past and I remained alone, I decided it was probably safe to get up and check out my surroundings.

The "vacation condo" vibe was even stronger in the primary living area, which had a dark beige couch and two matching chairs grouped around a travertine coffee table, along with a coordinating dinette set off to one side. Abstract art in beachy shades of tan and blue and soft coral adorned the walls. No windows, but the largest wall had a photo-mural of a tropical shore installed to keep the place from feeling too claustrophobic.

Or at least, I assumed that was the intention, but I still felt as though the walls were closing in. Then again, that was most likely my reaction to my current situation, and nothing to do with the suite itself.

No kitchen, but there was a mini-fridge and a microwave. An inspection of the cupboards revealed some instant oatmeal, hot chocolate packets, and a box of assorted herbal teas. No coffee or regular tea, which seemed like an odd omission. Did Lenz and the other people running the place think caffeine had some sort of effect on supernatural abilities?

Maybe. Not that I would bother to ask the next time I saw him. I doubted he would give me a straight answer.

The bathroom was larger than I'd expected, and done in natural stone tile. Expensive. Or at least, it seemed expensive to me, since all the houses my mother had rented either had chipped tile in colors decades out of date, or maybe some stained cultured marble at the most. Obviously, whoever had put this suite together hadn't been too worried about the cost involved.

My tax dollars at work, I supposed. I couldn't even really smile at the irony of the situation.

The closet contained the meager wardrobe I'd

put together for myself after fleeing Kanab. In a way, I had to admire Randall Lenz's resourcefulness. He'd swooped in to steal me from my rented house, but he'd still found the time to pack my things so he wouldn't have to source clothing for me.

Well, except for the black long-sleeved sleep shirt and capri-length leggings I wore. They weren't what I'd had on when I went to bed the night before—I'd been wearing the same T-shirt I'd bought in Las Vegas at a Walgreen's there, panties, and nothing else—and I found I really didn't want to think about who had changed my clothing while I was passed out thanks to the drug Lenz had shot me up with. Most likely, a female nurse or some sort of medical assistant had taken on that task, just because he didn't seem like the kind of person who cared to have that kind of intimate contact with a test subject, but I couldn't know for sure.

Just the mental image made me want to shudder.

Since I decided I really didn't want to get caught with my pants down—so to speak—I locked myself in the bathroom and changed into jeans, my favorite pair of flats, and an embroidered blouse I'd bought in Flagstaff when I went shopping with Laurel. I'd showered right before going to bed back in Riverton, so I didn't see the point in showering again, especially when I didn't know when someone might come barging into my fancy prison cell. One of the bathroom drawers contained the makeup I'd purchased on that same shopping expedition, so I went ahead and put on something of a face, more because I didn't know what else to do with myself than because I was trying to impress anyone.

Once I was done getting myself more or less presentable, I wandered back out to the living room. A TV had been mounted to the wall that wasn't covered by the mural, and a remote sat on the coffee table. I picked it up, wondering what sort of entertainment my jailers had decided to thoughtfully provide for their prisoner.

Not Netflix or HBO or Disney Plus, but the menu I scanned through offered a lot of the same stuff, movies and shows I recognized even if I'd never had the chance to watch them for myself. It looked like whoever was running the place had collected an assortment of popular entertainment, enough to keep a person occupied for years if necessary.

That wasn't a very comforting thought, actually.

No news programs, though, or even documentaries. From what I could tell, the point was to keep people entertained, but also to make sure they didn't have any access to timely information about what was happening in the world outside. Once again, I thought of the dossiers Jake had found, how some of the people at the facility had been kept there for months or even years. Did they have any idea how long they'd been held in this place? Or did they watch the canned shows provided for them and not notice how the fashions in them changed, how the cars and the phones and other bits of technology grew more advanced?

Maybe…or maybe not.

I turned off the television without selecting anything from the menu. It wasn't as though I had any desire to actually watch something—I'd just wanted to see what was being offered. For some reason, it felt as though I was surrendering if I sat down and allowed myself to be entertained by the prepackaged fare Lenz and his people had provided.

After putting the remote back down on the coffee table, I went to the door. It was guarded by some kind of sophisticated lock, something with a keypad and a small screen. For scanning a thumbprint, or maybe a retina? That seemed like the sort of security measure they'd have in place there, although I honestly didn't even know whether retinal scans were a real thing or just a device I'd seen in the movies.

Even as I stood by the door, staring at the

keypad and the smooth, blank screen above it, a chime sounded. I jumped, my heart beginning to pound, until I realized that the chime was only some kind of doorbell.

A female voice emerged from a hidden speaker. "Ms. Grant?"

I didn't answer right away. Instead, I scanned the room around me, trying to figure out exactly where the speaker had been installed, but I couldn't find any obvious signs of one. It was creepy, knowing that disembodied voices could address me any time they wanted. And that probably wasn't all; as much as I didn't want to acknowledge such a thing to myself, I had to believe I was under surveillance, that there were also hidden cameras placed around the suite to see what I was up to.

For all I knew, that was exactly why this unknown woman had spoken up at that particular moment. If they were watching me, then they'd know I was up and dressed, was wandering around the suite and taking stock of my surroundings.

A little shiver inched its way down my spine, but I ignored it as best I could and said, "Who's there?"

"My name is Dr. Michelle Richards," the woman's voice said. "I'm a researcher here at the facility."

"You work with Randall Lenz?"

Just the slightest hesitation before she replied, "Yes, he's the director of this program. However, I handle most of the day-to-day work with our guests."

Guests. There was a joke. I had a feeling they used that euphemism because no one really liked being referred to as a "subject," and calling us "prisoners" would have been just a bit too on the money.

I didn't respond—mostly because I didn't know what I was supposed to say—and she went on, "Would you mind if I came in?"

Of course, I did mind, but I doubted my feelings counted for much around there. I said, "Be my guest," and took a couple of steps away from the door.

It opened a second or two later, swinging inward like your usual garden-variety door. For some reason, I'd thought it might go whooshing into the wall like something from *Star Trek*, but apparently, they weren't quite that high tech at the SED.

The woman who entered the suite looked as though she might be in her early forties, crisply attractive, with sandy brownish-blonde hair in a shoulder-length bob and dark eyes. For some reason, I'd expected her to be wearing a lab coat, but instead she had on tailored dark trousers and a light blue collared shirt. Actually, with her silver hoop earrings and high heels, she looked more like a real estate agent than a researcher in a secret government facility.

She smiled at me. "It's good to see you up and around, Adara."

"Addie," I corrected her, an automatic response. While I liked my given name, was glad to have something unusual and pretty, my mother had always called me Addie, and it felt strange when someone addressed me by the far more formal "Adara."

"Addie," Dr. Richards repeated with a smile. "How are you feeling? Any side effects from the drug you were given?"

She sounded so matter-of-fact about the whole thing, as if it wasn't any kind of big deal that Randall Lenz had broken into my house and administered some kind of knock-out drug to make my kidnapping that much easier. For just a moment, I thought about calling her on the whole thing, then decided it was probably better not to get on her wrong side within a few minutes of our first meeting. I had no idea what she had planned for me, but I realized it was most likely smarter to go with the flow for a bit until I had a better idea of what my future might hold. If I antagonized Dr. Richards right from the start, she'd be more on her guard, and I might have fewer chances at escape.

"I'm fine," I said, which was only the truth. While I'd been a bit dizzy when I first woke up, once some time had passed and I'd been able to get up and walk around, I felt pretty much normal. Whatever that drug had been, it seemed clear that it was designed to ensure a quick recovery for whoever it was administered to.

Another smile, and she made a quick notation on the iPad she held. "Good. I need to take you for a few tests, but I promise it won't take long."

"Tests" didn't sound very appealing. "What kind of tests?" I asked.

Her smile didn't waver. "Just a few standard things. Nothing more than you'd do in a normal physical."

I'd never had a physical in my life, so I had no idea what that might entail. "Needles?"

"We'll take a blood sample, but I promise that our phlebotomist is very good. You'll hardly notice."

For a second or two, I didn't respond. I didn't have a phobia about needles; I'd donated blood before and didn't mind. However, I thought there was a huge difference between volunteering to donate blood at a community blood drive and having people at a secret test facility take it whether you wanted them to or not.

Problem was, even though it seemed Dr. Richards was doing her best to act pleasant and put me at ease, I knew that when you got right down to it, she was in charge and I wasn't. If I refused, I'd probably get hauled into the lab by a couple of orderlies and forced to comply.

"Okay," I said.

"Perfect. This way."

She led me out of my "apartment," and into a hallway that was vastly more industrial-looking than the suite we'd just left. No nonsense about travertine and mellow beach-toned furnishings there; the walls were painted pale gray, and the floor under our feet was gray vinyl. Cold-hued LED fixtures blared down from overhead. We passed several doors, all of them guarded by the same keypads and biometric scanners that watched over the entrance to my suite. However, the hallway wasn't that long, and soon enough we stood in front of an elevator, which also had a scanner mounted on the wall next to it.

Dr. Richards pressed her thumb against the scanner, and immediately, the elevator doors opened. It was as gray and industrial as the hallway we'd just traversed, the pale light overhead making my companion look downright sickly, even though otherwise she appeared healthy and rosy-cheeked enough. She leaned forward and entered some kind of code in a control panel just inside, and the doors shut behind us.

A moment passed, and another, and then the elevator stopped. There was no indicator to show how many floors we'd ascended; I assumed that the code she'd entered had specified our destination, which seemed to me like a good way of ensuring that the facility's test subjects didn't know for sure how many levels underground they were housed.

Not a question I could ask, however. Instead, I followed Dr. Richards out of the elevator and down another hallway, this one painted in the same gray tones as the one where my suite was located. She brought me into what looked like a standard examination room, with one of those elevated exam tables and a blood pressure monitor and a scale. The sharp scent of rubbing alcohol hung in the air.

A woman who appeared about a decade older than the doctor came into the room. Her dark hair was pulled into a tight twist at the back of her head, and she wore a set of mint green scrubs. A nod from Dr. Richards, and she came over and wrapped a blood pressure cuff around my arm, took a reading, and noted it on a tablet she'd brought in with her. A temperature reading from a digital thermometer she placed in my ear, and then she said, "On the scale, please."

Under different circumstances, I might have taken off my shoes before stepping on the scale. This wasn't about my vanity, though, and so I went ahead and stood on the thing, and waited while she moved the little weights around to get an accurate reading. After that, she asked me to sit on the exam table and proceeded to extract a total of three vials of blood from me. By the time she was done with the third one, I was wondering if I needed to revise my opinions on needles. She'd been careful, but having to sit there with a needle stuck in me while she kept filling up vials was definitely no fun.

Eventually, though, we were finished, and Dr. Richards said, "That wasn't so bad, was it?"

I wanted to tell her to donate three vials of blood and see how she felt about the whole thing. But I figured it was probably best to act cooperative. Until I had a better idea of exactly what was going on in Randall Lenz's "program," I needed to make them think I wasn't going to cause any trouble.

"It was fine," I said shortly. "What now?"

"Would you like to get out and take a walk?"

For a second, I could only stare at her. Was she joking? Trying to gauge my reaction to promised treats, and my reaction again when they were taken away? It seemed like the sort of maneuver Randall Lenz and his compatriots would pull.

"'Get out'?" I repeated. "Get out where?"

"We have quite a nice park here," she replied. "We want to make sure our guests get plenty of fresh air. Wouldn't you like to see a bit of the sky?"

Of course, I would. Because if she really was going to take me up where I could see clouds and the sun, then maybe I could use my gifts to call a storm and get myself the hell out of there. Yes, Michelle Richards had seemed pleasant enough so far, which meant absolutely nothing. It seemed much more likely that she and Randall Lenz had some kind of good cop/bad cop scenario going on, and if that was the case, I wouldn't hesitate to call down the thunder if necessary. No, I didn't like resorting to violence, but at least I knew that Lenz seemed to have survived my attack just fine.

Because the Wilcox healer made sure he was okay, I reminded myself, and for a second, I hesitated. How could I be sure that Dr. Richards would come out of such an encounter mostly unscathed?

But since they had nurses working at the facility, I guessed they must have doctors on staff as well, and anyone I attacked with my powers would get immediate medical attention. Besides, why should I worry about their well-being when it was clear they didn't give a damn about trampling on my rights?

"That sounds great," I said, hoping she hadn't noticed the way I hesitated. "It would be good to get some fresh air."

"Then we'll head outside."

Back out into the hallway, retracing our steps to the elevator. This time, it felt as though we were in it a bit longer than we'd been during our trip down to the exam room, although once again, I couldn't be sure how many floors we were passing. Eventually, though, the elevator slowed to a stop, and we came out into a hallway that felt wider and brighter than the ones I'd seen previously. Up ahead of us, I spied a set of glass doors, and beyond them, a flash of green.

"Here we are," Dr. Richards said, once again using a thumb scan to open the doors.

Warm, damp air met me as I walked outside, blinking at the contrast of the bright, sunny day to the cold artificial light indoors. The air smelled of fresh-cut grass, and I took a quick glance around, noting that the "park" she'd described was really more an enclosed courtyard, with walkways traversing the lawn and a number of trees breaking up the space. On all sides were the glass-fronted walls of the structure we'd just left. Honestly, if I hadn't known better, I would have said I was in the courtyard of a professional building, the kind of place that housed the offices of insurance agents and mortgage brokers, something like that.

Well, in a way, that made sense. Jake had said Agent Lenz's headquarters were someplace in Alexandria, Virginia. I didn't know much about Alexandria, but I knew enough to guess that the area was pretty built up, and therefore the facility would have to look completely innocuous to the outside observer.

"It's nice," I said, since Dr. Williams was watching me, apparently expecting me to make some sort of comment. "A little humid, though."

Was it my imagination, or did her pleasant expression suddenly seem just a bit tight? "Well, that's Virginia in June for you," she replied. "I suppose you're not used to it—you're from the Southwest, aren't you?"

I supposed that was as accurate a description as any, considering I couldn't call any particular place home, not with the way my mother and I had moved so often. If circumstances in the form of Randall Lenz hadn't intervened, maybe Flagstaff could have been my home, or even Riverton, although I understood now that had been only a pipe dream. Jake and I couldn't have been safe that far away from our clan, not really. It had been a mistake to leave me alone—I should have gone with him, to a place where the Wilcoxes could have protected me.

If I managed to survive all this, I'd have to let him know that the only place we really could be certain of our future was in Flagstaff.

"Yes," I said. "Mostly western Colorado and Utah. It's a lot drier there, except during monsoon season."

"Oh, yes—your famous summer storms." A pause, and then she added, "Do you think observing those storms helped you to control your powers?"

Obviously, she'd decided it was time to get past the preliminaries and on to the real meat of why I was there at the SED facility. I drew in a breath, trying to figure out the best way to respond to her question. The true answer was that I hadn't known how to control my powers at all, which was why I had so much misfortune following me wherever I went. I'd only gained control over that strange gift of mine after Joanna Wilcox, the clan's other weather-worker, had given me the guidance I needed.

However, I couldn't tell Michelle Richards about Joanna, or that I possessed my weather-working abilities because I was the daughter of a very powerful warlock and not because something in my genetic makeup had decided to take a left turn at Albuquerque.

I shrugged and said, "I don't think 'control' is the right word to use. It's more like the storms respond to my emotions."

There. That was nothing more than the truth…or at least, it had been the complete truth up until a few weeks earlier. Now, my reality was just a little more complicated.

"Was that what happened to Agent Lenz?" Dr. Richards asked then. Something about her tone sounded almost hesitant, though, as if she didn't know for sure what exactly had happened to him, and she wanted to see how I responded.

Which meant they still hadn't figured it out. I had a feeling whatever doctor or doctors had examined him had most likely found traces of injuries that might have been attributed to a lightning strike, but since Eleanor, the Wilcox clan's healer, had fixed Randall Lenz up as best she could, those injuries would have appeared long healed, not something that had happened to him only a few days earlier.

No wonder Dr. Richards sounded hesitant. She didn't know what might set me off, although there wasn't anything about our current situation to signal she was in immediate danger; we stood in a welcoming green space and were speaking in civil tones. Nothing there that should invite an attack, even if I was technically being held against my will at the facility.

"Um…I guess so," I allowed. "I wasn't really thinking. It just sort of…happened."

Her fingers tightened on the iPad she still held, as if she wanted to pick it up and make a quick notation but decided against it because she wanted to maintain the façade of the two of us having a friendly conversation and nothing more. "And that happened a lot with you, isn't that right?"

I shrugged. "I don't know about 'a lot.' That was the first time lightning ever got that close to someone when they were around me. A couple of near-misses, but…."

My words trailed off as Dr. Richards gave me a sympathetic nod, although she didn't appear as if she planned to respond, was instead waiting to see if I had anything else to add. I didn't…mostly because I had something far more important to occupy my mind.

The clouds that floated lazily above us were rich with moisture, even though they didn't seem to show any indication of actually raining. Still, I knew it wouldn't take much for me to call out to them to grow even heavier with water vapor, to become restless and full of potential energy just looking for a place to strike.

And I knew exactly where they should strike. Someplace close by Dr. Richards—not enough to hit her like I'd made the lightning strike Randall

Lenz, but near enough to stun her, knock her off her feet…maybe even render her unconscious for a few seconds. A few more strikes on the building, like on the doors to disable the biometric locks, and I'd have a pretty good chance of getting away.

Only…as I stood there under the other woman's watchful gaze, I suddenly realized I couldn't do it. Maybe I was being overly scrupulous, but it seemed to me that it was one thing to strike down someone who was being actively threatening, and quite another to attack a person who only stood close by and wasn't acting in the least bit menacing. What if I miscalculated, and the lightning bolt actually struck her? Michelle Richards was around my height and very slender; the same force that had nearly killed Randall Lenz, a man taller than six feet and certainly a good forty or fifty pounds heavier than the doctor, might prove to be lethal for someone so much smaller in build.

And that didn't even take into account anyone who might be standing near the doors when I targeted the lightning to hit the biometric locks. There might have been some who would consider any employees of the facility to be enemy combatants, and therefore not deserving of much consideration, but I didn't think I could be that callous. For all I knew, most of the people who worked in the place didn't even know exactly what sort of research was being conducted there. Did I really want to take that risk with innocent employees?

I pulled in a breath. The whole time I'd been wrestling with myself, Dr. Richards had stood quietly by, waiting for me to continue. Since I knew I had to say something, I told her, "Actually, I think that's enough fresh air for now. The humidity's giving me a headache."

At once, her expression grew concerned. "Then we'll go inside. I'd like you to meet the others, if you feel up to it."

I stared at her in feigned surprise. Or maybe not so feigned. Yes, I knew about the other test subjects, but I was startled that she'd mention them to me so early in the game. "'Others'?" I repeated.

"Oh, yes. I mentioned our 'guests' earlier. There are fifteen of you now, all very special people with very special gifts."

Right. Yes, she had mentioned them, and I'd been startled then as well, a little shocked that she saw no reason to conceal the presence of other supernaturally talented people at the facility when Randall Lenz had been so coy on the subject. In my mind, I'd just naturally assumed that Lenz and his staff would have made sure to keep everyone separate so there wouldn't be any chance of them collaborating somehow, maybe figuring out a way to work together so they could get the hell out of there.

But it seemed that assumption had been dead wrong.

What else might I have been wrong about?

"Sure," I said, finding my voice. "I definitely want to meet everyone."

5

RANDALL LENZ PAUSED THE VIDEO OF DR. Richards and Adara Grant once again. Yes, there it was—Adara hesitating for a scant few seconds, gray-green eyes flickering toward the partly cloudy sky overhead before she returned her attention to the woman who stood a few feet away. It seemed obvious enough to him that she'd considered reaching out with her gift to tap into the energies within those clouds, and then apparently had thought better of it.

The little test had played out precisely as he'd imagined.

Michelle Richards hadn't been overly thrilled to be part of his experiment, but he'd assured her she wouldn't be in any real danger. Yes, he had a feeling that Adara Grant had injured him badly, even if he couldn't remember exactly what had happened, and yet he guessed there wouldn't be a repeat of that particular incident. After all, even though he couldn't claim to know Adara very well, he doubted she would direct a violent attack at another woman.

Some sixth sense told him that Adara had far more control over her peculiar gift than he'd originally thought. She'd been frightened when he came to collect her from her mother's home in Kanab, Utah, and although a violent storm had descended on the property, it hadn't hurt him. The injuries he'd sustained had come later, during the blank time that had left such a hole in his memories. If she had such a weapon in her arsenal, why wouldn't she use it?

Well, apparently when she didn't think her current circumstances warranted such an assault. She'd held back with Dr. Richards, for whatever reason.

He'd hoped for such an outcome, since it meant she could make the lightning and the weather obey her commands. At the same time, he realized he would have to tread cautiously. Adara was not the sort of person to be coerced into cooperation; he'd have to make her believe it was in the country's best interests that she explore the full extent of her abilities and learn the sort of fine control that would make her a valuable asset.

Because he and Dr. Richards and the rest of

their team had seen encouraging levels of success with their other subjects, he had no reason to believe they wouldn't experience that same success with Adara Grant. People wanted to feel valued, to think they were making a contribution to their country, to their world. All he had to do was determine the correct angle of approach, and soon enough, Adara would realize she was in a unique position to make a very valuable contribution indeed.

For the moment, though, he knew it was probably best to sit back and let Dr. Richards handle things. She'd advised early exposure to the rest of the test subjects, simply because being around other people with singular gifts made those involved realize they weren't freaks, but rather a member of a special population. Lenz wanted Adara to adopt that mindset, to understand that she was now a part of a uniquely talented community. Once she saw herself as one of them, she'd be far more likely to cooperate.

His smile faded as he recalled the story she'd given him about the mysterious "Jake" being a Russian operative. He'd known at once that she was lying—her gaze had shifted away from his, and she'd tucked her hair behind her ears and licked her lips several times during the narrative, all distinctive tells he'd been trained to watch for.

Exactly what she was hiding, Lenz still didn't

know, thanks to the way any information about Jake or his activities had been scrubbed from their databases. He'd had Dawson search on "Jake Wilcox," just because Adara had used that surname when purchasing a car and setting up her bank accounts, but the only Jake Wilcox Dawson had been able to find within five hundred miles of Kanab was an individual at least forty years older than the man Lenz had confronted at the house Adara shared with her mother.

As with so many aspects of this case, they were effectively back to zero.

Randall Lenz told himself it didn't matter. While of course he would have preferred to track down Jake so he could discover exactly what his connection to Adara Blake actually was, having the man in custody was of lesser importance when contrasted with the value she brought to the organization.

And to his place in it as well. Lenz knew he was young to occupy a position with so much responsibility, and he worked tirelessly to ensure the under-secretary knew that his confidence in him hadn't been misplaced. In fact, he needed to get back to the report he'd been writing on Adara's capture, because he wanted to make sure his superiors knew that a prized asset had been safely brought into custody. His preliminary write-ups on her had garnered a good deal of interest, mostly because—unlike the majority of the subjects currently being held for study—her gifts had immediate offensive use.

If, of course, she could be convinced to use them.

All in good time. For the moment, he would have to trust in Dr. Richards…and hope that sooner rather than later, Adara Grant would understand that everything he did, he did for the good of his country.

Hanging around the house with nothing to do would have driven Jake crazy, so after he made sure Taffy had fresh water in her bowl and that she'd be okay until he came back to check on her at lunchtime, he headed over to the Trident Enterprises HQ across from Wheeler park. Yes, Jeremy would be buried in cracking the code that protected the SED's security system and wouldn't be thrilled to be interrupted, but Jake figured Laurel would be there as well, watching over the computers that tirelessly searched the world's news for any sign of individuals with special witchy talents. He could hang out with her and stay out of Jeremy's hair—mainly because Jeremy would be working in the PC room, while he and Laurel could stay in the repurposed living room that housed all of Trident's Mac Pro computers.

The day was bright and beautiful, with just a few clouds drifting around Mt. Humphreys, the highest of the San Francisco Peaks that towered above Flagstaff. In a perfect world, Jake would have packed a picnic lunch and taken Addie to see some of his favorite spots nearby—Lockett Meadow, on the north side of the peaks, or Aspen Corner, a little bit closer to town.

But since she was being held in a government research facility roughly three thousand miles away, there wasn't a damn thing he could do about it until Jeremy could get into the system and pull up some visuals for Connor and Angela to work with. In the meantime, Jake figured he might as well at least pretend to be doing something useful.

When he walked into the main room at Trident, he noticed immediately that the pocket doors separating the space from the dining room next door had been pulled shut. Laurel sat in front of one of the computers but didn't appear to be paying much attention to what was on the screen, since she had her phone out and was busily texting with someone. As soon as she spotted Jake, however, she set down the phone and said, "Sorry —it's just that the computers really don't need much babysitting."

"I know," he replied, speaking quietly so his voice wouldn't carry beyond the pocket doors and possibly interrupt Jeremy while he was in the middle of his hacking blitz.

Laurel paused, her gaze moving toward the doors before she looked back over at Jake. "Jeremy told me what happened," she said. "I'm really sorry about Addie."

"It's okay," he said. Not that any of this was okay, but what had happened certainly wasn't Laurel's fault. "Jeremy's working on it."

"I know. After he let me know about Addie, he went in there and shut the door, and hasn't come out since."

And probably wouldn't until late that night, if even then. When Jeremy went on a tear, he could be glued to a screen for up to twelve hours before he surfaced. Most of the time, he would remember enough of the world to order in some food, but not always. Well, since Jake planned to go home at lunch to check on the dog, he figured he'd bring back takeout for everyone. What else did he have to do with his time?

"He knows our hands are tied until he hacks that system," Jake said. "But once we have something to work with, Connor and Angela can go in and get her."

Laurel shook her head. As usual, she wore a brightly colored top—this one hot pink—and her overall look was just a bit too cheery, considering their current circumstances. But he knew he couldn't really blame her for that. It wasn't as if she'd known when she got dressed that morning that her newfound cousin had been captured by a rogue branch of the federal government.

"It's kind of wild to think Connor can do that sort of thing," she said. "I mean, I know he and Angela teleported before, but most of the time, they're both so low-key about their talents that you kind of, I don't know…forget they're capable of all that crazy stuff."

"I know what you mean," Jake replied. "I suppose it's a good thing that they don't really throw their weight around, so to speak. But in this case, even they have their limits. If they were all-powerful, they could just zap themselves right into the SED facility and get Addie out of there without us having to wait on Jeremy to crack the system."

And wouldn't all their lives be made easier if Connor and Angela really could do something like that? But, amazing as their combined talents were, even they couldn't teleport to a place they hadn't seen. Since he doubted that the employees of the facility were busy posting Instagram photos of themselves for the world to see, about all he—and Angela and Connor and Laurel—could do was wait and pray that Jeremy's own magical gifts would bail them out sooner rather than later.

"Well, Jeremy'll figure it out," Laurel said with a smile. No doubt she was just trying to be encouraging, but something about his cousin's smile grated on Jake right then. He didn't want false cheer; he wanted Addie back.

"Anything interesting pop up?" he asked then, abruptly changing the subject.

Although sometimes Laurel could be a little too bubbly for his taste, Jake would never accuse her of not being smart. At once, her smile disappeared, and she looked downright businesslike. "Nothing worth following up. A ping from some kind of faith healer in Oklahoma, but it turned out to be nothing. Another scam."

Which was just part of the territory. Whenever you were out fishing for people with extraordinary abilities, you ran the risk of catching a lot of charlatans in your net. The sad truth was, even though witches and warlocks existed, had been woven into humanity's history for hundreds and probably thousands of years, there were plenty of ordinary human beings out there who'd realized there was a lot of money to be made from people who desperately wanted to believe in their supernatural gifts. Jeremy had set up the algorithms to filter out fakes, but if someone was especially good, sometimes the Trident team had to take a second or even third look before determining that the person in question wasn't any more a witch or warlock than they were a unicorn.

"Too bad," Jake commented. "We can always use more healers."

He'd said the words in an almost off-hand tone—after all, one thing most of witch-kind could agree on was that healers were valuable and necessary to a smooth-running clan—but Laurel still frowned at him. "So, what…I'm wasting my time sitting here and babysitting your computers?"

Oops. He'd been so preoccupied with Addie that he'd forgotten his cousin could be a little touchy about her healing gifts, since she hadn't been doing all that much with them lately. She'd trained with Eleanor, the clan's healer, to make sure she had proper control over her talents, but it was clear to everyone that Laurel really wasn't terribly interested in delivering babies or fixing broken bones or managing someone's diabetes, or else she probably would have majored in biology in college rather than computer science, would have done something that might have assisted her in taking on some responsibilities as a clan healer. Eleanor had covered for her, saying that she was on top of the situation and really didn't need an assistant—especially when a lot of Wilcoxes saw civilian specialists to handle their minor health issues—but Jake could tell that was just Eleanor being kind. For the time being, the status quo worked just fine, since Eleanor was a healthy fifty-four and certainly had no intention of retiring any time soon. But eventually….

"That's not what I said," he responded, doing his best to keep his tone mild. The last thing he wanted right then was to get in an argument with his cousin, especially when he knew he was on edge, nerves frayed with worry over Addie. "If I thought you should be working with Eleanor, I wouldn't have asked you to come work here at Trident."

Laurel slumped against the back of her computer chair, expression now contrite. "I know. I'm sorry, Jake. There's just been way more drama the past few weeks than I'm used to dealing with."

Truer words were never spoken. While Jake might not have said he'd been precisely happy the past few years, not with Sarah, his former fiancée, torn from his life so unexpectedly and tragically, at least he'd settled into a sort of groove, working summers for the Forest Service and winters at the Snow Bowl ski resort. Neither of those jobs paid all that well; he didn't need them to, thanks to the Wilcox clan stipend he received every month. And then when he dreamed up Trident Enterprises and its mission, he had plenty to occupy him, but the work had been undemanding most of the time. It wasn't until Addie Grant entered his life that everything hit the fan.

Not that he would have changed any of it. Well, all right—if he suddenly was granted the ability to go back in time and alter past events, then he would have used his telekinetic abilities to make Agent Lenz's gun jam, or at least shoot straight up into the porch roof so that Addie's mother escaped the confrontation unscathed.

Unfortunately, he didn't have that kind of power. Hell, even his own telekinesis was limited in its own way, since he could only affect inanimate objects and not people. Otherwise, he could have used his gift to push Lyssa Grant out of harm's way.

Or make Randall Lenz aim his damn gun at himself, Jake thought bitterly, although he knew deep down he wasn't cold-blooded enough to take that kind of lethal action against another human being. The agent might deserve to meet that sort of fate, but Jake wouldn't be the one to deliver it.

"Well, we all knew we'd probably run into problems we couldn't plan for," he said diplomatically, and Laurel gave him an odd little grimace of a smile before reaching for a water bottle that sat on the computer desk in front of them.

She unscrewed the cap and took a swallow of water before replying, "I suppose so. But we were thinking about how we might have to jump through hoops to convince people they were actually witches and warlocks, or deal with the politics of reuniting our 'orphans' with their clans. Not even Jeremy mentioned the possibility of getting into it with the federal government."

Jake couldn't argue with that assertion. Yes, Jeremy tended to be the sort of person who came up with contingencies for his contingencies, and yet, even in all his worst-case scenarios, he'd never dreamed up a situation like the one they currently found themselves embroiled in.

"No plan survives a battlefield," Jake commented, and Laurel raised an eyebrow.

"Is that a Jeremy quote?"

"No…Winston Churchill, maybe?" Honestly, Jake couldn't be sure who'd said it, or if he'd even gotten the quote right. The important thing was the sentiment behind it. You could plan and plan, but the second you put those plans into action in real life, everything changed.

"Oh." His cousin was silent for a moment as she sipped some more water, then replaced the cap and set the bottle back down on the desk. "You seem pretty calm about all this."

About all Jake could do was shrug. "What else *can* I do? Until Jeremy hacks that security system, there isn't much any of us can do except wait. There's not much point in wasting my energy on freaking out, is there?"

"No, I suppose not." Laurel played with the ends of her long ponytail, which had slipped forward over her shoulder. "Still…."

He understood her hesitancy. In a way, it was easier than he'd thought to act calm, because he really didn't want his cousin to see him lose control. If nothing else, he was supposed to be in charge at Trident, although the setup was pretty loose and he honestly would never dream of telling Laurel to do something she didn't want to do. However, that didn't mean his mind wasn't still churning away, wondering what was happening to the woman he loved as he sat there and quietly talked to his cousin. Jake tried to reassure himself that Addie obviously was valuable to Randall Lenz, and so he wouldn't do anything to hurt her…but did he know that for sure? The man was driven, and maybe he'd already decided that a little painful coercion might be the ticket if she proved to be uncooperative.

No, he needed to push those sorts of thoughts away. Otherwise, he'd end up driving himself crazy.

Still, he would have given everything he owned to know what was happening to her right then.

6

Dr. Richards took me back inside the building and to the elevator. This time, it felt as though we traveled downward for a long while, although without a digital indicator to count off the floors or the little *bing* that informed an elevator's occupants each time it passed a floor, I honestly couldn't tell how many stories we'd descended. Farther than the floor where my suite was located, farther than the level where I'd gone to the examination room to have my blood drawn, telling me that wherever we were going, it was pretty deep underground.

I'd been expecting another industrial-looking hallway, but instead the elevator opened onto a reception area of some sort, although no one was sitting at the large metal and glass desk placed off to one side. Immediately in front of us was a set of double doors guarded by a biometric lock; Dr. Richards walked over to the panel, waited while her right eye was scanned, and then turned toward me, one hand on the door handle.

"We have a sort of common area on this floor," she explained. "We call it the multipurpose unit. Most of our guests like to spend their time here when they're not working with me or one of my assistants. There's a reading area, several televisions, a music system. Oh, and plenty of e-readers —we can get you any book you like. There's a basket where you can put your requests."

For a second or two, I was tempted to ask when we'd be finger-painting or braiding plastic lanyards for keychains, but then I decided it was probably better to keep the snark to a minimum. Although I had absolutely no idea how I was going to get out of the place, I reminded myself that it was in my best interests to at least seem as if I was going along with the flow and cooperating.

"Great," I said. "I have a lot of books I'd like to catch up on—between school and work, I never seemed to have enough time for pleasure reading."

That comment elicited a quick flash of a smile, maybe with just a hint of relief. Had Dr. Richards worried that I might be difficult? Maybe; I had a feeling Randall Lenz probably hadn't painted a very flattering portrait of me.

Not that I really cared one way or another.

"Perfect," she said. "But in the meantime, let's get you introduced to everyone."

She opened the door and led me inside. No wonder they called it the "multipurpose unit"— my first impression was of a large open space similar to the multipurpose room at an elementary school I'd attended briefly during my mother's and my first stint in Utah, since there were tables set up to either side, and dedicated spots for reading or watching TV. Unlike that multipurpose room, though, this space had a large conversation pit in the center, with lots of overstuffed couches and chairs. Sitting there was a group of nine people, men and women who appeared to range in age from their mid-twenties to their early fifties. I knew there were supposedly fourteen other "guests" besides myself at the facility, but I figured that the others were off being put through their paces by the members of Dr. Richards' staff, or possibly just hanging out in their own suites if they weren't into the whole togetherness thing at the moment.

Years of constantly enrolling in new schools should have accustomed me to meeting large groups of strangers at once, but I still experienced a flutter in my stomach as they paused their conversation to look over at Michelle Richards and me. I had to fight the impulse to flee through the door I'd just entered…not that it probably would have opened without the doctor's retinal scan.

"Hi, everyone," she said brightly, sounding more like a chirpy kindergarten teacher than a government-funded scientist. "This is Addie Grant, our newest guest."

"Hi, Addie," everyone replied almost in unison, reinforcing my feeling of being in some kind of surreal kindergarten class.

"Hi," I managed, knowing how limp that one syllable must have sounded. Right then, I was seriously reconsidering my decision to come meet everyone, even though I'd told myself that it was important for me to see who else was being held at the facility and—with any luck—learn something of what their talents might be.

One of the men stood up. He looked as though he was probably in his early thirties, with thin, intense features that somehow managed to be appealing without being exactly attractive. "Glad to have you as part of our group," he said, his voice a warm, friendly tenor. "I'm Ethan Sitko."

"Hi, Ethan," I replied, doing my best to smile. At the same time, I wondered how long he'd been held at the facility. He seemed almost too pale, as if he hadn't spent much time getting sun in the open courtyard area Dr. Richards has shown me a few minutes earlier.

Sitting next to him was a pretty woman probably around my age, with the kind of long, gloriously curly dark hair that I, with my straight brown locks, had always envied. Her skin was a warm shade of light brown, making me think that one of her parents must have been African American. Were there even African American witches? Probably, just because the Castillo and the de la Paz clans were both obviously Hispanic, and it seemed silly to think there wouldn't be various ethnicities represented in other witch families.

I'd have to ask Jake when I saw him again... and I made sure to emphasize the "when" in my mind, just so I wouldn't feel too overwhelmed by my current situation.

"And I'm Natalie," the woman said. A quick glance up at Ethan, and he smiled down at her, the warmth in his expression clearly echoed in hers. Maybe I was imagining things that weren't there, but I got the distinct impression the two of them were close...or at least as close as their standing as "guests" in a government facility would allow them to be.

But I didn't have time for much speculation after that, because the rest of the group started introducing themselves as well, and I tried to focus on names and faces—Lorna was the pretty, slightly plump woman who reminded me of Angela's Aunt Rachel, and Matthew the guy who looked like he was around my age, maybe a little younger, with gingery hair and a dancing light in his eyes that made me think he was glad to see an unattached female show up.

Well, I was most definitely attached, even if none of my current companions could know anything about my relationship with Jake Wilcox, or the world he represented. I had to hold that secret close to my chest, because as much as I would have liked to let all of them know they weren't genetic freaks, were instead lost members of various witch clans, I knew I didn't dare let slip such an important piece of information, not when I had a feeling everything we did and said was being recorded.

"Hi, everybody," I said, and attempted what I hoped was a natural-looking smile.

"I'll leave you all to get acquainted," Dr. Richards put in then. "But Andrew—it's time for our afternoon session. You can come back up to the lab with me."

A slim man with graying dark hair got up from one of the couches, gave me a nod, and headed over to the door, the doctor at his side. They exited the room, and the rest of us were left to stare at each other. My feeling of being back in some kind of strange kindergarten class only intensified, but I forced myself to say, "So…what are all your powers?"

Ethan grinned. "Cut right to the chase, huh?"

"Are you supposed not to talk about it?" I asked. I'd sort of gotten the impression that witches and warlocks generally didn't ask about one another's abilities, and instead waited for an acquaintance to volunteer the information, but I didn't see why the people who surrounded me would follow the same rules, not when they didn't even know witch society was a thing.

"No, that's not it," Natalie responded, sending a half-exasperated glance up at Ethan, albeit one that was tinged with fondness. "They've never told us that we can't discuss our powers. But usually we tell each other a little bit about ourselves before we get into all that."

I shrugged. "There's not much to tell. My mom and I moved around a lot because of my power. I was going to start my senior year of college at the University of Utah in August."

Ethan raised an eyebrow. "So…what *is* your power?"

"Weather."

He and Natalie exchanged a glance. Lorna, who hadn't spoken yet except to introduce herself, gave a nod, and a few of the others murmured amongst themselves.

"What?" I asked, not sure how to respond to their response...or rather, lack of. "Is that a common power? Do some of you have it, too?"

"No," Ethan said. "But some of us got the impression that it was something Randall Lenz wanted specifically."

Probably because it could be so easily weaponized. I thought again of the bolt of lightning I'd summoned, how he hadn't been able to offer any kind of defense against something so innately powerful. No wonder he wanted to use it as a weapon.

I did my best to push away the stir of unease that rose inside me and kept my tone light as I asked, "So, he has a shopping list of gifts he wants?"

"I wouldn't exactly say that," Matthew put in. During the previous exchange, he'd inched a bit closer to me, although not so close that I could accuse him of getting in my personal space. Still, I wondered uneasily if he was going to be a problem. "It's just that some talents are more useful than others."

I tilted my head. "What's yours?"

He hesitated. "Nothing special."

"Oh, come on," Natalie protested. "I think it's kind of cool."

"But it doesn't really *do* anything."

She put her hands on her hips and shot him a

direct look. Apparently deciding it wasn't worth arguing over anymore, Matthew let out a breath and then raised his hands. At once, a warm glow began to emanate from his palms, growing stronger and stronger until it was bright enough that I had to look away.

Then it disappeared, and he shoved his hands in his jeans pockets. "That's my gift. But I don't know what I'm supposed to do with it, except find work in a coal mine or something."

From the deprecating tone of his voice, I guessed he'd made the same remark many times before. And honestly, I didn't know why he would have such a talent, either, except that I supposed there was some value in having a light source that didn't require any fuel or outside energy.

"Can you do anything else with it?" I asked. "Like, charge your phone or something?"

My question elicited a few chuckles from some of the other people in the group, but Matthew appeared serious enough as he replied, "Actually, yeah, I can. I didn't even realize that until I started working with Dr. Richards and her team. Part of what they do is have us exercise our gifts, see what else we can do with them."

He didn't sound all that upset about being locked up in an underground facility and being put through his paces like some kind of glorified lab rat. Actually, as my gaze moved from him to

Ethan and Natalie, and on to Lorna and the others, I noticed that none of them looked terribly troubled by their current situation. What, were they actually *happy* to be there?

No, that was probably taking my speculation a bit too far. On the other hand, it seemed as though Dr. Richards wasn't too worried about some kind of mass breakout, or she wouldn't have left us alone down in the multipurpose unit without any adult supervision.

Well, without any adult supervision I could see. I knew I was fooling myself if I didn't think there weren't hidden cameras and microphones all over the place.

Which made me hesitate before I asked my next question. However, Randall Lenz knew damn well that I was less than happy to be plucked from the life I'd been trying to make for myself, so it wasn't as though I was giving away any state secrets.

"And you don't mind?" I asked. "Being here, I mean. Didn't you all have lives somewhere out there?"

I gestured vaguely toward the ceiling, indicating the world at large. For a moment, none of them said anything, although Ethan and Natalie traded an uneasy glance.

To my surprise, it was Lorna who spoke first. "Of course, we did," she said quietly. "But we also had spent most of our lives having to hide these things about ourselves. When we were approached by Agent Lenz and he explained to us that we were extraordinary people with extraordinary gifts, talents that could help our country, I think we all decided it was better to be someplace where we didn't have to hide any longer."

In a way, I could almost understand that particular motivation. It was exhausting to hide something that was an essential part of your being. On the other hand, I couldn't believe they'd be so willing to walk away from family and loved ones.

"And the people you left behind…?" I said, then stopped myself, wishing I hadn't asked.

Because what I saw on all their faces was a sort of pain I hadn't really expected. Ethan's fingers twined themselves with Natalie's, his skin pale against hers. At the same time, I got the impression he'd reached out for her subconsciously, that it hadn't been a calculated gesture at all.

"Most of us were pretty alone," she said. "I was a foster kid—never knew who my parents were, never had much of a connection to anyone. It was hard to get close to people when I knew I could do this."

At once, her face and form seemed to shift, and for just a second, I stared at myself. It was far more unsettling than I'd imagined to be confronted by someone who appeared to be my identical twin, the experience utterly unlike looking at myself in a mirror. A second later, and it was Natalie standing in front of me again.

I managed to find my voice. "Illusion, or do you really shapeshift?"

She chuckled. "Just an illusion. But a pretty convincing one, don't you think?"

"Very."

Ethan squeezed her fingers gently and let go, then said, "I had some family, but I never felt like I fit in anywhere. No real attachments."

"Your talent?" I asked.

In answer, he raised a hand, and on one of the iPads that had been sitting on the coffee table in the conversation pit rose into the air and dropped into his outstretched palm. "Nothing too big, or too heavy," he said. "And I know it seems like a useful power, but I didn't know how to control it until I got here. Things around me would move and shift, and I didn't know why. It just seemed safer to stay away from people whenever I could."

Since I'd done pretty much the same thing myself while trying to pretend all those crazy storms were none of my doing, I could relate to Ethan's avoidance of connections whenever possible. I wondered then whether Randall Lenz had purposely sought out gifted people who were mostly alone in the world. Not out of any particular altruism, but simply because there would be far fewer questions asked if individuals like that simply…disappeared.

"But you can control it now because of the work you've done here?" I said, and Ethan nodded.

"It wasn't really that hard, once we had some guidance," he said. "Sort of like a mental flick of the wrist, if you know what I mean."

Since Joanna Wilcox had helped me figure out how to perform that same sort of mental maneuver, I knew exactly what he was talking about. Still, I couldn't help thinking that these people would all be so much better off if they could be with the witch clans they truly belonged to, rather than isolated here by an organization that valued them only for what their powers represented.

"Once you start working with Dr. Richards, it'll be a lot clearer," Lorna put in.

I looked over at the older woman. "So, you work with her most of the time?"

"Her, or her assistants—Dr. Keegan and Dr. Woodrow. They share responsibilities, although Dr. Richards is the one in charge."

And where were those two assistants now? Working with the members of the group who weren't present at our little gathering…or maybe watching the feed from the security cameras to see how their latest acquisition was faring?

"You don't work with Agent Lenz?" I asked next.

"Not usually," Natalie told me. "He's mostly in charge of finding us."

"But he interviews us once a month for his reports," Ethan said. "Otherwise, we don't see him much."

In a way, that particular piece of information was a relief. The fewer interactions I had with Randall Lenz, the better. On the other hand, if he was stuck at the Alexandria facility talking to the inmates, so to speak, then he wouldn't be out grabbing some other unlucky soul for his collection.

"Got it," I said, since I had the impression that none of my fellow test subjects appeared to share my antipathy for the man in question. Then again, I had a very real reason to hate him, while it didn't seem as though any of the other "captures"—for lack of a better word—had been nearly as violent as mine.

"You'll probably start working with Dr. Richards tomorrow," Natalie added. "We all got a day to sort of acclimate, and then she started measuring our talents, figuring out what we could and couldn't do."

While I was glad to know that I wouldn't have to start right away, I had to wonder exactly how Dr. Richards or her assistants planned to perform those particular measurements. It wasn't as if they could put me in a lab and ask me to summon a hurricane or something.

"But for now, you can just hang out," Ethan said. "There's a little kitchen area in the back, with a fridge and a microwave and snacks, drinks, that kind of thing."

"A six-pack of beer?" I asked, putting on a grin so he'd know I was joking.

"I wish. We get to have one drink once a week, but otherwise, they don't want alcohol messing with our abilities."

No, I supposed having a bunch of tipsy witches and warlocks wandering around and using their powers indiscriminately would play havoc with the facility's testing regimens. And although one drink a week sounded pretty austere, it was better than none at all.

Not that I planned to hang around for a week. I had absolutely no idea how I was going to manage it, but I knew I needed to get out of there.

No matter what.

7

MICHELLE RICHARDS ENTERED RANDALL Lenz's office, looking slightly irritated…probably because he'd called her in toward the end of the day as she'd been preparing to head home. Unlike him, she was married and had a child, and tried her best to ensure her work hours weren't too irregular and didn't interfere with her home life. Most of the time, Lenz didn't get in her way, since her support staff was certainly adequate to handle any emergencies that might arise in her absence, but that evening he hadn't wanted to wait until the following morning before he spoke with her.

"Tell me about Adara Grant," he said without bothering with a greeting, and the doctor raised an eyebrow.

"There isn't much to tell at this point," Richards replied. "She met the other subjects and appeared to get along with them. She asked about their talents and there was some discussion of their various gifts, and afterward she remained with the group until it was time for all of them to return to their individual suites."

"Any signs of friction with the others?"

"Not so far," the doctor said. "She also asked about you."

"What did she ask?"

"Whether any of the others worked with you on a regular basis here at the facility. She appeared somewhat relieved when they replied in the negative."

That particular revelation didn't surprise him. While he hadn't planned what had happened to Lyssa Grant, he knew Adara wouldn't easily forgive him for her mother's death, nor did he expect her to. He might not have been a psychiatrist, but even he could see the writing on the wall there.

At the same time, he allowed himself a small inward smile at the irony of the situation. Although it wasn't standard practice for him to be involved with the day-to-day routines of the test subjects, he'd already planned to make an exception in her case. Of those currently participating in Project Daedalus, her talent was by far the strongest and the most spectacular…and was also the only one that couldn't be tested in a laboratory. Their earlier interaction had proved that she needed to be somewhere outside, or at least with easy access to the outdoors, in order for her to utilize her gift, and he'd decided that he needed to be present to oversee those particular experiments.

"I hate to disappoint her," he said easily, "but that isn't exactly the truth. I'll be working with you tomorrow when you start putting her through her paces."

His announcement didn't provoke much of an outward response—Michelle Richards was too much of a professional for that sort of thing—but he could tell from the brief startled flicker of her eyes and the way her mouth tightened slightly that she wasn't especially happy to hear of his proposed involvement in those tests.

"I don't think that's necessary—" she began, but he cut her off before she could continue.

"I think it is. If nothing else, I've seen her powers in action and know what to expect. You'll be starting at nine, correct?"

Just the barest hesitation before Dr. Richards replied, "Yes. I'd planned to have Dr. Woodrow observe as well, just because we were going to be working in the north field rather than the lab. But I can ask him to work with one of the others if you'd prefer."

"No, he can attend," Lenz told her. Possibly having all of them present would be overkill—

especially since he knew the doctor would also have an armed escort to ensure that Ms. Grant didn't try to escape during the experiment—but he didn't see any reason to keep Alec Woodrow away. "I'll see you on the north field at 9 a.m. tomorrow."

"Very good, Agent Lenz," she said. "Anything else?"

"No, that's all. Enjoy your evening."

She didn't bother to return the sentiment, only gave him the barest nod before she turned on her heel and left his office. The clack of those heels on the linoleum in the hallway outside came to his ears briefly before the door shut behind her.

Clearly, Michelle Richards was less than happy with him. However, since he was the program director, he didn't require her approval to attend Adara's session the next morning. He'd suffered far too much in his pursuit of that troublesome young woman to step aside and let the scientists handle things. He wanted to see for himself exactly what she was capable of.

After that…well, after that, he would make his own recommendations as to how best the government could utilize her extraordinary gifts.

Jeremy showed no signs of emerging from the PC

room, so at a little after six, Jake told Laurel to go home. "Just because he's killing himself in there doesn't mean you have to as well," he said, and she frowned slightly.

"I can hang if you want me to," she replied. "I don't have any plans for tonight."

Although he was touched by the worry he saw in her face, he didn't see any reason for her to stick around Trident HQ. Probably in an hour or so, he'd order some pizza in the hope that the aroma of pepperoni would lure Jeremy out and convince him to take a break, but Laurel might as well try to go home and have a normal evening.

"It's fine," Jake said. "Nothing is going to change until Jeremy gets into that security system, and I have no idea when that's going to happen. If there's an update, I'll text you."

"Okay," she replied, although the reluctance in her tone told him she still wasn't happy about abandoning him to go back to her apartment and watch Netflix, or whatever it was she planned to do with the rest of her evening. To his surprise, she put her hand on his arm and gave it a quick, reassuring squeeze. "It's going to be okay, Jake. Jeremy will figure it out."

"I know he will," he responded. He couldn't even say he was lying, because deep down, he knew his brother would get into the SED's security system eventually. The real problem was how long it might take him to accomplish that goal… and what might be happening to Addie in the meantime. "Have a good night, Laurel."

His cousin sent him one more dubious glance, but she didn't argue, only retrieved her purse from where she'd slung it over the back of a chair, gave him a quick "good night," and went out the door. The sound of it closing was curiously final, even though he knew she'd be back at nine o'clock the next morning.

Unless Jeremy cracked the system and things swung into high gear right away.

Jake settled himself back down in his office chair and stared at the screen in front of him. There really wasn't much for him to look at; a multitude of images, interspersed with streams of code, flowed across the large cinema display, but it wasn't until one of the algorithms flagged a piece of anomalous data which needed to be analyzed that the flashing images and code would stop, would display the scrap of information that merited a closer look. In fact, the display was really mostly for show, since of course Jeremy's formulas could have functioned quietly in the background. But he'd thought this setup might be a little more reassuring to Jake; at least that way, he'd have something to look at while the algorithms churned through those enormous piles of data.

Of course, it would be just his luck to have something pop up while he was asleep, or far enough away that he couldn't get back to HQ in a timely fashion.

Luck....

The word seemed to stick in Jake's mind, and he frowned for a second, wondering why luck should seem so significant. Then it came to him, and he wanted to clap his hand against his forehead for not thinking of it sooner.

His cousin Lucas' gift was luck. Luck that applied to him particularly, but still. If—*when*—Jeremy broke into the system and discovered where Addie was being kept, then if Lucas came along on the rescue mission, his presence would guarantee a successful breakout, since his talent would make sure that nothing bad happened to him...and, by extension, anyone in his immediate vicinity.

Almost without thinking, Jake reached into his pocket and got out his phone. A quick glance at the closed door to the PC room told him he should probably make the call someplace where he wouldn't risk disturbing his brother's work with a phone conversation.

Well, the back porch seemed as good a place as any. The yard was big enough that there wasn't much chance of any neighbors overhearing him, so Jake went out the French doors that opened on the porch and took a seat on one of the Adirondack chairs placed there. The outdoor furniture had been Laurel's idea, and he hadn't argued with the expenditure because he figured there would probably be times when they needed to take a break from crunching data and get some fresh air.

It was almost six-thirty, and Jake hoped he wouldn't be disturbing Connor just as he and his family were sitting down to dinner. Still, he didn't want to wait; if Connor went along with his idea of having Lucas come along on the jailbreak, it would be up to him to reach out to their cousin and let him know what they were considering.

The phone rang three times, and Jake feared it might go straight to voicemail. However, at the last minute, Connor picked up, sounding breathless.

"Did Jeremy get in?" he asked.

"No," Jake replied, then added, "I didn't catch you in the middle of something, did I?"

"Just a game of tag with the kids. What's up?"

If they'd been playing in the yard, then they definitely weren't having dinner yet. Most likely, they'd been eating later than usual because of the long, lazy summer days. "I had an idea," Jake said. "What if we brought Lucas along as a sort of lucky charm?"

Connor didn't bother to ask where Jake wanted to take Lucas. Instead, he said, "That might work. I mean, as far as I've been able to tell, his gift protects him no matter what, so if he's around, then it stands to reason nothing will go wrong. Only...."

"Only what?"

"Well, Angela and I can only take one person each when we're teleporting. If we have Lucas with us and are going to bring Addie back at the same time, then you can't come along. Even our powers have limits, you know."

Damn. Jake supposed he should have thought of that, but although he knew the *primus* and *prima* had used their gift of teleportation to bring some Castillo witches with them to help in the fight against Joaquin Escobar's people, he hadn't realized they'd only been able to bring one person each. He didn't much like the thought of not being there to help Addie escape from Randall Lenz's prison, but he told himself that it was far more important to guarantee the success of the jailbreak than to have him there when it happened. After all, Connor and Angela's gift of teleportation was basically instantaneous. It wasn't as though he'd have to spend hours and hours waiting for them to return to Flagstaff.

"That's all right," Jake said, hoping he sounded casual and unconcerned, and guessing that instead his cousin could all too easily hear the tension in his voice. "The important thing is to get Addie out of there."

"True. Well, let me give Lucas a call and see if he's game. Hang tight."

Connor ended the call there, and Jake set his iPhone down on his leg as he stared out into the backyard—green and manicured, with cheerful pansies and snapdragons and hollyhocks in the flowerbeds along the borders, thanks to a couple of weekends of hard work by the entire Trident HQ crew—and tried to reassure himself that of course Lucas would go along with their plan. The guy was generally up for anything that sounded remotely entertaining.

No, the real problem would probably be Lucas' wife Margot. She'd never been anything but friendly the few times her path had crossed Jake's, but he knew that, thanks to her being a McAllister clan elder for years before she married Lucas, she was also used to getting her own way. There was a very strong possibility that she'd declare the entire scheme way too dangerous and put her foot down.

Well, Lucas was his own man, and Jake had to hope that he'd put his own foot down and inform Margot that the safety of a fellow clan member—especially the daughter of a former *primus*—was more important than a few niggling concerns about his safety. Anyway, Connor and Angela weren't exactly helpless, even if there were a few limits on their powers. If the worst happened and their intrusion was discovered, they could use their magic to drive off any civilian attackers and still be able to get Addie away.

But as the minutes ticked past and his phone remained silent, Jake couldn't help but experience a growing trickle of unease. Maybe Connor wasn't getting back to him because simply making the request had been enough to instigate a confrontation between Lucas and his wife. They'd never seemed anything but crazy about each other when they were in public together, but people tended to present their best face to the public no matter what might be going on at home.

Just as he was about to give up and go back inside, his phone rang. At once, he scooped it up without even looking at the screen. "Connor?"

"Lucas is in," the *primus* said. "I had to wait for him to call me back because he and Margot had gone out to dinner. Luckily, she went to the restroom, and he checked his phone while she was gone."

Random luck, or Lucas' power exerting itself because it knew he needed to come along on the rescue mission? Jake honestly couldn't begin to guess—all the ramifications of his cousin's magical gift could get pretty crazy when you stopped to really puzzle them out—but right then, he didn't care. The important thing was that Lucas had agreed to come along, and all of Jake's worry that Margot might try to interfere had apparently been unfounded.

"Great," Jake said. "Now we just have to wait for Jeremy to work his magic."

Literally.

"Any updates from him?"

"No. He's cloistered in the PC lab and hasn't come out for hours. When he gets like this, it's better to stay out of the way. As soon as he has something, he'll let me know."

"Got it." Connor paused, then added, "Well, Angela's yelling at me that dinner's about to hit the table, so I'd better go. Just call when you hear something. Even if it's the middle of the night."

Actually, a midnight raid would probably be a good idea. Even though the government facility where Addie had been hidden away was under video surveillance, there would probably be a lot fewer people out and about in the dark watches of the night.

"I will," Jake said. "Have a good evening... and thanks."

"No problem. Hang in there—we'll get this sorted out."

Connor ended the call there, and Jake got up from his chair and slipped his phone into his pocket. As soon as he was back inside, he sent a hopeful glance in the direction of the PC lab's door, but it was still closed.

A sigh escaped his lips. He knew he shouldn't have been hoping for much right then, but....

With a shake of his head, he got his phone back out. Time to order that pizza.

8

MAYBE IT WAS THE REMNANTS OF THE KNOCK-out drugs in my system, or maybe it was simply that I'd just lived through a very long, very strange day, but I actually slept far better in my luxurious prison than I'd thought I would. I'd spent a good chunk of the afternoon with the rest of the test subjects, but we were all sent to our individual suites for dinner and whatever entertainment we wanted to use to fill up the rest of the evening. Why Dr. Richards and her staff saw the need to separate us when we'd already spent hours and hours together, I didn't know. Some kind of psychological torture? I wouldn't put it past them, although the arrangement could have simply been for logistical reasons. People came and went over the course of the afternoon, depending on whether they had any "tests" scheduled with one of the three doctors assigned to Project Daedalus, and so having us all share a cafeteria-style meal might have been impractical.

Whatever the reason, I had to sit by myself and eat a simple meal of grilled chicken breast, rice, and steamed vegetables on my own, and I had no choice but to maintain that solitary state when I relocated to the sofa and watched several back-to-back episodes of *The Mandalorian* on TV before I decided I was tired enough to crash. And crash I did, so hard that when I woke up, I had to lie in bed and blink at the smooth white ceiling overhead for a few seconds before I remembered I wasn't in the little house I'd rented in Riverton, but buried underground in a place that hardly anyone even knew existed.

A digital clock sat on the bedside table. The readout told me it was a little after seven, meaning I'd slept for nearly nine hours. However, I didn't feel particularly rested, but rather keyed up, nervous, my brain already racing with possibilities about what Dr. Richards and her team had planned for me that day.

Since there wasn't much I could do about their schemes, I resolved to take care of myself as best I could and worry about Michelle Richards when the time came.

At least I wouldn't have to deal with Randall Lenz.

Despite getting nine hours of sleep, I really could have used some coffee that morning, or even some strong tea. But the only thing available was herb tea, so I heated water in the microwave and made a cup of Lemon Zinger. The cupboard had been stocked with multiple varieties of instant oatmeal, seeming to indicate that I was on my own for breakfast. While the tea was steeping, I made myself some cinnamon and spice oatmeal, and after I was done with my breakfast, I went ahead and took a shower. All of my toiletries from the house in Riverton had been transferred to the suite, so, while I didn't have to worry about using unfamiliar shampoo or moisturizer, I still couldn't quite prevent myself from getting creeped out at the thought of Agent Lenz and his team efficiently looting my house while I lay there, unconscious. Or had they spirited me out right away, and gone back later to fetch my things?

Hard to say, and I doubted the man in question intended to give me any straight answers about what had actually happened that night.

But I had to admit I felt a little better with some tea and food inside me, my hair and face and body clean. I didn't know what the doctor and her team had planned for me, so I dressed simply in a pair of jeans and a dark green V-neck T-shirt, my favorite pair of black flats on my feet.

Only about five minutes after I was done

getting dressed, the door chime sounded. This time, I wasn't caught quite so off guard, was able to walk calmly over to the door and say, "Dr. Richards?"

Her voice emerged from the same hidden speaker as the day before. "Good morning, Addie. Are you ready to get started?"

I really wasn't, but I guessed that answering in the negative probably wasn't an option. "Sure."

The door opened to reveal Dr. Richards standing outside the hallway, a man probably some ten years younger next to her, with a couple of burly guys who looked like they lifted tractors in their spare time waiting a few paces beyond. Guards, I assumed, so I wouldn't attempt a jail break.

"This is Dr. Woodrow," she said, pointedly leaving out any introductions to the two body-guards. "He'll be working with us this morning."

"Hi, Addie," he said, offering me a quick smile. He had light brown hair and bright blue eyes, and his overall demeanor seemed almost too relaxed for this sort of setting. I could much more easily imagine him in a T-shirt and board shorts rather than the blue button-up and tie he wore under his white lab coat.

For all I knew, Dr. Richards had hired him precisely because she'd wanted someone on her team who would put the test subjects at ease.

However, I pushed the notion aside and allowed myself to send him a smile in return. "Hi, Dr. Woodrow."

"We'll be asking some questions, getting some of your history to supplement the physical tests we performed yesterday," Dr. Richards said then in her brisk, no-nonsense way. "After that, we'll head up to one of our outdoor areas for some practical tests."

Practical tests? I didn't think I liked the sound of that. Was she really expecting me to produce tornadoes on demand?

I didn't ask. No doubt, I'd find out soon enough.

She gestured for me to come into the hallway, and I did so, trying not to show how reluctant I was. Even though all of the other test subjects had reassured me the day before that the tests of their abilities weren't a big deal, were even sometimes sort of fun, I didn't know whether I could entirely believe their assessment. For one thing, none of the others possessed a gift as big and as ferocious as mine. Even though Joanna had shown me how to control it, my magic still held within it the power to cause a great deal of destruction, and I didn't want it used as a weapon against innocent people.

The three of us headed to the elevator, then ascended several floors. We emerged on a level that looked just as institutional as the others, although the hallways there were more crowded, had quite a few people going to and fro. Some wore white lab coats, like Dr. Woodrow and Dr. Richards, while others were dressed in corporate-looking attire, the men in dress shirts and ties, the women in slacks and blouses and the occasional skirt. To tell the truth, if I hadn't known I was in a subterranean government lab, I would have thought I was walking the halls of a medical complex somewhere.

Dr. Richards led me into a large office furnished with a shiny metal and glass desk and several metal bookcases filled with what appeared to be scientific texts. She sat down behind the desk, while Dr. Woodrow took one of the chairs placed in front of it and then inclined his head toward the other one. The guards remained outside in the hall.

"Go ahead, take a seat," he said.

There wasn't much for me to do except sit down. The chair's seat wasn't very well padded, and I had a feeling it would start to get downright uncomfortable if I had to perch there for very long. Maybe that was part of the plan.

Dr. Richards opened up a sleek laptop that sat on her desk. "I just need to get a little bit of your history," she said, brown eyes narrowing behind her glasses as she began to enter something into the computer. "How old were you when you first began to notice your unusual connection with the weather?"

I could have lied, but I honestly didn't know how much data they had on me. Some of the comments Randall Lenz had made previously led me to think they'd been tracking me for some time. Maybe not all the way back to when I was a kid, and yet it didn't take a genius to realize that the pattern of my life had shifted abruptly in my tenth year. Before then, we'd only lived in two different towns, Truth or Consequences and Tucumcari, both in New Mexico, but as soon as the weather started going haywire around me, my mother and I had moved about twice per year on average, mostly in Utah, with a few forays into the western edges of Colorado and the southeast stretches of Wyoming.

"I was ten," I said. "Around ten and a half."

"And how long did it take for you to realize that your emotions were having a direct effect on the weather?"

Jesus. I didn't even know how I was supposed to answer that question. It wasn't as though I suddenly woke up one day and realized that every time I got horribly upset about something, tornadoes appeared from nowhere and hundred-year storms rained down destruction wherever I lived. No, it was more like a gradual, sneaking suspicion, a dread which only gained more power as I saw the growing fear in my mother's eyes, the hideous worry that something was horribly wrong with her only child.

"I don't know for sure," I said. "My mother and I really didn't talk about it at first."

"And yet she started moving you almost right away."

I could only shrug in response to her statement. A few feet away, Dr. Woodrow was listening intently, but unlike Dr. Richards, he wasn't taking any notes. His expression appeared sympathetic, although I didn't know whether I could really trust his reactions. They also could have been playing some kind of good cop/bad cop game, although to what end, I had no idea.

"I think she was scared," I said. My hands tightened on the knees of my jeans, but I kept my tone steady as I added, "I'd say you could talk to her and find out firsthand what she was thinking…except you can't do that now, thanks to Randall Lenz."

For a long moment, Dr. Richards didn't reply. She only sat there at her desk, eyes opaque behind the lenses of her glasses. Next to me, Dr. Woodrow shifted uncomfortably in his chair, although he remained quiet, as if he knew better than to say anything before his boss had spoken.

At last, she said, "That was…unfortunate. I

can assure you that Agent Lenz had absolutely no intention of causing any harm to you or your mother."

"Maybe he didn't," I returned, "but that's what happened. And, as far as I can tell, it doesn't seem as if any of you are too concerned about what his supposed 'accident' did to my mother, or to my life."

"We can discuss compensation at a later date —" she began, and my eyebrows lifted in disbelief that she would be so callous as to even think that was an appropriate response.

"What, you're trying to pay me off for murdering my mother?"

"It was an accidental discharge," Dr. Richards said. Her voice was nearly as flat as mine. "The incident has been investigated, and Agent Lenz was found not to be at fault. A tragic accident, of course, but you need to understand that of course he didn't intend for any of that to happen."

He'd said pretty much the same thing to me. And I'd believed him, mostly because I couldn't see how it was in his best interests to make me hostile toward him from the outset. No, his life would have been much easier if he hadn't given me any reason not to be cooperative.

As far as the supposed "investigation" Dr. Richards had mentioned went, I had no idea whether she was telling me the truth or not. True, usually there was some sort of internal review when a federal agent was involved in a deadly shooting, and yet the agency Randall Lenz worked for was so secret, I didn't know whether they were bound to the same rules as the FBI or your standard police department. It wasn't as if anyone had asked me, as an eyewitness, for my input on what had happened.

"Anyway," the doctor went on, her tone a bit gentler as she seemed to realize I wasn't going to offer any further protests on the subject, "you moved quite a bit from the time you were ten years old to the time when you ended up in your last home in Kanab, Utah. Can you tell me why things were more stable there?"

Damn it—I already felt exhausted, and I knew it wasn't even nine o'clock in the morning yet. I gave a weary shrug and said, "I don't know. No major upsets, I guess. I was going to the local U of U campus in Kanab and working at the same diner where my mother worked. I had my head down and was just trying to finish my coursework so I could graduate."

"But on the afternoon of June fifth, something did upset you," Dr. Woodrow said, speaking for the first time.

I nodded, even as my gut clenched at the recollection. The letter from the student aid office…the dark clouds that had formed over our tiny rented house as the anger and worry swirling in me had reached out to the skies and disturbed the air currents there.

"They denied my student aid," I said. "I was angry." *And that anger painted a nice big target right on me and my mother....*

Dr. Richards typed something into her laptop. "Understandable. So, that was the first time you were extremely upset during your time in Kanab?"

"Yes." Sure, I'd had minor irritations to deal with, but nothing that had caused the level of anger the letter from the student aid office had instigated. I couldn't even say exactly why I'd been so furious. After all, once I'd calmed down, I realized I had several options to explore, even if none of them were exactly optimal. Problem was, I'd wasted so much time and energy going back and forth with the people in the school's student aid department that the thought it had all come to nothing in the end was enough to make me blow a gasket.

"Are you angry with us now?" Dr. Woodrow asked.

I shifted on my chair to look over at him. His expression showed nothing except lively interest. Mouth curling a bit, I said, "Take me out where I can talk to the weather, and we'll find out."

His jaw clenched slightly, and I thought I saw a flicker of worry in those bright blue eyes.

"Now, Addie," Dr. Richards said, her tone just this side of scolding. "There's no need for that."

"I was just making a suggestion," I replied without blinking.

Something shifted in her expression, but I couldn't say exactly what. She obviously had years of practice keeping her thoughts to herself, and I doubted she would allow an amateur like me to see anything more than what she wanted me to see. "A good suggestion, actually," she said as she shut her laptop, then got to her feet. "I think it's time to go outside and see what you can do."

"Great," I replied, although inwardly I wasn't very thrilled at the idea of being put through my paces like some sort of show pony. Besides, I'd intimated to Randall Lenz that I didn't actually have very much control over my gift. Despite the veiled threat I'd made just a moment earlier, I didn't want to hurt anyone. On the other hand, I also didn't want to make it seem as if I knew what I was doing. I'd have to walk a very fine line, and I honestly didn't even know whether I was up to the task. It wasn't as though I'd had many opportunities to actually work with my ability. Mostly, I'd done my best to keep it in check and prevent it from causing any further calamities.

But there didn't seem to be any way to wriggle out of my current predicament, so I got up from my chair while Dr. Woodrow rose as well, and the three of us left Dr. Richards' office to head to the elevator once again, burly guards tagging along for the ride. This time, it rose all the way to the surface, once again disgorging us in an anony-mous-looking lobby. However, Dr. Richards didn't lead me to the same courtyard as before, but instead took me down a long corridor, one that opened on a large grassy field enclosed in a high cinderblock wall. On the other side of the wall, tall trees waved in the wind, their leaves glistening in the bright sunlight. If anything, the air was even warmer than it had been the day before, hot and damp and smelling of grass and something else I couldn't identify, thick and heavy, moist as the air itself.

However, all thought of my surroundings quickly vanished as I focused on the tall figure standing off to one side, his dark suit an incon-gruous note against all that bright green.

I turned on Dr. Richards, not bothering to hide my irritation. "I thought you said Agent Lenz didn't work with the test subjects."

Just a hint of a smile on her mouth, which was coated in a neutral pinkish-brown lipstick. "No, that's what our other guests told you. As a rule, they were correct. But he wanted to observe this session."

Anger flared in me, sharp and hot. Almost immediately, I could feel the currents in the air pick up, beginning to swirl above us. Had that been their plan—to provoke me with Randall Lenz's presence, knowing I would react negatively?

Well, if that was the case, I'd have to make sure I disappointed them.

At once, I took in a breath and fixed a neutral expression on my face as he approached. The air around me calmed, and I allowed myself a hint of inner satisfaction. I might have been worried and upset…but I hadn't lost control. So far, it seemed as if Joanna's teachings were sticking with me.

"Good morning, Adara," Agent Lenz said. "Did you sleep well?"

"Very," I responded coolly. "So, you're going to observe today? I would have thought you'd prefer to maintain a safe distance when I'm working with my power."

Like Dr. Richards, Randall Lenz was a professional. The pleasant expression he wore didn't shift an inch, although I noticed he squinted slightly, as if his pale blue eyes couldn't handle the bright glare of the June sun overhead. "Not at all," he said. "I'm quite eager to see what you can do in controlled circumstances."

I glanced over at Dr. Richards and Dr. Woodrow. He stood about a foot behind her, obviously deferring to his superior. "But I don't have any control," I told him. "Not really. That's the problem."

"And that's what we're going to work on," Dr. Richards said. "But first, I'd like a demonstration of raw power." From inside the pocket of her lab coat, she brought out a photograph and handed it to me. "How does this make you feel?"

Mystified, I took the photo from her and stared down at it. For a second, I didn't even recognize what I was looking at—I saw flowers, and green grass.

And a bare patch in that grass, about six feet long and three feet wide. No headstone yet, of course; it took time to order those things and have them engraved with the proper information.

I was looking at my mother's grave.

An aching mixture of anger and sorrow rose within me, and once again, I could feel the air begin to waken and stir as those emotions rode the current of my magic all the way into the sky. This time, though, I didn't try to hold it back, to allow the wind and the weather to continue undisturbed by the storm raging within me.

They wanted a demonstration?

Fine…they'd get one.

From nowhere, clouds came boiling toward us, building up even as we watched, darkening the sky so that day seemed almost night. A furious wind tore at our clothes and hair, mussing Dr. Richards' precise bob and rippling the hem of Dr. Woodrow's lab coat. Randall Lenz's hair was cut too short to be much disturbed, although his tie whipped in the wind before he reached up to calmly hold it against his chest until the tempest had passed.

Thunder growled, and the damp air grew even more moist, thick and heavy against my skin. A cold drop hit my cheek, then another.

And a bolt of lightning flashed from the heavy clouds, striking the grass a hundred paces off. The sharp scent of ozone flared in my nostrils, and Dr. Woodrow muttered a curse under his breath, although both Agent Lenz and Dr. Richards remained silent as they watched the spectacle. A few feet away, the two guards watched the display with faces so impassive, they might have been carved from stone.

As quickly as it had come, the storm began to dissolve, the clouds blowing away on the wind. Within a minute, the day was bright again, the only sign that the clouds had been there at all a small charred patch on the green grass of the field where we stood.

"It made me angry," I said, and handed the photo back to Dr. Richards.

She took it from me and returned it to her pocket. "That was…very impressive."

"Glad to oblige."

Randall Lenz hadn't moved an inch. If he'd been at all disturbed by standing so close to a lightning bolt, he didn't show any sign of it. When he spoke, his voice was calm, almost amused. "I told you she was very strong."

"I can see that," Dr. Richards said. Her gaze flicked toward me. "Addie, what did it feel like when you were angry and the storm came?"

I shrugged. "I'm not sure if I can really explain it. Something upsets me, and it's like the emotions inside talk to the storm outside."

"So, you don't create the storms from nothing?" Dr. Woodrow asked then, even as a small flicker of irritation appeared in Dr. Richard's face. Apparently, she would have preferred to ask that question herself.

"I don't think so," I said. No point in giving everything away; I would have to do my best to be vague while at the same time providing just enough information that they wouldn't get frustrated by my lack of response. "I think I just kind of work with whatever's already there."

"The sky was clear," Dr. Woodrow pointed out.

"Well, it *looked* clear," I told him. "But there's always moisture in the air. Things are always moving on the wind. I guess my gift just works with that. Don't ask me how, though. I've spent the last fourteen years doing my best to not think about it, to keep it from taking over my life."

Dr. Richards' mouth turned down for just the

briefest instant before her expression smoothed itself again. Clearly, she didn't think I'd done a very good job at preventing my strange talent from affecting my life. In that one thing, I was inclined to agree with her.

"We'll figure out how it works," she assured me. "For now, let's try for a little control. With many of our other subjects, all that was required was some work on focus. Mindfulness techniques tend to work very well."

"'Mindfulness'?" I repeated. I knew I'd seen the phrase in some of the self-help books my mother always had lying around, but since I'd never read any of them, I honestly didn't know what it meant.

"Paying attention to the here and now," Randall Lenz said then. I was a little startled by that particular contribution to the conversation, since I'd gotten the impression that he didn't have much to do with the day-to-day training of the facility's inmates. However, I didn't say anything, only stood there and waited for him to go on. "Our minds like to jump ahead to the future, to imagining contingencies and worst-case scenarios. Mindfulness trains you to remain focused on what's in front of you."

Had he trained himself in that kind of mental focus? Was that why he'd fixed on me like some sort of guided missile and hadn't let go? I didn't dare ask him those questions, not with Dr. Richards and Dr. Woodrow listening to everything we said, but I had to wonder.

"I have some guided meditations that will help," Dr. Richards said. She might have been irritated by the way Agent Lenz had inserted himself in the conversation, or she might not. Her expression once again was pleasant, neutral, impossible to read. "You can access them from the entertainment console in your suite. They've been very effective for our other guests."

Prisoners, I corrected her mentally, but I only nodded. And all right, the rest of the test subjects didn't seem that upset about being trapped there, but that was simply because they had no idea who they really were, that they all had families in the witch world, connections they didn't even know existed. They'd lived such lonely lives…but it didn't have to be that way.

"Anything else?" I asked. "You want me to call a tornado or something?"

"Could you?" Dr. Richards responded with the slightest lift of an eyebrow.

Actually, I could, although I knew better than to answer with the truth. "I've done it in the past," I said, replying without really replying. "But only when I was really upset."

A nod as she absorbed that particular piece of information. "I don't think it's necessary at the moment. Better for you to learn some focus first. After all, we don't want a tornado flattening half the complex, do we?"

Probably not. Then again, although from the outside, the SED's facility looked like a normal office complex, I knew there was far more to it than met the eye. Even if one of my tornadoes managed to level all the visible structures, there would be far more that survived underground.

About all I could do was shrug in answer to her question, which I guessed had been mostly rhetorical.

"I'd also suggest that you should talk to our other guests," Dr. Richards went on. "I think they'll be able to provide a great deal of insight on how to gain control over your talent. Like you, they all had to come to that control gradually. It wasn't something they understood by instinct."

Again, pretty much the same thing both Jake and Joanna had told me about my powers. Dr. Richards and her team were on the right track, even if they had no idea that the people they were working with just happened to be a bunch of witches and warlocks.

"Okay," I said. "They were all very nice yesterday, so I'm sure they'd be happy to give me some advice."

"Oh, they will," Dr. Richards replied. "All you have to do is ask. In fact, I'll take you down to the lounge now. It's a little early, but most of them will be up and about." A glance over at Randall Lenz, and she added, "That is, if it's all right with you, Agent Lenz. Did you have anything else planned for Addie today?"

"Not at the moment," he said.

That response made me want to sag with relief. Although I thought I'd maintained fairly well during this particular go-'round, I definitely didn't want to spend any more time in his company than I absolutely had to.

He must have detected some shift in my expression, though, because almost at once he went on with a faint smile, "But that doesn't preclude another meeting later on. In the meantime, have a good day."

A nod at Dr. Richards and me—he basically ignored Dr. Woodrow and the two bodyguards—and then he turned and headed back into the building.

Damn it. I should have known Randall Lenz wouldn't let me off that easy.

9

RANDALL LENZ PAUSED THE VIDEO ONCE more at the exact moment when the lightning bolt speared the ground of the facility's north field. Its glare turned all their faces dead white—and quite clearly revealed the look of terror on Alec Woodrow's features. Even though the entire team had been briefed on what to expect from Adara Grant, it seemed obvious enough that Woodrow still hadn't been anticipating quite such a display...or at least, not one in his immediate vicinity.

Well, he'd know to be a bit more on his toes in the future.

However, Dr. Woodrow wasn't his immediate concern. The man was generally competent, although he didn't take matters quite as seriously as Randall Lenz would have liked. No, he instead kept replaying that scene with Adara in his mind, the way she'd claimed she didn't know exactly how her powers worked, that she had no real control over them and they lashed out whenever she was troubled or angry or afraid. Her reaction to the photo Dr. Richards had shown her seemed genuine enough…but at the same time, he couldn't help wondering if Ms. Grant had manufactured the entire display, had given them what she thought they wanted from her.

Showing Adara her mother's grave had been a piece of casual cruelty he hadn't quite expected. While he couldn't entirely approve of Michelle Richards' decision to do so, he wouldn't argue that the stratagem had produced some interesting results.

He just wasn't sure whether he could trust those particular results.

His finger touched the mouse, and the scene continued. The north field's hidden surveillance equipment had picked up both sound and video, but on this replay, he'd turned down the sound, not wanting to be distracted by their words when instead he was focusing on the minute shifts in Adara Grant's expression, the subtle tells that might provide some clue as to what was going on inside her head.

For someone trapped in a situation that was none of her choosing, she appeared remarkably self-possessed, as if she held some secret knowledge within her that allowed her to believe her tenure in the Daedalus Program would be of short duration.

Something to do with the mysterious Jake? Very possibly, especially since the man seemed to have disappeared off the face of the planet. No one matching his description could be found in the government's databases of known foreign operatives, Russian or otherwise, but Dawson was still meticulously sifting through what data she had to work with, hoping against hope that just maybe, she might stumble across something useful. So frustrating to know the man was out there somewhere, and yet the best analysts in the world couldn't seem to pin down his location.

The video was nearing the end of the little convo they'd all shared while standing out in the north field. Once again, Lenz paused it, this time so he could study the expression on Adara's face. It was right when he'd informed her that he didn't see any need to work with her further that day. Yes, the relief that flashed in her eyes was obvious, although her features had gone still immediately afterward, as if she'd realized she'd given away too much. And then, a minute later, just as he offered the not-so-subtle threat of seeing her later on, he couldn't help noting the way her lips had pressed together and her slender body had gone rigid.

No, she had no love for him, that much was obvious.

Which was to be expected. He knew there was no point in protesting to her that he'd never intended her mother any harm. She wouldn't believe a word of it, and besides, her antipathy didn't necessarily need to create a barrier between them. The wound was still raw and new, but he hoped that once she'd settled into her life here at the facility, she'd realize she was in the only place she logically could have ended up. No worries about her gift causing harm to herself or anyone around her, all her needs provided for, similarly gifted people as her companions…everything that had been uncertain in her previous life would be taken care of here.

All the same, he thought they had better clear the air between them.

He reached for the phone on his desk and entered Dr. Richards' extension. It rang a few times, then made the faint click that told him he was being transferred to another extension. A moment later, a woman's voice answered.

"Corey Liu."

Corey was one of the lab techs who worked the overnight shift. Lenz glanced down at his watch and saw it was almost seven, telling him that Michelle Richards was long gone for the day. She rarely stayed past five-thirty.

Well, no matter. He certainly didn't need Dr. Richards' permission to conduct an interview with one of the test subjects.

"Randall Lenz here. Could you bring Adara Grant to my office?"

Not even a hesitation, which he appreciated. "Of course, Dr. Lenz. I'll have her up there in less than ten minutes."

"Thank you, Ms. Liu."

He hung up then, wondering if he was interrupting Adara in the middle of her dinner. All of the test subjects were given their evening meals sometime between six-thirty and seven-thirty, but he didn't know where she'd ended up in the rotation. However, it was a risk he was willing to take. She could always eat after he was done speaking with her, if she hadn't done so already.

Exactly eight minutes later, the intercom on his phone buzzed. "Corey Liu and Adara Grant to see you, Agent Lenz," came the voice of Lionel McGraw, the evening security guard on duty.

"Send them in," Lenz responded.

A moment passed, and then Ms. Liu and Adara Grant appeared at the open door to his office. Adara was wearing her studiously expressionless face again, which told him she was less than pleased by the summons.

"Here's Ms. Grant, sir," Liu said, quite unnecessarily. But she was young and energetic, and generally wanted to make sure she followed all the protocols, even if the current situation didn't call for them.

"Thank you, Ms. Liu," he replied. "I'll be in touch when it's time to take Ms. Grant back to her apartment. You can close the door as you leave."

The tech inclined her head. "Of course, sir."

She went out, shutting the door behind her as requested. Adara remained standing a scant foot inside the office, her expression now wary, slender form rigid, reminding him of a wild animal caught in a pair of headlights and trying to decide whether or not it would be safe to bolt.

"Please sit down, Ms. Grant," he said pleasantly.

For a second or two, she hesitated. Then she seemed to realize it probably wasn't worth the effort to challenge him on such a minor request, and she went ahead and took a seat in the chair that faced his desk. Her fingers gripped the armrests, pale against the black leather. He saw the way her gaze flickered around the office, apparently taking in the sleek modern furniture, the framed photos of black and white cityscapes— New York, Washington, D.C., Los Angeles, Chicago. Possibly the slightest flare of surprise as that gaze settled on the single personal item in the space, a photograph of Lenz and his parents from his freshman year of college...the last year the world could still be called normal.

"Is that your family?" she asked.

He'd already decided to be frank with her on some topics, mostly because he didn't see the harm...and also because anything he could do to establish some sort of rapport between them would, he hoped, make her more manageable as a test subject.

"Yes," he replied. "That was taken when I was just about to start school at Columbia University."

She appeared to absorb that information, inquiring, "You're from New York?"

"Yes. I grew up in Manhattan."

"You don't sound like you're from New York."

He allowed himself a smile. "Is that a compliment?"

"Just an observation."

So wary. He could see it in the tension in her shoulders, the way her gaze flicked from one side to the other. A beautiful girl, actually, he thought with some surprise, as if just noticing her appearance for the first time. He'd been so intent on making sure he found her and made her part of the program that he honestly hadn't paid any attention to her looks.

Not that she interested him sexually. She was far too young, and making any sort of advance on a test subject would be the very worst abuse of his power. Still, he could see why Jake—whoever he was—might have had an interest in her that wasn't entirely professional.

"Is your family still in New York?" she asked next. He could tell she was probing because she wanted to see when he would decide to shut her down.

Well, he would allow the questions…up to a point. "My mother is."

"Your father moved away?"

"Not exactly," Lenz replied, voice level. Odd how the pain was still there, so many years later. "He was working in the North Tower when the first airplane hit."

That comment only elicited a puzzled frown, and he had to remind himself of how young Adara Grant actually was. She would have been barely more than a toddler at the time.

"During 9/11," he explained, and the frown disappeared, replaced by a look of startled sympathy.

"Oh, I'm sorry," she said at once.

"It's been almost twenty years," he replied, which he knew wasn't much of a response but better than nothing. "But you can understand why I went to work for Homeland Security."

A nod. She let go of the chair's arms and settled her hands in her lap. "I still don't see how people who can move things with their minds or change their appearance or even summon storms have much to do with national security."

Was she really that naïve? No, a second passed, and he thought he noted a slight gleam in her eyes. She was only pretending to not understand in the hope that he might let something slip he didn't intend to.

Well, he'd been playing this game too long to make an amateur mistake like that. At the same time, he didn't see the harm in doing his best to make her understand why she was here…why all of them were here.

"You and your fellow guests have extraordinary abilities, Ms. Grant," he said. Her mouth twitched at his use of the euphemism "guests," but she didn't call him out on it, only sat there and waited for him to go on. "As I told you at our first meeting, those abilities can make a great deal of a difference when it comes to making this nation more secure. First, of course, you all need to become more acquainted with your talents, so they come to you as easily as breathing. This is why Dr. Richards suggested the mindfulness exercises. Have you tried any yet?"

"A couple of them," Adara replied. "Natalie and Ethan sat down with me and walked me through a few this afternoon." A lift of her shoulders, and he realized she'd put on a cardigan over the T-shirt she'd been wearing when she met him on the north field earlier that day. "I think I can see the benefit. I was going to try again after I ate." She paused there, frowning slightly. "Not that you gave me the opportunity. They'd just delivered my food when your assistant showed up."

"My apologies," he said. "You can have a late dinner when you go back, but I wanted to speak with you."

"About?"

"I thought we might revisit the subject of your benefactor Jake."

The frown deepened. "I've already told you everything I know."

"You told me a story, true. I'm fairly certain it wasn't the real one."

Her arms crossed, and she settled against the back of the chair. A protective gesture, although Lenz wasn't sure whether she was protecting herself...or the mysterious Jake. "You can think what you want, Agent Lenz," she said. "I told you what happened. I have no idea why he did what he did—why he came for me in the first place, or why he thought it was safe to leave me in Riverton for a few days. Or at least, I've already given you my possible explanations. You probably know a lot more about undercover operatives than I do, so you tell me."

The challenging note in her voice was clear

enough, but he didn't take offense. Actually, he thought he almost admired her for going on the attack and hoping the stratagem would take him off guard.

However, he knew better than to fall for a ploy such as that.

And whoever "Jake" was, Lenz could be almost certain that he wasn't a spy. There had been a flash of shock and worry in his eyes when Lenz confronted him on the doorstep of Adara Grant's modest rented home in Kanab. It had been the look of a man who'd run into something he hadn't been expecting. If Jake really was a Russian operative…or a mercenary…he would have known there was a good chance that other parties would be interested in someone with Adara's abilities, and would have planned accordingly.

He said, his tone mild, "We don't have to be enemies, Ms. Grant."

Her fingers tightened on her arm. An unconscious gesture, he knew, but one that gave away her worry, her inner fear that nothing she said or did would be enough to put him off the scent. Still, her voice was cool as she replied, "After what you did to my mother, I don't think we can be anything else."

There it was. He reminded himself that her grief was still very fresh—that terrible day was only two weeks in the past—and that he needed to give her more time.

"I'm sorry to hear that," he said. "I understand, however. Just try to remember that none of it would have happened if Jake hadn't intervened. You were planning to go with me peacefully."

Now her knuckles stood out white against the black cardigan she wore. Tone ragged, she said, "Is there anything else? I'm tired and hungry, and I want to go back to my room."

No reason to push things any further. He'd planted a seed in her mind, and now it was time to let it alone and see if it would eventually bear fruit.

"Of course," he said. "I won't keep you any longer."

He pushed the intercom button on his phone. "Ms. Liu, you can come and take Ms. Grant back to her apartment."

Almost at once, Corey Liu was at the door. She led Adara out—but not before he caught a glimpse of the doubt and worry in his test subject's eyes.

Good.

Time to wait.

His phone *bing*ed, and Jake startled awake,

dislodging Taffy, who'd taken advantage of his distraction to jump on the bed and fall asleep on his feet. She landed on the rug with an offended shake, then shook herself again before trotting out into the hall.

No time to worry about the dog, though. The display on his phone told him it was nearly two in the morning, and there was only one reason he'd be getting a text message at that hour.

I'm in, was all the message said, but that was enough.

Excitement sang through his veins, and his hands shook slightly as he texted back, *On my way. Be there in 10.*

Sooner than that, probably, but he knew he'd have to pause long enough to put on some pants.

His jeans were still slung across the chair where he'd left them when he went to bed, so he grabbed them and slipped them on, leaving his Lumberyard Brewing Company T-shirt untucked. Shoes and socks seemed like way too much of an effort, but there was a pair of flip-flops handy near the closet door, and he slid into them just before hurrying out of his bedroom.

Taffy was in the kitchen, getting a drink of water. The dog gave him some serious side-eye as he headed for the back door, as if asking what the hell he was doing going out at the time of night.

"No time to explain, kiddo," he said, although

he paused long enough to give her a brief pat on the head. "I'll be back to feed you, though."

After delivering that promise, he went out the back door and hurried down the path to the detached garage. For just a second, the boxy white shape of the Jeep Wrangler parked there took him aback before he reminded himself that he'd gotten rid of his Gladiator in exchange for the much more anonymous Wrangler.

At least he'd already gotten the seat and mirrors where he wanted them, so he didn't have to waste valuable time making adjustments. Within the minute, he was backing out of the driveway, reminding himself not to take off in a squeal of tires and thereby wake the neighbors.

The distance to Trident HQ had never felt so great, even though the place was only about five minutes away. Soon enough, he was pulling up to the curb, since Jeremy's Dodge truck was already parked in the driveway.

Jake got out of the Jeep and hurried along the front walk, then practically ran up the porch steps. When he entered the house, he saw that the front room with all its Mac Pros was still empty, but the door to the PC lab now stood open.

"Hey," Jeremy said as Jake stuck his head in the room. He looked like hell—shadows under his eyes, a darker scruff than usual obscuring his cheeks and chin, hair sticking out in all directions

—but at the same time, triumph was clear in his expression. "Take a look."

He pushed his chair away from the computer desk where he sat, allowing Jake a clearer view of the screen in front of him. It showed a quadrant of different scenes—a long hallway, what looked like a reception or guard desk with a pretty Asian woman seated at it, an elevator, a dimly lit room where a man appeared to be sleeping.

"This is the facility?" Jake asked.

"Yep," Jeremy replied.

"Who's the guy?"

"I think it's Ethan Sitko. He's one of the test subjects—you know, the guy who's been there for three years."

While that nugget of information was mildly interesting, it didn't answer the question foremost in Jake's mind. "Where's Addie?"

"Don't worry—she's there," Jeremy replied. "You need to be patient. This feed cycles through a bunch of different cameras, and I didn't want to start messing with the sequence and possibly alert someone that their system isn't quite as secure as they think it is."

While Jake could understand his brother's caution, he wanted to scream with impatience as the security feed traded one set of images for another, none of them showing Addie. At last, though, he caught a glimpse of her, lying soundly asleep on what appeared to be a king-size bed, dark hair spread out on the white pillowcase.

He remembered waking up to see those same silky tresses covering the pillow next to him, and his gut clenched with worry. But she seemed fine, as far as he could tell. It was hard to pick out many details because the room was dark, but the place where she was sleeping looked almost like a high-end hotel room or vacation condo. Clearly, his worries about her being locked in a cell or restrained in her bed had been unfounded.

"They all have suites like that," Jeremy remarked as he reached for the energy drink he'd left sitting off to one side. "Beats the hell out of the dorm room I stayed in my freshman year."

"So, they're taking good care of their prisoners," Jake replied, not bothering to keep the irritation out of his tone. "They're still prisoners."

A shrug. "Anyway, do you think that image is clear enough for Connor and Angela to work with?"

Jake had to hope so. But there was only one way to really find out. "I'll have to have them come over and take a look."

"Now? It's two in the morning."

"I know, but Connor told me to call him no matter what time it was."

His brother looked dubious. "Yeah, people always say stuff like that, but when you actually call them at 2 a.m., they're not quite so enthusiastic."

Maybe not, but it was a risk Jake was willing to take. He pulled his phone out of his pocket and went to his contacts list, then pressed the entry for Connor's cell phone. The matter was urgent enough that he didn't want to waste time with a text message.

The phone rang twice, and then Connor said, sounding sleepy, "Jake? Do you know what time it is?"

He really hated it when his brother was right. "Yeah, I know," Jake said. "But you said to call when Jeremy got into the system. Well, he's in, and we have a visual on Addie's position. We just need to know if it's clear enough for you and Angela to work with."

"Got it," Connor said, sounding much more awake than he'd been even a minute earlier. "I'll come take a look—we don't both need to be there for this, and it's better if Angela stays here with the kids. Otherwise, I'd have to wake someone else up to come watch them while we're gone."

Right. Jake tended to forget about all the logistics involved when children were included in the equation. Hopefully, one day he'd have to take those sorts of concerns into consideration himself, but for the moment, he needed to focus on getting Addie away from her captors. "No problem. We'll just hang tight until you get here."

"I'll be as fast as I can," Connor promised, then ended the call.

"He's on his way," Jake informed his brother.

Jeremy nodded. "I'll try playing with the resolution on this end. They have some good cameras, or the image wouldn't be as sharp as it is despite most of the rooms being dark, but there's always room for improvement."

He turned back to the computer and pulled up what looked like some kind of remote console, although Jake couldn't tell for sure what all the controls embedded in it were supposed to do. Apparently, Jeremy didn't have that sort of problem, because he fiddled with it for a moment and managed to make the picture both a little brighter and a little sharper. Now Jake saw that framed pictures hung on the wall—landscapes or seascapes of some sort—and a lamp with a rounded metal base sat on the nightstand.

More details…but would they be enough?

The image on the screen shifted, showing once again a hallway, empty at that hour. More of the prisoners' rooms. Somehow, even though Jake had seen their photos in the files Jeremy had unearthed on the SED's servers, catching a glimpse of them like this, asleep and defenseless, drove home to him even more that they were all individuals, people whose lives had been taken over by Randall Lenz's ruthless ambition.

"I hate this," Jake murmured, and Jeremy expelled a breath.

"Me, too. And maybe at some point, we'll be able to do something about it. For now, though, we need to worry about Addie."

True enough. He was about to reply to his brother's comment when a soft knock came at the front door, followed by Connor quietly easing himself into the house. "I'm here," he called out.

"In the PC lab," Jake replied.

The *primus* entered the room where the other two warlocks were waiting. His gaze went immediately to the screen in front of Jeremy. "Is that it?"

"Almost," Jeremy said. "We're waiting for it to cycle back to Addie."

Connor nodded and jammed his hands in his jeans pockets, tension clear in the set of his shoulders. He was wearing a pair of plaid flannel pajama bottoms, flip-flops, and a faded Northern Pines University T-shirt, and clearly had rolled out of bed without bothering to change or even comb his hair.

"There it is," Jake said as the image on the screen shifted once again to Addie's room.

The *primus* squinted at the image in question and rubbed at the dark scruff on his chin. "I don't know…there's not a lot of detail. I can't even tell what those pictures on the wall are supposed to be."

Exactly what Jake had been afraid of. "Are you sure? I mean, you can see the position of the bed and the table next to it. Shouldn't that be enough?"

"Not really. That could be any one of a thousand rooms. Without a really good look at the place, Angela and I would be putting ourselves at risk if we tried to teleport there."

Well, shit. Jake wanted to curse but knew it would be a waste of energy. He couldn't ask Connor and Angela to put themselves in danger because of his impatience. They had more to lose than most people.

"Hey, wait," Jeremy said then. "I think she's waking up."

Immediately, Jake's head swiveled back toward the screen. Sure enough, Addie had sat up in bed and was staring out into the darkened room as though she wasn't quite sure what she was looking at. Then she reached over and turned on the bedside lamp.

The light showed the soft tan paint on the wall, the watercolors of the seascapes, the muted beiges and blues and browns of the comforter on the bed. He looked over at Connor.

"Is that enough detail for you?"

"Definitely," he said, eyes fixed on the image.

Which shifted then to the next one in the rotation. That time, Jake went ahead and let himself curse.

"Fuck."

"It's all right," Connor said quickly. "I saw enough."

"I was just about to get a screen grab, too," Jeremy remarked, his tone morose. "Shitty timing."

"Really, it's okay." Connor scratched his chin again. "We don't both have to know where we're going as long as one of us does."

Jake didn't know whether he should allow himself to be hopeful. "Even when you're taking a third person along?"

"Even then."

"Still, we'll wait and see what happens when it swings back around again," Jeremy said.

That sounded a little too optimistic, but Jake didn't reply, only waited while the feed cycled through what felt like an interminable sequence of images before returning to Addie's room. The light was still on, allowing Connor to study the image once again and Jeremy to quickly perform a screen grab. A door in one of the walls opened, and Addie emerged. Although the space behind her was dark, Jake could make out just enough detail to realize it was the bathroom.

He supposed he should be grateful that there apparently weren't any surveillance cameras in there.

It hurt to watch her, though, to know she was standing there almost three thousand miles away and that there wasn't a damn thing he could do about it. She climbed back into bed and pulled up the covers. Something in her expression appeared almost resigned, and he wished he could reach through the screen to hold her and let her know she wasn't going to be a captive for much longer.

Connor seemed to detect something of his cousin's unease, because he clapped a hand on Jake's shoulder and said, "It's okay, Jake. We're going to get her. Now that we know where she is for sure, it won't be long. Tomorrow night, probably."

That felt like an eternity away, but Jake knew his cousin was only being cautious. Stealing Addie in the middle of the night seemed like the safest course, and Connor and Angela would have to make arrangements to have someone watch their kids while they were off making the rescue attempt. Probably, they'd have the kids stay with Margot, since they went over to play with Margot and Lucas' daughter Mia all the time. And since Lucas would be coming along anyway, doing so would make the arrangement that much neater.

The fewer people who knew what was going on, the better.

Still, a lot could happen in a day.

Hang on, Addie, he thought.

We're coming.

10

THE NEXT MORNING, DR. WOODROW CAME alone to take me to a small laboratory on the ground floor of the building. I didn't ask him where Dr. Richards was; something about her set my teeth on edge, and if I was going to be put through my paces, better to do it in the company of the much friendlier Dr. Woodrow. At the same time, I had to wonder about the third scientist on the team, the "Dr. Keegan" that Natalie had mentioned but who I had yet to actually meet. Was his area of specialty something that didn't mesh well with my particular talent, and so Dr. Richards had assigned me to Dr. Woodrow instead?

Maybe. I wouldn't bother to ask, since in the end, I supposed it probably didn't matter one way or another.

No, what mattered was that I got to sit in a room with real windows, and so I could see it was another sunny day there in Alexandria, Virginia. I wondered if the skies were just as blue thousands of miles away in Flagstaff. Probably bluer, if only because there wasn't much air pollution in northern Arizona, unlike the area around Washington, D.C.

"How are you today, Addie?" Dr. Woodrow asked. He had an iPad Pro lying on the table in front of him, presumably for taking notes.

"Fine," I replied, then added, "Getting sort of tired of oatmeal."

That response made his mouth quirk slightly. He actually was kind of good-looking, although even if I hadn't been with Jake, I would have considered him too old to be an object of interest, probably at least eight or nine years older than I was. Still, I realized he was still pretty young to be holding a position of such responsibility, and wondered how he'd managed to end up working for the SED.

"We'll have to do something about that," Dr. Woodrow said. "Actually, Dr. Richards should have shown you how to order breakfast and how to make special requests if you don't want the standard evening meal—there's a menu you can access through your entertainment console. I can show you how it works when I take you back to your suite."

"Thanks," I said. Why Michelle Richards had decided to let me eat instant oatmeal two days in a row—and didn't tell me that I could put in dinner requests—rather than giving me access to the same amenities as the rest of the test subjects, I wasn't sure. She definitely didn't seem to me like the sort of person who would overlook that kind of detail, which meant she must have done it on purpose. Testing me to see how long it would take for me to raise a stink?

Maybe.

"Have you had a chance to work on any of your mindfulness exercises?" Dr. Woodrow asked.

I nodded. "I had some time this morning after I finished getting ready."

This meeting was taking place much later than the one the day before, when I'd been taken out to the north field at nine in the morning. There had been a flashing message on the TV when I turned it on that informed me Dr. Woodrow would be coming to get me at eleven. Why so late, I didn't know, but the additional downtime had given me the opportunity to work through a couple of the exercises Dr. Richards had sent me. Actually, that might have been the whole point of giving me some extra space in my morning.

"Do you think they helped?" he asked.

I settled back in my seat and gazed across the table at Dr. Woodrow. His expression was open and friendly, but I didn't know whether he looked like that to put me at my ease or whether that was the way he always appeared. "There's really only one way to find out, isn't there?"

He didn't blink. "True enough. You can feel the weather from in here, can't you?"

"Sure. I'm not ten stories down…or however deep my room is."

I should have known he wouldn't rise to the bait. No reaction, no little twitches or tells to let me know whether my guess had been correct. He only gazed back at me, eyes as blue as the skies outside the window. "Well, then, let's see what you can do now that you have a little focus. You're not anxious or nervous this morning, are you?"

Maybe I should have been, but I wasn't. Just knowing I would be working only with Dr. Woodrow that morning had taken a huge mental weight from my mind. While I'd slept well enough the night before, except for one bathroom break, it had taken me a while to relax, to make myself stop thinking about my interview with Randall Lenz. I still couldn't quite figure out why he'd revealed so much of his personal history to me. To try to evoke some sympathy, to make me think he wasn't quite the villain he appeared to be?

Good luck with that. I wouldn't deny that he'd

experienced tragedy in his life, but a loss like the one he'd suffered wasn't enough to justify what he'd done to me, to my mother. I barely remembered anything about 9/11—I was a tiny kid at the time, and my main memories of the incident were of my mother being glued to the TV set afterward, her pretty face taut with worry as those horrific images of tall skyscrapers exploding into flames against a backdrop of an impossibly blue sky kept playing over and over again. It wasn't until I was much older and started learning about the tragedy in school that I realized how many people had lost their lives that day, how many families had been touched by those moments of terror.

Including Randall Lenz's family. It was horrible, but I wasn't about to feel sorry for him. If he really wanted to prove what a patriot he was, he could start with releasing everyone in the program…and I had a feeling that wasn't going to happen.

I crossed my hands on the tabletop and looked back at Dr. Woodrow. "No, I'm not feeling nervous or anxious."

"Good," he said. "Then I'd like to try something simple. Can you try reaching out to see if you can bring a cloud over the courtyard outside?"

Yes, that was a simple enough trick. Or rather, it was simple for me because Joanna had taught me how to let my powers go with the flow. Dr. Woodrow didn't know that, however, and I knew I had to make him think I was very new to all this.

"Well…." I hedged. Would biting my lip be too much? Probably, since it wasn't something I normally did.

"It's okay," he said, his tone soothing. "Think of your mindfulness exercises. Just be present in the idea of having a cloud move over us. There's no threat, nothing to worry about. Just let the weather talk to your gift."

The guy was good. Maybe Dr. Richards had chosen him for this kind of work because he had a nice voice, friendly, gentle. Even if I hadn't already been in control of my power, that voice of his might have convinced me I was.

Might as well give him some encouragement. I'd already determined that it was probably in my best interest to seem cooperative and to show some progress, so succeeding at this simple task really shouldn't be an issue.

The day was sunny, but there were a few clouds drifting lazily along a few miles to the east. I felt them in my mind, soft and cool and friendly, and coaxed one of them along, pushing it opposite the prevailing wind so that it came drifting overhead.

Outside, the bright sunshine beaming down

on the courtyard dimmed for a moment. Dr. Woodrow got up from his chair and went to the window so he could peer out. When he turned back toward me, he was smiling.

"Excellent, Addie."

"There's really a cloud?" I asked, my tone and expression as guileless as I could make them.

"See for yourself."

I stood up as well and went to the window. Sure enough, a small cloud floated directly overhead, just thick enough to block some of the sun. The leaves on the trees in the courtyard fluttered, telling me the wind was brisk enough that the cloud should have already started to move on... but it didn't, and instead remained fixed in position as though someone had pinned it to the bright blue sky above.

"Wow, it worked!"

"Of course, it did. You need to trust in your talent, Addie."

"I know," I said. "It's just...."

"Just what?"

"It's just that I've never had any control over it. It always scared me. But this...." I looked up at the cloud again, soft and innocent and white, as it floated overhead. "This is just fun."

"It can be fun," Dr. Woodrow said earnestly. "I'm not saying that our work here isn't important, but there's no reason why you can't enjoy what you're doing."

I nodded. "Okay. Anything else?"

"Can you make it rain? Just here in the courtyard and nowhere else?"

Again, that was a simple enough trick. But I made myself shake my head. "I don't know…."

"Try," he urged me. "It's just the two of us here. No one else is going to know if you tried and failed."

My glance moved to the iPad he'd left sitting on the table. "What about all the notes you're taking for Dr. Richards?"

"I won't mention it. I'll just write up the way you successfully moved that one cloud over here."

"Won't you get in trouble for falsifying a report?"

"I wouldn't call it falsifying. I'm only omitting a single piece of data."

He looked so earnest, blue eyes shining down into mine, that I couldn't help giving a reluctant chuckle. "Maybe you should have been a lawyer instead of a scientist."

That remark made him laugh outright. "I actually thought about it for a bit, but then I decided science was more up my alley."

"What kind of scientist are you, anyway?"

His smile faded slightly. "Behavioral psychologist. Of course, the work I do here is a bit far afield from the subject of my dissertation."

I could only imagine. Somehow, I had the feeling they weren't handing out many doctorates in ESP and telekinesis. "Well, most people end up doing something that doesn't have much to do with their degree."

"True enough. Give it a try, Addie."

"Okay."

I pulled in a breath and closed my eyes. Actually, I didn't have to do either of those things to reach out with my talent, but I figured I might as well put on a bit of a show for the doctor.

The cloud wasn't a big one, and yet I knew I wouldn't have any problem coaxing the water vapor within to coalesce, to form into drops of liquid. Not too much, nothing that would drench someone crossing the courtyard to get from one wing of the building to another. Just enough to show Dr. Woodrow that I'd learned how to control this small part of my talent.

Rain fell from the cloud, gentle, misty, beginning to dampen the concrete walkways outside. His eyes lit up with wonder as the paths grew wetter, although it still was a very gentle rain.

"Can you stop it now?"

I nodded. That would be much easier, actually, because the cloud really should never have dropped any rain at all. I could tell it was eager to ride with the wind and rejoin its brethren, so I let it go and watched as the shadowed courtyard grew bright with sunlight again, the spatter of rain on the walkways already beginning to dry out.

Dr. Woodrow was beaming. I honestly never thought I'd actually see someone smile broadly enough that "beaming" could even be applied to them, but I had the feeling if he'd been any happier about the results of our little experiment, he probably would have danced a jig. "That was excellent, Addie, excellent," he said. "How do you feel?"

"Fine," I told him, which was nothing more than the truth. Using my talents didn't appear to take any mental or physical toll—well, except for the times when I'd been rightfully worried about the consequences of bringing those powers to bear.

"No headache? Fatigue?"

"Nothing like that."

"Then I'd say those mindfulness exercises have worked out very well for you." He stepped away from the window and went back over to the table, although he didn't sit down, only picked up his iPad and touched something on the screen. "It's almost noon—would you like to go down to the multipurpose unit to spend time with the others? There'll be sandwiches for lunch."

"That sounds great," I said. Again, only the

truth. I didn't know what kind of sandwiches were being provided, but my meager meal of a small bowl of instant oatmeal hadn't done much to satisfy my appetite, and I was hungry.

"Then let's go."

He led me out of the lab, pausing only to secure the door behind him. His smile disappeared as soon as we were out in the hallway, almost as if he didn't want anyone we passed to know what a successful session we'd just had. Why, I couldn't guess, except I supposed it was possible that he simply wanted to avoid any conversations with his fellow researchers until he'd seen me safely down to the level where the rest of my fellow test subjects were currently residing.

After all, even though the small tests I'd just passed with flying colors had been innocuous enough, Dr. Woodrow knew all too well that my power was a dangerous one until I was safely underground.

Since he hadn't told me not to discuss those successful tests with the rest of the group, I cheerfully answered their questions as we all gathered in the multipurpose unit's conversation pit and chowed down on some of the best deli sandwiches I'd ever eaten. I didn't know who was doing the

SED's catering, but clearly that was one instance where my tax dollars were being put to good use.

"You're making quick progress," Natalie observed after swallowing a bite of pastrami on rye. "I didn't have that much control over my gift until I'd been working with Dr. Keegan for almost a week."

I gave a deprecating shrug. "Well, pushing clouds around probably isn't as much work as making yourself look like someone else."

"Don't sell yourself short," she said, then paused to take another bite of her sandwich. "You're doing really well."

"Thanks to you and Ethan helping me with those mindfulness exercises."

Ethan had been in the middle of swallowing some potato salad, so he couldn't reply right away. When he did, he sounded thoughtful. "I'm kind of surprised they helped so much. I mean, just like Natalie, I'd been doing the work for days and days before I had any sort of real control."

So much for trying to take it easy. Apparently, my attempt at subtlety hadn't been a very successful one. But I'd already done the work, so there wasn't much I could do except shrug and act as though none of it was a very big deal... although Natalie's and Ethan's reactions went a good way toward explaining why Dr. Woodrow had been so startled and happy with my accomplishments that morning.

"You're lucky you got to work with Dr. Woodrow," Lorna put in. She'd already finished her sandwich, but eyed a container of pasta salad wistfully before giving a small shake of her head, as if mentally scolding herself for wanting to eat anything else. "He's a real cutie. If I were twenty years younger…."

Natalie grinned, while Ethan and Matthew and a few of the other guys looked distinctly uncomfortable. "I think they call that fraternizing, Lorna," she said. "Big no-no."

"Maybe so, but a girl can still dream."

I had to smother a smile of my own. Yes, I'd already admitted to myself that Dr. Woodrow was attractive, and he seemed like a pretty nice guy… but he sure didn't compare to Jake Wilcox.

Then again, who could?

Right then, I ached for him so badly that I had to pick up my glass of iced tea and take a large swallow, hoping I could distract myself with the flavor of the cool, astringent liquid slipping down my throat. It didn't help much, unfortunately; I wanted to hear the sound of his voice, wanted to look into those velvety brown eyes with the friendly crinkles at the corners, needed to feel his strong arms holding me close, letting me know that I wasn't alone, that he would be there for me just as he'd promised.

He will *be there for you,* I told myself. *You know he's working on getting you back. Just don't get mopey in front of the others, or someone might start asking questions.*

Those bracing inner words helped to smother my need…or at least tamp it down to a manageable level. Later, when I was alone, I could allow myself a good cry if I thought it might help. Or maybe not; I knew there were surveillance cameras in my room. The last thing I wanted was to give Randall Lenz the satisfaction of knowing he'd worn me down.

I took a bite of my honey ham and cheddar sandwich, then said, "More importantly, Dr. Woodrow seems like a nice guy." I paused, then figured I'd go ahead and ask the question, since it seemed natural enough to me. "Do any of you know why I'd be assigned to work with him instead of Dr. Keegan or Dr. Richards?"

Ethan shrugged. "Usually, Dr. Richards just works with us in the beginning, and then we're assigned to one of her two assistants. I honestly don't know why we're assigned to one or the other. I've always worked with Dr. Woodrow."

"And I got Dr. Keegan," Natalie said. "Which I'm not too happy about, because he's a real grump compared to Dr. Woodrow. Luck of the draw, I guess."

Maybe…or maybe not. Ethan's talent, like mine, worked on objects outside him, while Natalie's was more self-focused. That could have been the deciding factor, or maybe it all was completely random.

Either way, I hoped I wouldn't be sticking around long enough to find out.

"Do they ever let you out of here?" I asked next.

Natalie's mouth twisted in a lopsided grin. "What, you mean like on a field trip?"

As soon as she made that response, I realized it had been a pretty silly question. I somehow doubted Randall Lenz would be cool with letting his valuable specimens free to have a day at the beach or something.

"No, we never go anywhere," Matthew put in. He'd been watching and listening quietly up until that point, but it seemed as though he wanted to insert himself in the conversation. "I mean, we sometimes can go out in the courtyard or out to the north field if the weather is decent, but that's about it."

Oh, well. So much for the vague notion that maybe if I was allowed out of the facility at some point, I could use my weather talents to assist me in making a jailbreak. It sure looked as though I wasn't going to be allowed that opportunity.

I supposed I shouldn't have been too surprised.

"Well, at least you get some fresh air," I said.

He shook his head. "Not enough. But it is what it is."

I didn't like the note of resignation in his voice. Yes, they all pretended to themselves that they were there at the facility voluntarily, but it seemed to me they realized deep down they were never getting out of the place. Would they even flee if given the opportunity?

Yes, I thought fiercely. *Because I'll tell them who they really are and all about the world they'll be able to live in…if they're brave enough to leave this place.*

I had to hope I hadn't misjudged them, that they'd be able to save themselves when the time came.

And that I'd be able to save myself.

11

BECAUSE OF THE TIME DIFFERENCE, THEY didn't have to plan the raid for the middle of the night Flagstaff time. No, Connor and Jake decided that eleven o'clock should work just fine, since that would make it two in the morning in Alexandria.

"Hopefully, that means we'll be more on our game," Connor said. He set down the color laser-jet printout of the image from Addie's room, and Angela picked it up so she could study it once more.

"Yep, now that Miranda's three, we're kind of out of the habit of being up at all hours of the night," she said with a grin. "My biggest problem will be staying awake until midnight or whatever. These days, we crash pretty early since the kids get us up at o'dark thirty."

"I doubt you're going to have too much trouble staying alert," Lucas put in. They were all gathered at the dining room table in his showplace of a house in University Heights, since Angela and Connor had brought their kids over to spend the night. Ian and Emily and Miranda had been thrilled at the prospect, since they loved coming over to spend time with their cousin Mia. "Considering you're about to teleport into a secret government facility."

"Well, there's that," Angela said. Her big green eyes were sparkling; Jake could tell Lucas was a favorite of hers. Then again, Lucas was pretty much a favorite of everyone. He just had that knack with people.

Margot entered the room, a plate full of fun, snacky hors d'oeuvres in one hand. "Last-minute fortifications," she announced. "And the kids are finally asleep, so try not to make too much noise down here."

"We'll be silent as the grave," Lucas promised, then added, as Margot gave him a truly epic side-eye, "Sorry…bad choice of words."

"It's going to be pretty simple," Jake said, figuring he'd better try to smooth things over… especially since it was his girlfriend who needed rescuing. Could he even call Addie his girlfriend? It seemed like such a trite phrase for the woman who'd suddenly become his entire world.

He supposed when you felt that way about someone, the exact words involved didn't matter so much.

Margot lifted an eyebrow as she set down the plate, and he went on, "I mean, Connor and Angela know exactly where they're going, and they teleport so fast that even if they're picked up on the facility's security cameras, no one will get there in enough time to do anything about it."

"And Jeremy's back at Trident HQ, ready to jam those cameras so there's no chance they can get a good look at any of our faces," Connor added. He picked up a mini quiche and popped it in his mouth. "It's going to be totally surgical, Margot."

"So you've said." None of those reassurances seemed to have mollified her; she had her hands on her hips and was frowning. "That doesn't mean I like it."

"You don't have to like it," Lucas said reasonably. He, too, grabbed a quiche, but he waited to take a bite so he could add, "You just have to not say no."

"I already told you I wouldn't say no," she returned. "I just don't like it."

"I don't, either," Angela said. "But we can't leave one of our own behind. That's not how any of the witch clans operate."

Margot's lips pressed together, but she didn't

protest. After all, what Angela had said was only the truth—clans stuck together and looked out for their own. Otherwise, there was far too great a chance of their existence being discovered, putting them all at risk.

"Besides," Lucas said, "the whole reason I'm going along is to make sure that nothing goes wrong. So sit down and have a snack, Margot. It's going to be fine."

For a moment, she didn't reply, only stood there looking uncertain, which was definitely not Margot's usual demeanor. Then she let out a sigh and went ahead and sat down next to her husband. He leaned over and gave her a quick kiss on the cheek. In response, she shook her head... but she also reached for a miniature pig in a blanket, seeming to signal that she'd given up the argument for the time being.

"Is there anything else we need to be watching for?" Angela asked. "I mean, the images off the security cameras make it seem as if the room where Addie is being kept is pretty normal, but for all we know, these people have all sorts of extra security measures in place."

"I don't think so," Jake replied. That was one thing he could feel fairly confident about, considering the way he and Jeremy had spent the last twenty-four hours scrutinizing every square inch of Addie's prison suite as revealed by the security camera footage. "I suppose there's always a chance we've overlooked something, but other than the surveillance system and the biometric locks on the door, the place pretty much looks like a normal condo. After all, they're not going to do anything that might endanger a prize specimen like Addie."

While he hated to think of her like that, Jake knew he had to look at the situation the way Randall Lenz would. And although they had standard security measures in place, it wasn't as if they'd have her suite set up to belch out poison gas or something at the first sign of an intruder. Anyway, the raid was going to happen so quickly that no one at the SED would even have time to react.

Angela gave a thoughtful nod, and picked up a mini quiche and took a bite. "Well, that's good to know. At least we don't have to worry about any kind of wards or traps set out to catch witches and warlocks."

"I'm sure Agent Lenz doesn't believe in witches," Connor remarked. "Which is kind of ironic, considering he's holding a bunch of them captive right now. But honestly, I don't care what he believes in. The important thing is that he won't see us coming, and he won't know where we've taken Addie. It's going to seem like she's vanished into thin air."

Which was exactly the outcome they wanted.

Since Angela and Connor had erased all his memories from the time when Jake showed up at Addie's house in Kanab to the time when Lenz awoke alone in a motel room in that same town five days later, there wasn't any way for him to connect her to the Wilcoxes in Flagstaff.

Or so they all fervently hoped.

"Vanishing into thin air is pretty much exactly what's going to happen," Jake said. He glanced down at his phone, which he'd left lying on the tabletop. Ten fifty-two. Almost time.

God, he wished he was going along. He wanted to be the one to wake Addie, to bend down and let her know help had arrived. But since that wasn't feasible, he was just glad that Angela and Connor would be there. She knew them, would probably be glad to see that her brother had come to rescue her.

"Getting close," Connor said. He glanced over at Lucas. "You're going to teleport with me, since it'll be easier for me to move someone who's heavier."

"Hey," Lucas said, looking offended. "Who're you calling heavy?"

"*Relatively* heavier," Angela told him. Her lips twitched with amusement. "That's why I'll be teleporting back with Addie. Our weights are closer."

"Ah," Lucas said. "Glad you're not accusing me of getting chubby in my old age."

"Not yet," Margot said crisply, an amused lift at the corner of her mouth. "Good thing you've been playing plenty of golf lately."

His brows drew together, as if he was working through her remark and attempting to see whether there had been a backhanded insult buried in there somewhere. Then he gave a philosophical shrug and reached for another mini quiche, dark eyes glinting at his wife as if challenging her to comment on his snack choices.

However, she seemed to have decided it wasn't worth teasing him on the subject any longer, because she reached for a quiche of her own and took a bite. "You're sure it's not going to be jarring for Addie to be brought back here, a place she's never seen before?"

"It'll be fine," Jake said. "I'll be here, and she'll be with Connor and Angela." He'd already hashed this over with the *primus;* Connor had suggested that Jake wait at his own house and that he and Angela would bring Addie there, but Jake shot down the plan. There was no way in hell he was going to sit alone at his place, not knowing what was going on. Better to wait here with Margot. At least he wouldn't be by himself, even if Margot Wilcox wasn't exactly the most comforting person in the world. "And I'll take her home right away."

Those words seemed to satisfy Margot; she

nodded and reached for her glass of water, then took a sip.

The alarm on Jake's phone went off, and he quickly shut it down. "Eleven," he said unnecessarily.

Connor and Angela looked at each other, and they both rose from the table at almost the same time. Lucas got up as well, his expression not one of worry or resignation, as might have been expected, but almost eagerness. It seemed he was looking at this rescue mission as just another adventure to be experienced.

Well, with any luck, it wouldn't be an adventure, but instead just a quick trip, no complications, there and back and nothing more...and luck was the entire reason why he was there in the first place.

"Ready?" Connor asked, and both Angela and Lucas murmured a quick assent.

Connor grasped Lucas' hand, and Angela took her husband's free one. Her eyes caught Jake's for just a second, and she offered him an encouraging smile.

"Back before you know it," she said, and then the three of them were gone.

Margot pushed the plate of hors d'oeuvres toward Jake and shot him a weary smile. "Might as well eat something," she told him. "If all goes well, they'll be back before you've even finished chewing."

He picked up a bit of puff pastry stuffed with feta. "I'll eat to that."

A quick, worried nod, and then they both settled down to wait.

Randall Lenz had felt restless all evening. Why, he couldn't really say, because if Dr. Richards' reports were correct—and he had no reason to believe they weren't—everything seemed to have gone very well that day. Adara Grant's weather-control experiment with Dr. Woodrow had surpassed everyone's expectations, and she appeared to have spent a pleasant day after that, socializing with the rest of the test subjects before it was time for her to return to her suite and settle down for the night.

Absolutely nothing had occurred to cause the unease which prickled the back of his neck, that made him pick up his phone and inspect it multiple times in case he'd overlooked an important message. However, there were no missed calls or texts, and even when he checked the email on his home computer, rather than his work laptop, he didn't see anything more urgent than an email from his mother reminding him that he needed to

RSVP for his cousin Theresa's wedding no later than the end of next week.

He shook his head, then sent off a quick reply saying that he doubted he'd be able to get away from D.C., but that he'd send a gift and his congratulations. The same back-and-forth they'd shared far too many times over the years, even though Barbara Lenz never seemed willing to admit defeat and accept that her son had no intention of attending family festivities. He tried to go back to New York once a year, either at Thanksgiving or at Christmas, but otherwise, his work kept him in the D.C. area.

That duty handled, he got up from his desk and wandered through the house, fingers kneading the back of his neck as he tried to ignore the low-grade headache that had been plaguing him most of the day. By that point, he was almost used to never feeling quite in tiptop shape, to always having some sort of strange ache or twinge present no matter what he did. The doctors said he should be getting past the worst of it, but Lenz wasn't sure he believed them.

Eventually, he came to the couch in the family room and sat down, more because he didn't know what else to do with himself. He rarely watched television, but he picked up the remote anyway and turned on the TV, thinking perhaps he'd catch a bit of the evening news. An exercise in futility, probably, since he knew better than most how filtered and carefully censored that news actually was, but the sound of other people's voices helped to fill some of the silence in the house. It was a large Colonial-style home that would have been better suited to a growing family than a single man who was rarely there; he'd bought the place because he wanted something close to work, and the house was a steal because the people selling it were going through a nasty divorce and needed to unload it—and their expensive mortgage—as quickly as possible. More than once, Lenz had wondered if he should sell it as well and move to a more manageable condo, but he'd never gotten around to committing to such a course of action.

At any rate, watching the news and the late night program that came on afterward didn't seem to help much. He couldn't shake the feeling that he'd overlooked something vitally important, even though he mentally revisited his day multiple times and reassured himself that there didn't seem to be anything out of place.

The late night show wound up, and the late late show came on after that. He turned off the television and got up from the sofa, knowing that if he didn't go to bed soon, he'd pay for it the next day. Many times, he'd been forced to function on only three or four hours of sleep, but such a situation wasn't optimal. Besides, there was no emergency keeping him awake now, only the sensation that something had gone awry in the world, even if he couldn't put his finger on what it might be.

He brushed his teeth, splashed water on his face, and headed toward the walk-in closet so he could get out of his dress trousers and shirt—he'd hung up his coat and tie when he'd gotten home hours earlier—and found himself stopping dead in the middle of his bedroom.

You need to go in to work.

The disembodied voice in his head didn't sound like himself. No, that voice sounded almost like his father, brisk and authoritative. A voice he hadn't heard for nearly twenty years.

Now you're hearing things? Lenz mocked himself, but he knew that wasn't quite the case. No, it was more that he'd heard his father's voice because he was more likely to pay attention to it than he might to his own.

Go in to work, though? Why?

Something was wrong…or at least, his brain had somehow latched on to the notion that something *might* be wrong. Which didn't make any sense. If any of the test subjects had suffered some sort of mishap, then the guards on duty would have reached out to him immediately. Anyway, it was the middle of the night, and they should all be safely in their beds, even Lorna Johnson, who was an insomniac and often got up in the middle of the night to read for a while in the hope that doing so would make her drowsy enough to go back to sleep.

Well, it couldn't hurt to make a call, just to be safe. Lenz reached for his phone but then paused.

Don't call. Go.

And what a fool he'd be making of himself, to show up in the dead of night, acting on a hunch he couldn't explain.

Then again, his hunches had gotten him out of sticky situations more than once. He'd be tempting fate to ignore this one, especially since it had come on so strong.

No point in bothering with a tie, but he slipped his suit jacket back on and put his cell phone in his pocket. Back downstairs, and through the door in the kitchen that led to the garage. Inside was a dark gray Audi RS 5 coupe, his one true indulgence. Right then, however, he wasn't thinking about the growl of the engine or the way the leather seat cushioned his body, but only of how quickly the powerful car could get him from his home to the SED facility, not quite three miles away.

He didn't have to worry about being stopped —or rather, he knew if he was stopped by local law enforcement, one flash of his Homeland Security badge would send him on his way.

However, even a quick traffic stop would slow him more than he wanted, and so he did his best not to exceed the speed limit by more than ten miles an hour. Soon enough, he was approaching the guard shack at the entrance to the facility. He didn't recognize the man on duty, but clearly, the man recognized him, because he got a startled, "Evening, sir!" and was waved on through the gate without even having to reach for his I.D.

At that hour, the parking lot was nearly deserted. Lenz pulled into his designated parking space and hurried out of the car, barely breaking his stride as he came through the entrance and offered a curt greeting to the two men sitting at the front desk. They, too, looked surprised to see him there, but they knew enough not to ask any questions, but only nodded and gave him a "good evening, Agent Lenz" as he sailed past.

His office was located on Subfloor Two. Nothing amiss there; not that he'd expected there to be. He picked up the phone and contacted Conrad Ostrow, the chief analyst on duty during the overnight shift.

"Anything to report?" he asked.

"No, sir," Ostrow replied, doing his best to sound brisk, although Lenz could almost hear the questions in the other man's voice. "All quiet. Is something the matter?"

"No," he replied. "At least, not that I'm aware of. I just came in to follow up on something."

He hung up then, and turned on his office desktop computer. It woke up and requested his login and credentials. Once he was in the system, he brought up the feed from the security cameras, figuring that was as good a place to start as any.

The cameras showed quiet corridors, unoccupied elevators. Each of the test subjects was asleep in his or her bed—yes, even Lorna Johnson, who had an e-reader parked on her bedside table but who appeared to be down for the count. There was absolutely nothing here to support the hunch that had brought him back to the SED, to tell him that the strange feelings of unease he'd been experiencing all evening were anything more than generalized anxiety with absolutely no basis in reality.

Except—

The feed shifted to the view from inside Adara Grant's bedroom, and he watched in shocked disbelief as three strangers materialized out of nowhere to stand by her bed. One of them, a woman, leaned down to shake her awake.

Lenz didn't wait to see Adara's reaction. Although his brain was singing with disbelief at the sight of three people appearing out of thin air in a room that was more locked down than Fort Knox, he knew he didn't have a moment to waste.

Instead, he bolted from the office and ran for the elevator, pulling out his phone as he did so.

"Intruders on Sub-level Five," he barked into the phone. "Adara Grant's suite."

At least he didn't have to worry about the guards on duty asking any unnecessary questions. "On our way," came the reply.

He shoved his phone into his pocket, then decided that waiting for the elevator was foolish, considering he only had to descend three floors to reach his destination. Besides, the entrance to the stairwell was much closer.

The metal stairs clanged under his hasty feet as he pounded down the stairway. In less than a minute, he'd emerged on Sub-level Five and was running toward the suite where Adara Grant was supposed to be sleeping. No sign of the guards yet, but Lenz wasn't about to wait for them. He had no idea how someone could have gotten inside her rooms—the alarms should have sounded the second someone entered the facility without clearance—and yet he realized the time for figuring out exactly what had happened was later, after the rescue attempt had been foiled.

Because he somehow knew that was exactly what was going on.

Just the briefest pause to allow the biometric lock to scan his eye, and then he was inside, running toward the door of her bedroom, which stood open. From inside came a jumble of voices, both male and female.

He reached for the light switch and flipped it on. Immediately, the lamp on the nightstand flared to life, showing him Adara, who'd climbed out of bed and now stood next to it, and the three strangers he'd glimpsed on the security feed. Two men, one woman. The men looked as though they could be related, both tall with dark hair and strongly marked features, although one of them was probably at least ten years older than the other. The woman was dark-haired as well, with brilliant green eyes that stared at him in shock as he came through the doorway, his service pistol already in his hand.

Something about the woman and the younger of the two men felt oddly familiar, although Lenz couldn't say why. He knew he'd never seen them before; while he didn't have an eidetic memory, he never forgot a face, and he should have been able to put a name to them if he'd truly encountered them in the past.

Another puzzle he'd have to put aside for later. Voice steady, he said, "I'll have to ask you to step away from Ms. Grant."

The strange woman with the green eyes shook her head, even as the older man standing behind her stared at him with a frown, expression puzzled rather than worried. Odd reaction, but Lenz didn't have time to worry about that at the moment.

"No, we're taking Adara with us." The woman's voice was firm, somewhat low-pitched. No real trace of an accent, making him think she had to be from somewhere in the West or Southwest. "And I'm afraid that's not going to help you, Agent Lenz."

A flick of her finger, and his gun was torn from his grasp and landed on the bed.

Impossible…unless you were dealing with someone who had the same kind of extraordinary abilities as Adara Grant or the rest of the facility's test subjects.

He lunged for the gun, but some sort of invisible force seemed to catch him, to propel him back against the wall, where he was pinned in place, unable to break free. Had the woman done it? He hadn't seen her hands move. Not that it mattered so much, since he'd been rendered basically useless. Panic flared through him, accompanied by the same kind of helpless sensation he'd experienced the day the towers fell…the sort of reaction he'd worked very hard to make sure he never felt again.

"Let's go," said the younger of the two men. At once, the green-eyed woman reached out for Adara's hand, while the older man, the one who hadn't said anything but still stared at Lenz as if he wasn't sure he should believe the evidence of his eyes, took the hand of the other man.

Adara's gaze met Lenz's for just a moment. Her face was pale, her expression one of utter relief.

"Goodbye, Agent Lenz," she said.

And they all disappeared. No sound, no light, nothing to show how they'd managed such a feat. There one minute, gone the next.

The invisible hand holding Randall Lenz against the wall seemed to disappear as well. He fell to the ground, knees cracking against the tile floor. A muttered curse escaped his lips, but he forced himself to his feet and stared down at his gun where it lay on the empty bed.

He had no idea how he would ever begin to explain what had just happened.

12

THE INTERIOR OF A WARMLY ELEGANT HOUSE materialized around me—high ceilings paneled in wood, amber-toned lights glowing against smoothly plastered walls. I blinked, and realized Jake was coming toward me, arms outstretched.

That was all I needed. I fell into his embrace, wanting to feel the strength of those arms around me, the beating of his heart against my cheek. If it weren't for Connor and Angela's presence—and the presence of the other man, someone I didn't know but guessed had to be another Wilcox warlock—I would have pressed my lips against Jake's, would have tasted him over and over to reassure myself that it really was him and I wasn't just having some kind of insanely vivid dream.

As it was, I let him hold me for a moment.

Then he let go and said, "Do you need to sit down?"

Right then, that sounded like a good idea. Everything had happened so quickly—Angela waking me from a deep sleep, scrambling out of bed, being suddenly confronted by Randall Lenz —that my legs felt a little rubbery.

I nodded, and Jake led me over to a dining room table and stepped aside as I lowered myself onto one of the chairs next to it. Belatedly, I realized there was another person in the room, a darkhaired woman who somehow managed to look elegant in a scoop-necked gray T-shirt and a pair of black yoga pants.

"I'm Margot," she said. Her gaze flicked toward the man who'd accompanied Angela and Connor on their rescue mission. "I'm your cousin Lucas' wife."

"Hi," I said shakily.

Lucas stepped forward. "Hello, Addie. You doing okay?"

I managed to nod.

"How about something to drink?" Margot asked. "Tea? A glass of water?"

Since it was the middle of the night, anything with caffeine didn't sound like a very good idea. "Water would be great," I told her.

She nodded and left the room. Jake continued to stand next to me. He put his hand on my shoulder and squeezed gently, letting me know he was close, that he wasn't going anywhere.

"Well, that went pretty well, I think," Angela said. Her hand stole into Connor's, and he twined his fingers with hers as he sent an encouraging smile in my direction.

"Definitely, since we got Addie back safe and sound."

Lucas frowned then. I'd only just met him, but I somehow got the feeling that he wasn't the sort of person who frowned too often; his face had the friendly lines of someone who found much more to smile about in the world than frown.

"You didn't tell me about this Agent Lenz of yours," he said, his tone faintly accusing.

"Tell you what?" Connor replied. His brows drew together, as if he was trying to figure out exactly what his cousin had meant by that particular remark. "We told you he was dangerous."

"Oh, that." Lucas waved a hand, as if having a gun pointed in his direction was nothing to be worried about. "No, I meant that you didn't tell me he was a warlock."

"*What?*"

The same startled syllable burst from all our lips. Margot, who'd just reentered the room, glass of water in hand, gave us all a quizzical look. "What's going on?" she asked.

I'd already felt off balance, despite sitting

down, but Lucas' crazy remark made me feel as if the entire planet had just tilted slightly on its axis. "Randall Lenz isn't a warlock," I said, my tone flat. "Connor explained to me how we all get that tingle or itch or whatever you want to call it when we meet a witch or warlock for the first time, and I never felt anything like that when I met him."

"Neither did I," Jake added. "I mean, we were only a few feet apart when I faced him on Addie's front porch. Didn't feel a damn thing."

Connor and Angela glanced at each other. Her shoulders lifted ever so slightly, and he reached up to push an over-long piece of hair back off his forehead. Both of them looked just about as flummoxed as I was feeling right then.

"We didn't feel anything, either," Angela said. "I mean, yeah, he was lying unconscious on the floor, but that shouldn't have made a difference…should it?"

That last question was accompanied by an inquiring glance in Margot's direction, as if she hoped the other woman might be able to provide some clarification on that particular point. Why she was asking Margot's advice, I didn't know. Simply because Margot was older and might be better equipped to provide some insight?

She crossed her arms and frowned slightly. "I don't know for sure," she said after a long pause. "That is, what the 'tingle' simply means is our own witch natures recognizing the spark, the magic, in another person. It's something inherent in each of us, which means it probably doesn't matter if the warlock in question is conscious or not. What's very odd is that none of you felt it, but Lucas somehow did."

Her tone had remained carefully neutral, but I could tell that Lucas didn't look too thrilled by the insinuation buried somewhere in her statement. "What," he said, "you think I'm imagining things?"

"That's not what I said," she responded, her tone still cool, calm. "I wasn't there, but I can imagine that it must have been a fairly tense scene. Don't you think it's possible you experienced a twinge of nervousness or doubt that might have felt like the tingle you feel when you meet a strange witch or warlock, but was actually something completely different?"

He was silent for a moment, considering her question, hands shoved in the pockets of his khakis. For the first time, I realized Lucas was wearing Dockers and a dark blue polo shirt, and looked as though he should have been out on the golf course or something, rather than assisting in a midnight raid on a secret government facility.

At length, he shrugged and said, "Maybe. I mean, anything is possible. But it didn't feel that way."

Connor's eyes widened, as though he'd been struck by a sudden thought. "And then there's what Genoveva told me."

"Genoveva Castillo?" Margot asked, and Connor nodded.

"Yeah, when I talked to her a couple of days ago, she told me about how Randall Lenz came to see her at her house in Santa Fe. She mentioned how she felt a bit of a twinge when she met him, but she brushed it off because it was very slight and nothing to be concerned about. Still, when you add her experience to what Lucas is telling us now...."

The words trailed off, and we all were silent for a moment as we stared at one another, grappling with the idea of Randall Lenz possibly being a warlock. The notion seemed completely ludicrous to me. All right, the man was scary as hell in a variety of ways, but I'd never seen him show the slightest sign of possessing any sort of magical powers.

"It's crazy," I said then, wondering even as I spoke whether I might be protesting a bit too much. Still, there didn't seem to be anything to do except continue, so I went on, "How could it be possible that neither Jake nor I—or Connor or Angela—could sense anything special about him, but Genoveva and Lucas somehow did? What could have changed between then and now?"

Again, we all lapsed into silence…until Jake's fingers clenched on my shoulder. I looked up at him, startled, and watched his eyes widen as some sort of idea seemed to suggest itself to him.

When he spoke, his voice was almost hushed. "You struck him with lightning."

I stared at him, not sure what he was hinting at.

Then Angela's eyes widened and she said, "Oh, my God." As all our gazes fixed on her, she added, "It makes sense, in a horrible kind of way. What if Agent Lenz was basically a *nunca*—a witch or warlock who barely has any powers," she explained quickly as I gave her a blank look. Maybe someday I'd be up to speed on all the ins and outs of the witch world, but at the moment, I was just feeling fried. I managed to nod, and she went on, "Then Addie zaps him with lightning, and his magical gifts wake up. That would explain why none of us felt anything special about him… yes, he'd been zapped by the time we encountered him, but his powers might not have really started to grow yet. However, by the time Genoveva met him—and Lucas met him—they'd have woken up enough to be detectable."

In a way, what Angela was saying made a horrible kind of sense. Or at least, it made as much sense as any of the rest of this craziness. I still knew so little of this strange new world, and so I honestly had no idea whether it was possible to have your powers sleep until something came along to give them the nudge they needed. Judging by the shocked silence around me, I had a feeling none of the others were quite sure, either.

"Well, let's agree on that as a theory for now," Margot said in that brisk way of hers. "It's plausible, if nothing else. But if we accept the idea of Randall Lenz being a warlock, what do we do next?"

"Nothing," I said, my tone flat. Everyone stared at me, and I drew a breath and made myself go on. "Look, I get that you're doing what you can to find orphaned witches and warlocks and return them to their clans, but you can't include Agent Lenz in that same group. For one thing, this is all only a theory. Something else entirely could be going on. And second, the man's life has been devoted to tracking down people with special powers and turning them into guinea pigs. You think he's going to be thrilled to find out he's actually been one of the lab animals all along?"

For a long moment, no one said anything. Then Jake shifted slightly so he stood next to me, rather than behind. His eyes met mine, and I found myself wishing desperately, fervently, that we could be alone together. After all, I'd been jolted out of a deep sleep by the sudden arrival of Angela and Connor and Lucas Wilcox, and I was still doing my best to come to terms with the sudden change in my status. All I wanted was to crawl into Jake's arms and stay there for about a hundred years.

"We don't have to make a decision about anything tonight," he said. His gaze moved from me to the rest of the people gathered in the dining room. "Addie's exhausted, and I want to take her home. We can hash all this out tomorrow."

"You're right," Angela said. I got the feeling that she'd cut in before anyone else could speak so she could lend her support to Jake. Maybe she'd seen the same thing in my face that he had. Whatever the reason, I was very glad of her unexpected support. "It's almost midnight—let's all meet at Jake's place tomorrow to discuss this further. If that's okay with you," she tacked on quickly, as if realizing that maybe she shouldn't have volunteered his house as the location for their meeting.

"That's fine," he replied. "Eleven o'clock?"

Margot's mouth pursed. Possibly, she was thinking about protesting that we should meet earlier than that, given the gravity of the situation, but a sideways glance from Lucas was enough to keep her from commenting.

"Eleven is great," Connor said. "That'll give the rest of us time to scrounge up babysitters. And probably you should have Jeremy there, too."

"And Laurel," Jake added. "I know she wasn't

part of the rescue effort, but she's a member of the Trident team, so she should be included."

"Sure." My brother—I wondered if someday it wouldn't feel strange to think of him that way— looked around at everyone. "I know this is something we didn't even imagine could happen. But the important thing is that Addie is safe."

For now, I thought, although I didn't voice those words aloud. Yes, my brother and sister-in-law had called on their incredible magical gifts to effect my rescue, but would it be enough? I'd come to think of Randall Lenz as a force of nature, something inexorable as the tide. How could we ever stop him?

Somehow, I managed to shove those worries aside as I got up from my chair and gave Connor and Angela a quick hug, then murmured a thank-you to Lucas as well, even though I wasn't quite sure what his part in the whole rescue operation had been. A quick goodbye to Margot, and then Jake was guiding me out the front door and into the cool night air.

A bright moon, nearly full, hung overhead. However, I didn't have time for much more than a quick glimpse before Jake opened the passenger door of a white Wrangler parked in the driveway and helped me in.

Right. He'd sold the Gladiator because he thought it was too conspicuous. A pang of guilt went through me, even though I knew he would only wave it off if I made a comment about the vehicle. Instead, I sat quietly in the passenger seat as I waited for him to come around to the driver side and slide into his own seat.

As he began to back down the long, curved driveway, he said, "You okay?"

I nodded. "Just a little shell-shocked, I guess."

"That's understandable. But we'll be home soon."

Home. Had that been a slip of the tongue, or had Jake already acknowledged to himself that our dream of settling in Riverton had been merely that—a dream, a fantasy that couldn't possibly come true? I didn't know, and I sure as hell wasn't going to ask right then. The day had been a long and crazy one, and I only wanted to fall asleep in his arms and sort out everything else once I wasn't so damn tired.

Lucas and Margot's house was about ten minutes away from Jake's, so it wasn't too long before he pulled into the driveway of the big Victorian and then into the detached garage. Soon enough, we were inside, with an ecstatic Taffy dancing around my feet, her tail wagging like crazy.

"Looks like someone missed you," Jake said with a smile.

I wouldn't have said I'd been around Jake's pet

long enough for her to form that kind of an attachment, but I also would have been the first to admit that I didn't know much about dogs. Without answering, I bent down and scratched Taffy behind the ears, and did my best to blink away the odd little pricks of hot tears behind my eyes. I didn't know why, but something about the dog's joyous reaction to my homecoming made me worry that my fragile self-control was about to start shredding itself apart.

"She's a good dog," I said, not directly responding to his comment.

He seemed to realize I wasn't mentally ready for any kind of in-depth dialogue, because he also bent and gave the dog a couple of affectionate pats, telling her, "We're wiped out, Taffers. Time for all of us to go to sleep."

She cocked her head, one ear erect while the other flopped adorably to one side. But she seemed to understand this wasn't the time to beg for treats or cajole a good belly rub out of her master, since she then trotted out of the kitchen and headed for the stairs.

Jake looked at me. *Really* looked, eyes so dark and deep, I was pretty sure I might drown in them. "I was so worried about you," he said quietly.

"I was worried, too," I replied. "But it actually

wasn't nearly as bad as I thought it would be. I'll tell you about it tomorrow."

Silence for a few seconds as he seemed to assess my current condition. Whatever he saw in my face must have reassured him, because he seemed to nod to himself. "Okay. Let's get you in bed."

We headed upstairs, but when we got to the landing, he gave a worried little look in the direction of the master bedroom, as if he didn't know for sure whether I really wanted to sleep in his bed or if I would have preferred the guest bedroom. True, we'd slept together in my rented house in Riverton, but that felt like a lifetime ago.

Even so, a lifetime wouldn't change my feelings about Jake Wilcox. I said quietly, "I want to sleep in your room."

No words, just his arms reaching for me, pulling me close. Our lips touched, and despite my weariness, heat awoke in me, my body telling that this was what I'd needed so desperately—Jake's mouth on mine, his arms a strong, protective circle, the scent of fresh air and pine somehow caught in his thick, dark hair. We stood that way for a long time, until at last he let go…but only to twine his fingers with mine.

"God, Addie," he said, voice husky, hardly more than a whisper. "I was so scared I'd never be able to do that again."

That confession made tears start to my eyes once more. Was it because he'd stated the truth so simply, hadn't worried about admitting his fear to me? I didn't know. All I knew was that I loved him more than I'd ever thought I would love anyone. That love was an ache inside me, the knowledge that, while I might be able to live without him, I sure as hell didn't want to think what such a life might be like.

"But you did," I said softly. "Because you rescued me."

"Angela and Connor rescued you," he pointed out, but I shook my head.

"Don't try to tell me you didn't have a lot to do with that."

"Okay," he said, relenting. "The plan was my idea. But Angela and Connor and Lucas had to actually execute it, because it was their magical gifts that would be the most useful in that situation."

It seemed the right time to ask. "Why Lucas?"

"His gift is luck, Addie. With him there, the rescue had a much greater chance of succeeding."

Of course. Jake had told me about his cousin's talent, but it had completely slipped my mind. Naturally, Jake and everyone else would have done whatever they could to ensure their plan worked the way they'd intended. "Which it did," I said. "Although I have to wonder if Lucas' gift is slipping a little. I don't think it was all that lucky to have Randall Lenz come in and catch us in the act."

"But he couldn't stop us," Jake replied. "That's the important thing."

I supposed he was right, and yet a little flicker of doubt stirred within me. If Lucas Wilcox's talent for luck was so great, why hadn't our getaway been completely clean?

However, it was late and I was tired, and I told myself that we could try to hash out all those details the next day after I'd had a chance to get some sleep. "Yes," I said as my fingers stole into Jake's. "That is the important thing."

He kissed me on the cheek, and we went into the bedroom together. Taffy had already curled up in a little ball in the oversized dog bed in the corner, and a small smile crept onto my lips as I looked down at her. It was as if she'd known it was okay to settle down and wait for us, that we'd be along very soon.

I was already wearing a sleep shirt and a pair of capri-length leggings—and had washed my face and brushed my teeth hours earlier—so it wasn't as if I had to do anything to get ready for bed. Jake pulled off his T-shirt and unbuckled his belt, letting his Levi's slide to the floor. For a moment, I allowed myself to once more admire the hard lines of his body.

And yet, I knew I was too damn tired to do anything about it.

He seemed to sense my mood, because he came over and kissed me again, this time softly on the lips.

"It's all right," he said as he pushed a lock of hair away from my face. "We can just sleep."

"I'm sorry—" I began, but he only shook his head.

"Don't you dare apologize. We have all the time in the world."

And while I still wasn't sure about that—not with the specter of Randall Lenz hovering uneasily in my mind—I didn't protest, only allowed Jake to lead me over to the bed so we could slip beneath the covers and snuggle up against one another, his arms holding me close, the steady beat of his heart telling me that it was all right, that we were together, and nothing else mattered.

Holding that thought in my mind, I slept.

13

THE UNDER-SECRETARY OF THE SCIENCE AND Technology Directorate within Homeland Security was Wallace Bryant, a man who had worked his way up into the position from being a field agent and someone who was widely regarded as a fair, no-nonsense manager. Randall Lenz had always enjoyed a good working relationship with Bryant, mostly because his superior knew enough to stay out of the way and allow Lenz to do what was required for maximum results. At the same time, Bryant had always appeared to respect Lenz's zeal for the work and the professionalism he demanded of all his subordinates.

At that exact moment, however, Bryant was staring at Lenz with roughly the same mixture of astonishment and derision he might have directed at someone who'd just announced that they'd seen a flying saucer hovering over the White House.

"Are you trying to tell me, Agent Lenz," he rasped—thirty years of smoking two packs a day had done their work on Wallace Bryant's vocal chords—"that your newest subject, the one you claimed was more valuable than all the others, has vanished into thin air?"

That was exactly what had happened, but Randall Lenz fervently wished the man could have come up with a slightly less sensational phrase to describe the abduction of Adara Grant. "That seems to be the case, sir," he replied in his driest, most neutral tone. "The people who took her did not appear to have circumvented our security measures, either coming or going."

Bryant leaned against the back of his seat. He was in his early sixties, thinning hair iron gray, eyes dark and shrewd. Nicotine stains showed yellow on his fingertips. "How did they get in?"

A very good question. Lenz had surmised that the operatives who'd carried out the rescue attempt had to be gifted, just like Adara and the rest of the test subjects still residing in the research facility. If those strangers truly had the ability to transport themselves through solid walls, then their talent was insanely powerful—and, by extension, exceedingly desirable.

But although Under-Secretary Bryant was of

course privy to all the details of Project Daedalus, asking him to believe that people existed who could teleport was probably straining credulity a bit. It was one thing to accept the idea that there were individuals who could control the weather or move objects with their minds or alter their own appearance. Believing that somewhere in the world there were those who could treat solid matter as if it didn't exist was something else entirely.

There was also the frustrating fact that, even though the security cameras in Adara's suite should have caught the entire episode, every detail of that scene had been conveniently erased from the facility's servers. All Lenz had to go on were his memories of the incident, and he knew better than anyone else that trying to explain exactly what had happened made him sound like a madman...especially since there was no corroborating evidence to back up his story.

"We're still working on that, sir," he said.

"So, what you're trying to tell me is that you don't have anything at the moment...except a missing test subject."

Succinct, if damning. "Unfortunately, no. Of course, it's very early in the investigation, and I'm confident that we'll have answers soon enough, including the identities of the culprits and the current whereabouts of our missing woman."

From the way Bryant's mouth thinned, it was clear enough he didn't agree with his subordinate's optimistic view of the situation. "I hope you do, Agent Lenz," he said, the rasp in his voice now distinctly ominous. "I've continued to approve funding for your program because it showed promise, but incidents like this? It's damn sloppy."

"Yes, sir," Lenz replied, shoulders straight and voice level, although the threat in Bryant's words had sent a chill of dread down his spine. "I'll send you real-time updates with any new developments."

"See that you do."

No other dismissal, but Lenz knew the interview was over. He got up from his chair, nodded at Bryant, and headed out into the hallway. Although no one appeared to be looking at him, he wouldn't allow himself to reach up and touch his forehead to see if any nervous sweat had beaded there. Just in case he was being observed, he wanted to make sure he appeared in control at all times.

He left the under-secretary's office in the Pentagon, got in his Audi, and drove back to the SED facility. As soon as the interlopers had left with Adara Grant in their clutches, he'd contacted Dawson and told her to get to work at once. No matter that it was two-thirty in the morning; he needed his best analyst on the job, and damn the time of night.

Now, nearly eight hours later, Dawson was still at her workstation. She'd put on work clothes before coming in—gray dress slacks and a white button-up shirt—but she still gave the impression of someone who'd rolled out of bed to come to the office, thanks to her messy ponytail and complete lack of even the minimal makeup she usually wore to work.

"Anything?" he asked as he came into the analysts' room.

She shook her head. "I've analyzed and scanned the security feeds backward and forward and upside down. There's absolutely no sign the footage has been tampered with…except that it shows Adara Grant sleeping at the time of the intrusion, and continuing to sleep through the night. Eventually, it goes blank, as if to make it seem that the camera itself has malfunctioned."

"But it hasn't."

"No. We had a tech come in and test every camera in Adara Grant's suite, and every one is operating optimally."

Which was exactly what he had figured, but Lenz still wanted to grind his teeth in frustration. However, he didn't want to display that kind of weakness in front of Agent Dawson, and so he made himself ask, "What about biological evidence of the intrusion?"

"Marginal. Several hairs that belonged to Ms. Grant. A few traces of dirt on the floor—we're having it analyzed. And that's all we have to work with currently."

He supposed he should be glad the investigators had found even that little bit of dirt. It might be a clue—or it might have been something Adara herself had tracked in after her outing in the north field the day before yesterday. Still, he would allow himself to hold out hope, simply because otherwise, he had very little to go on.

"I think it's the same hacker," Dawson went on, and he lifted an eyebrow.

"What makes you think that?"

"Just that it's all so...seamless. Whoever these people are, they're very good at covering their tracks. And although possibly I'm flattering myself, I'd like to think that there aren't too many people in the world who could gain access to our system."

"So, they're all working together."

"It would make sense, sir."

Yes, it would. Perhaps he was simply grasping at anything that would give some meaning to the chaos which seemed to surround Adara Grant, but Lenz wanted to believe her rescue and the continuing eradication of any evidence that might provide an actionable clue had to be part of a concerted effort. Once he found the clue that tied everything together, he'd be in a much better place to unravel the whole mess.

"I'll be in my office," he told his assistant. "Contact me at once if you find anything."

"Of course."

He left the analysts' room and went to his office. Usually, the spare lines of the furniture there and the cool elegance of the black and white photos on the walls were enough to allow him to center himself, to practice the mindfulness he'd explained to Adara Grant only two days earlier. At the moment, however, he found his thoughts darting this way and that, no matter what he did to get them to settle down. As much as he wished he could have ignored the veiled threat in Under-Secretary Bryant's words, Lenz knew he needed to take it to heart. Although the program might not be expendable, Randall Lenz definitely was.

All right. He sat down, then picked up the coffee mug of water that sat on his desk and took a sip. It was tepid and didn't do much to refresh him, but he'd drunk the liquid as much to center himself as to quench his thirst.

It didn't seem to be helping much.

Jaw clenched, he reached in his desk drawer and brought out a blank piece of paper. He'd described the scene in Adara Grant's room to

Dawson, but he thought he'd sketch it out for himself to see if doing so might help him recall something that had previously slipped his mind. In the past, he'd engaged in similar exercises whenever he found himself blocked. He wouldn't call himself an artist—although he'd taken several studio art classes at Columbia as a break from his political science studies—but he thought he might be considered a halfway competent draftsman.

Anyway, there was the rectangle of the bedroom where Adara Grant had slept, with the king-size bed up against one wall and the single nightstand on the left side of the bed. Framed prints on the walls, dresser opposite the bed. Adara standing next to that bed, wearing the long-sleeved night shirt and leggings that had been provided for her. The three strangers close by, both the men tall. Several inches above six feet, because he himself was six foot one, and they were both slightly taller than he. The strange woman around Adara's height, possibly a little shorter, with wavy dark hair and eyes that had flashed brilliant green when he flipped the switch next to the door.

Those eyes....

Randall Lenz blinked. It was there and gone in a flash—a sudden image of those eyes staring down at him, as if he lay on the floor and was gazing up at her.

Had he seen the woman before?

Pain lanced through his head, and he reached up to rub his temple. Although he'd certainly gone through enough that day to bring on a headache, he had no time for one. Hand shaking slightly, he picked up his mug of water and sipped from it again. Maybe he was just dehydrated.

The water seemed to help a little. After he'd drunk half the mug's contents, he set it back down and stared at his sketch. The strange woman was pretty, with a cloud of wavy dark hair that surrounded her face and delicate, slightly sharp features.

A relative of Adara's? That had actually been his first impression, but when he closed his eyes and did his best to analyze their features side by side, he realized they didn't look much alike, except for the superficial resemblance in their coloring. Adara Grant's hair was a silky brown, not wavy at all, and several shades lighter than the strange woman's. Also, her face was a near-perfect oval, her chin more rounded.

It would have been a good theory, but he had a feeling it was a false one.

The two men were more fodder for conjecture. Lenz had a strong suspicion they were related, because of the wavy near-black hair and the similarities in their height and build. The younger man had had greenish-gray eyes, not nearly as bright as those of the woman who'd accompanied him. He'd only caught a glimpse, and yet Randall Lenz felt he'd seen those eyes before as well—not because of the flash he'd just experienced when considering the strange woman's appearance, but because they reminded him of someone.

Reminded him, actually, of Adara Grant.

Could theirs be the real connection in this twisted, knotty puzzle?

He turned to his computer and pulled up her file. From the screen, her face from her Utah driver's license stared at him, intent, not smiling, gray-green eyes meeting the camera squarely.

Gray-green eyes….

Right then, he thought he would have killed for a single still shot from the surveillance system. His recall was excellent, though, and he shut his eyes and imagined the face of the younger stranger. Chiseled, handsome. Mid-thirties, so around ten years older than Adara Grant. Not much similarity in their features, but the color of their eyes had been nearly the same, highlighted in both of them by luxuriant dark lashes and strong brows.

The stranger certainly wasn't old enough to be her father.

Brother?

She had no siblings, though.

No known siblings, Lenz reminded himself.

He'd seen a facsimile of her birth certificate for himself and noted that her mother had left the sections pertaining to the biological father conspicuously blank. At the time, he'd thought Adara must have been the result of a one-night stand with a man her mother hardly knew, and that was why Lyssa Grant had never provided the information. Maybe that was still the case, but maybe…just maybe…Adara had a half-brother out there who'd somehow managed to track her down.

If that turned out to be the actual scenario, then it didn't seem so odd that the stranger with the gray-green eyes would also possess extraordinary talents. Were those talents genetic? Was that the connection?

He thought that theory seemed very plausible. None of the test subjects had any known gifted siblings, but that was because they were all adopted, or, like Natalie Delacroix, were orphans who had been brought up in the foster care system.

Which meant they all might have brothers and sisters out there in the world with their own unique talents.

How many people might be involved in this?

Randall Lenz had no idea, but he knew he had to find out.

No matter what.

~

It was beyond wonderful to wake up in his own bed and have Addie sleeping there next to him, her hair a fall of brown silk over his bare arm. She stirred almost as soon as Jake moved, her eyes widening for a second or two before she seemed to remember where she was.

"Sleep well?" he asked, and she nodded.

"Really well. It helped so much to have you here next to me."

"I know the feeling."

Those were the only words they shared, but they both seemed to reach the same understanding, because in almost the same moment, their mouths met in a kiss much hungrier than the ones they'd shared the night before. Addie had needed that time to sleep, to heal, but it seemed obvious to Jake that now she knew she was home and safe, she needed to be with him in every way possible. Her fingers reached for the waistband of his underwear, and a moment later, she had taken him in her hand, was stroking him up and down.

Damn. He'd been wanting her, of course, but for some reason, he hadn't thought she would be quite so…forward. With low growl in his throat, he took hold of her nightshirt's hem and drew the garment over her head, then followed up by pulling down her leggings and the panties beneath.

His fingers dipped into her, and he could feel how ready she was for him.

"Oh, God, Jake," she moaned, and he continued to stroke her even as she slid her fingers up and down his shaft.

Oh, God, was right. He knew if she kept up with that for much longer, he was going to come then and there. His hands wrapped around her waist, and he pulled her on top of him, let out a moan of his own as he sank into her. She began to move her hips, sliding up and down, and he thought then that nothing could be as amazing as being able to feel her surrounding him as she looked down into his face with those glowing agate-hued eyes of hers.

The climax arrived faster than he would have liked, but to his relief, she came only a few seconds later, her head tipping back as she cried out in ecstasy, her hair brushing against the bare skin of his thighs. Afterward, she lay on top of him, breasts warm and welcome against his chest.

"What was that charm again?" she murmured, and he smiled.

"*Blessed Brigid, now is not the time. Bestow your blessings elsewhere.*"

A nod, but then Addie pushed herself up slightly to gaze down into his face. Her skin was glowing, her eyes bright, but something in her expression seemed almost troubled. "It's okay, isn't it?" she asked. "To say the charm?"

"Of course, it is," he assured her.

"Because I don't want you to think that I don't —that I don't want—"

"It's fine," he said, knowing he needed to disabuse her of that notion right away. "I want a future with you, Addie. And I want everything a future like that might hold. But it's like the charm itself says—'now is not the time.' We have so much going on. I don't expect anything more than just being with you right now."

She smiled at him, relief clear in her expression. A whisper of the charm's words, and then she carefully eased herself off him so she could lie pressed up against his side. "I love you, Jake."

"I love you, Addie," he said. "Never doubt that. And never doubt that this is all going to work out all right."

A second or two passed as she lay there in silence. For a woman who'd just been reunited with the man she loved, she looked very troubled. "I want to believe that," she said. "But I can't stop thinking about Randall Lenz out there somewhere. He's like—he's like the goddamn Terminator or something."

That comment made Jake chuckle, even though he thought he understood what she was trying to say. "He is kind of relentless, I'll give him that. But he's just a man. He's not some unstoppable machine. And we just threw a big monkey wrench into his efforts, so I think he'll be sidelined for a while."

"You really think so?"

His arm tightened around her, pulling her close. There had been such a note of plaintive hope in her tone, a need to believe everything was going to be fine…even while she feared it definitely would not.

"Well, if nothing else, he's going to have a lot of explaining to do to his superiors," Jake said. "He may be running the show at his project, but he's a government employee, and that means he's got plenty of people above him in the food chain."

Her full mouth curved slightly as she appeared to assess that statement. "I think I'd pay money to watch Randall Lenz try to explain how one of his test subjects vanished right in front of him."

While that might have been fun, Jake thought he was just fine with having several thousand miles separating them from Agent Lenz. With any luck, he'd stay out of their orbit indefinitely.

He pushed a lock of glossy brown hair away from Addie's brow and marveled at the silky feel of it under his fingertips. "I have a better idea. We've got the rest of the morning free—let me take you out for breakfast, and then we can come back and wait for everyone to arrive."

"I thought you weren't big on breakfast," she replied, her green-gray eyes glinting with amusement.

"I'll make an exception in this case. It'll be a celebration of having you back."

Her expression sobered, and she nodded. "I think I'd like that. But we need to do something else first."

"What?" he asked, mystified. Maybe she needed him to make some coffee before they headed out— they'd been up pretty late the night before.

The glint returned to her eyes. "How big is your shower?"

Ah. His body warmed as he realized what she was asking. "Big enough," he responded, then bent down to kiss her, taste her sweet mouth.

"Let me show you."

14

Jake took me to a little hole-in-the-wall place just a few doors down from the Blendz tasting room where we'd mixed our own custom wine. That night felt as though it had taken place a century earlier, in another lifetime, but I realized, as I counted out the days on my fingers, that it had only been two weeks ago. So much had happened, I barely could process all of it, but amongst all the insanity, I knew I was sure of one thing.

I loved Jake Wilcox, and he loved me back. Everything else would get worked out in time.

Or at least, that was what I tried to tell myself as I sat down at the shabby booth with its worn red vinyl seats and cracked Formica tabletop. I wanted to raise an eyebrow at Jake's choice of our breakfast location, since he had only taken me to nice places so far, and, it being a Sunday, I assumed there were other venues where we could have gone and gotten a nice brunch.

But the coffee was excellent, strong and rich, and once the food came, I realized that this was one case where you really couldn't judge a book by its cover—my omelette was bursting with farm-fresh tomatoes and crisp bacon and pepper-jack cheese, and the hash browns that accompanied it were crisp and moist at the same time, perfectly golden.

"How did you know about this place?" I asked.

His brown eyes seemed to laugh at me from across the table. "This is my hometown, Addie. I know every restaurant here. Wilcoxes have been coming to the Downtown Diner for years—generations, probably, since it's been here since the 1950s. It's not fancy, but it's great for breakfast…if you're into that sort of thing."

After our…energetic…morning, I was definitely into breakfast, even though generally, I was a grab-and-go kind of girl. But I thought there was something to be said about relaxing and eating a hearty meal at the beginning of the day, especially if the food was that good.

"Well, let's just say I may be changing my mind about breakfast," I said.

"Good thing the diner's so close, then."

Which it was. The day had started out bright and sunny and showed no inclination to change from that model, so we'd walked the few blocks from Jake's house, hand in hand, not talking, simply enjoying our closeness and the time spent together. In those precious moments, I realized once again how I'd never thought it could be so easy to be with someone, to talk when we wanted to talk, to be silent when no words were necessary, breathing in the other person and letting them surround you and fill you.

I had that with Jake, and I knew I wasn't going to let anyone take it away.

"We'll have to come back soon," I said. "I liked walking over here."

"Might as well enjoy it while we can," he said. "The walking's not so easy in the winter."

No, I supposed it probably wasn't. Right then, the snows of December and January felt as though they were years away, thanks to the beautiful weather I'd been able to enjoy since I'd come to Flagstaff. But walking in the winter could be fun as well, although I supposed if the sidewalks got icy enough, it would be safer to drive.

Was it crazy to be thinking of a future six months away when I knew that Randall Lenz was still out there, most likely plotting how he could track me down? Maybe, but I understood that I needed to believe in a shared future with Jake

Wilcox. Otherwise, everything else I'd gone through so far would be too difficult to bear.

"That's a long ways off," I said. "There'll be plenty of beautiful days between now and then."

His eyes caught mine and held. "Yes," he said, "I know there will."

We didn't say much after that, content to eat our breakfasts and bask in the miracle of one another's company. After we paid the bill and walked back to the house, I helped Jake tidy up a bit and then made a big batch of iced tea in preparation for the meeting with Connor and Angela and everyone else. He got some wooden folding chairs from the basement and mixed them in with his regular furniture, since his dining room table didn't have enough regular chairs to accommodate everyone we were expecting.

Still, we had everything ready a good twenty minutes before eleven, and so we headed out to the backyard to sit in the sun for a bit before the crowd started to arrive. It was the first time I'd really had the opportunity to relax there and look around, and I liked everything I saw. Nothing fussy, just a large flagstone patio and a green lawn that maybe needed a bit of mowing, surrounded by beds of old-fashioned flowers—pansies and snapdragons and hollyhocks. Their cheerful blooms made me feel a bit better about the world. In surroundings like those, it was hard to imagine that someone like Randall Lenz even existed.

"Feeling better?" Jake asked, and I nodded.

"Much," I said. "How did you know I needed this?"

He was silent for a few seconds, and then he smiled. "Because I did."

We were sitting at a patio table, glasses of water in front of us since we were saving the iced tea for when everyone arrived. I reached over and touched his hand, which rested on the tabletop next to his glass, and his fingers clasped themselves around mine.

"What was it like?" he asked, and I found myself tensing. I really didn't want to think about those few days I'd spent at the SED facility, even though I'd been able to escape relatively unscathed.

"Maybe I should wait to talk about that until everyone's here."

Jake didn't seem upset by my unwillingness to talk. Instead, he nodded, then asked, "So…what do we do now?"

I guessed that he didn't mean the collective "we." Whatever Connor and Angela and everyone else decided was the best thing to do about Randall Lenz, I'd probably go along with their plans, if only because I'd tried to go my own way already and it hadn't worked out so well. Wanting to be independent was one thing; walking into danger a second time just because I refused to follow the advice of those who were older and more experienced than I was a recipe for disaster.

No, I understood that Jake needed to figure out where we stood, if only because we needed to present a unified front before we sat down with our clan's *primus*. It felt odd to think of the situation in those terms, and yet I realized that I needed to start looking at it that way. I needed to accept myself as a Wilcox, as the half-sister of the man who was running things. True, most of the Wilcoxes had absolutely no idea who I was, just because Connor had held off on making any announcements about our relationship until the situation was more stable, but that didn't change the truth at the heart of the matter. I was a Wilcox, and therefore whatever I did would affect the clan as a whole. It was an odd feeling, when I'd spent most of my life completely disconnected from any family other than my mother. At the same time, though, I welcomed knowing I was part of the Wilcox clan. It meant I had someplace I belonged.

"Well, we can't go back to Riverton," I said. I figured I might as well lay it out on the table so Jake would know I'd abandoned that particular pipe dream.

"Probably not," he agreed, and left it there, as

if he knew I was the one who had to feel her way through this particular maze.

Part of me wanted to sigh, but I told myself it was silly to feel much of a sense of loss over a place I'd only lived for a few days. No, it was more what Riverton represented—a place to get away from who I was, the path that I'd found myself on.

But since I'd already learned that running away didn't solve a damn thing, I put the fantasy aside. Anyway, as cute as Riverton was, it didn't compare to Flagstaff. My days spent in the Wilcox clan's hometown had told me it was the only place I wanted to be.

Then again, possibly that had a lot to do with the man who currently sat next to me, watching me with quiet dark eyes as I sifted through everything that needed to be done.

"So, I need to get in contact with Tracy and tell her I'm moving out," I said. "At least I didn't sign a lease, and she's paid through the end of the month, so I'm not leaving her totally hanging."

"She'll understand," Jake said, but in that one thing, I didn't know whether he was right. After all, it wasn't as if I could tell her any of the truth behind my sudden departure. I'd seem like a flaky girl who'd thought she could start over in Riverton and then had decided it wasn't for her after all.

"And I need to call Leona at the casino and tell her I'm quitting."

Jake shook his head. "She already knows what's going on, Addie," he told me. "Or at least, I think Carson has told her as much as is safe. She knows there are extenuating circumstances and that it's not like you walked off the job without telling anyone because you didn't care."

Well, that was something. I knew in the grand scheme of things, it probably wasn't a big deal—people took off from minimum-wage jobs like that all the time without giving notice—but my mother hadn't raised me to act like that, and I didn't want Leona to think I was a total flake.

"Okay," I said, and left it at that. "So...I'm back in Flagstaff for good. No matter what happens."

"Here with me."

He spoke the words without any of the rising inflection of a question, and yet I knew he was asking all the same. We'd made love twice that morning, first in bed, hard and fast, and then later in the shower, reacquainting ourselves with one another's bodies, and yet we hadn't made any promises to each other, except the promise implicit in our murmured words of love.

"Yes, Jake," I said. "Here with you. If that's all right."

"'If that's all right'?" he repeated, surprise clear

in the words. "God, Addie, that's all I want. I know it hasn't been easy, but I keep pushing on, telling myself that there's a future for us here if we do our best to see it through." He paused there, dark eyes scanning my face. "Unless…unless it would be strange for you to live in a house Sarah and I bought together. We'd only shared the place for a few months before—well, before it happened —but I can understand why you might not be comfortable here."

The last thing I wanted was to make Jake leave his home. And all right, maybe at first glance, it would seem strange for me to be okay with living there, but I loved the house, already felt safe there in a way I hadn't in a very long time…if ever. It was okay that he'd bought the place with the woman he thought he was going to marry. I'd rather live in a house that had been bought with love, with the expectation of shared hopes and dreams coming true there, than one where the previous occupants had fought all the time and left their own negative energy behind.

"I want to be here with you, Jake," I said. "Yes, in this house. We can make our own future here. Not to erase the past, but—"

"But to look forward to something new," he finished for me, the worry in his eyes fading as if it had never been there at all.

We leaned in, mouth brushing against mouth.

However, we didn't have the opportunity to deepen the kiss, because from somewhere inside the house, a doorbell rang. The sound made us both startle and pull apart like a couple of kids sharing an illicit embrace at a high school party rather than a pair of adults who could do anything they liked.

"Sounds like the troops are arriving," Jake said, and I nodded.

"Go ahead and get the door—I'll bring the glasses into the kitchen."

He kissed me again, just a quick brush of his lips against my cheek. Then he was moving quickly inside, while I scooped up our water glasses and followed at a more sedate pace. A quick pause to deposit the glasses on the kitchen counter, and then I went on to the entryway, where Jake was exchanging greetings with Connor and Angela.

"Everything quiet around here?" Angela asked, but there was a twinkle in her big green eyes, as if she'd guessed that Jake's and my reunion had been anything but quiet.

"Oh, yeah," Jake said, a lift at the corner of his mouth seeming to suggest that he understood exactly what she'd been asking.

Luckily, no one expected me to give any gory details, not with my brother standing right there and listening to the exchange with slightly raised eyebrows.

"I slept like the dead," I volunteered. "And this morning, we went out and had a great breakfast."

"Sounds like your outlook on life has definitely improved," Connor said, and I nodded.

"I'm doing much better today," I told him. "Thank you again for coming to my rescue—and for somehow getting my stuff."

I still didn't know exactly how they'd managed it, but when I'd gotten ready that morning, I found all my clothes hanging in the closet and my toiletries safely stowed in the master bath. Maybe at some point, I'd stop being amazed by my brother and sister-in-law's apparently boundless talents. I sure hadn't gotten there yet.

Connor looked almost uncomfortable, as if he thought I was being overly grateful for something he'd taken as a matter of course. "Like we would have done anything else. You're family, Addie— never forget that."

Not much chance of that, when everything and everyone around me seemed intent on reminding me that I was now a part of the Wilcox witch clan, no longer the rootless girl who wandered from place to place, trying to escape a reality that wouldn't let her go. And that was okay. Honestly, after a lifetime of never feeling as if I fit in anywhere, it was nice to be surrounded by people who only wanted me to be myself.

The doorbell rang again. This time, the arrival was Jake's brother Jeremy, who tilted his head at me in a casual way, acknowledging my presence without making a big deal about it.

"Hey, Addie."

"Hey, Jeremy. Thanks for cracking the surveillance system at the SED."

A lift of his shoulders. "No biggie. Actually, I'm sort of annoyed with myself that it took so long."

I wanted to tell him it was kind of amazing how he'd cracked such a secure system in less than forty-eight hours, then decided to let it go. Not that I'd ever take Jeremy's astonishing computer talents for granted—it was still hard for me to believe just one person could manage so much on his own—but I knew he pushed himself hard and probably wouldn't be reassured by my compliments.

"You got it in the end," I said. "That's the important thing."

Another shrug from Jeremy, and Jake said, "I figured we'd all sit down at the dining room table. There's iced tea and water, and I can make coffee if anyone wants it."

"Tea is great," Angela told him.

It turned out everyone wanted tea, so Jake and

I poured for those present, and then Margot and Lucas showed up, followed by Laurel a minute or two later. She looked a little puzzled, as if she could tell events had been moving so quickly that no one had had a chance to get her caught up on everything that had happened. Well, I hoped our meeting would help her get filled in on all the details.

Eventually, we were all seated with our beverage of choice in front of us—although I could tell Lucas probably would have been happier with a mimosa or a Bloody Mary. To be honest, I wouldn't have turned down a glass of white wine right about then. Although I'd met everyone in the room before, this was the first time I'd faced them *en masse,* so to speak, and I found it a little overwhelming to be surrounded by so many Wilcoxes at once. And okay, I knew that Margot and Angela weren't Wilcoxes by blood, but they were married to Wilcoxes, so that amounted to roughly the same thing.

I told myself I had no real reason to be nervous. After all, I had Jake at my side, and everyone there probably wanted the same thing I did—to live a quiet life in Flagstaff without any worry about what Randall Lenz might attempt next.

To my surprise, Jeremy spoke first. His fingers tapped against the glass of iced tea in front of him, and I noticed how he didn't quite meet anyone's gaze, as if he didn't really like having to talk in front of such a large audience but knew he needed to provide some important information.

"I was able to scrub your images from the facility's surveillance recordings," he said. "So, even though Lenz got a good look at you, there's no real physical evidence he can use to back up his personal observations."

"That's great news," Connor said. He offered all of us a reassuring smile. "I was worried about that, even though I knew it was a risk we'd have to take."

Jeremy settled against the back of his chair, looking relieved that he'd managed to deliver his message and now only had to worry about some back-and-forth with the *primus*. "No, about all Lenz can do is call in a sketch artist or something, and that's probably not going to help much. It's one thing when you already have a suspect in mind and need some corroboration from a witness. In this case, he'd be trying to match a sketch to a database of the entire U.S. population. I doubt that's going to work."

No, probably not. Of course, Randall Lenz knew exactly what I looked like, but with Jeremy's dutiful little algorithms chasing down my likeness wherever it appeared so it could be scrubbed before it popped up on someone's radar, I didn't think I had much to worry about on that front. And since it seemed that the memory wipe Connor and Angela had performed on him was still holding, I also didn't have to worry about him suddenly recalling my connection to Flagstaff and making a beeline for the mountain town.

"So, we're in the clear?" Angela asked.

"As far as I can tell," Jeremy replied. "They're doing their damnedest to kick me out of their system, but my countermeasures knock out their countermeasures before they can take hold, and so I can still get a pretty good read on what's happening behind the scenes. Right now, they don't have anything to go on, except that a trio of unknown intruders somehow managed to get past all their security and then vanish into thin air with one of their test subjects. I think as long as we all lie low for a while, we should be able to skate out the other side without any problem."

Next to me, Jake shifted in his chair. "Does that mean I can go back to being Jake Wilcox?"

"I'd wait a while," Jeremy said. "Just because we've managed to give them the slip so far doesn't mean we should get careless. I know it's a pain not being able to use your debit card or whatever, but if it's that big a problem, just have Bethany get the bank to issue a dummy card under your alias. That'll hold you until we know you're definitely in the clear."

I glanced up at Jake, trying not to frown. What alias? Clearly, I'd missed out on a lot, and Jake hadn't had time to bring me up to speed because we'd been focused on other things…like figuring out what exactly a future together was going to look like. I had to surmise that Jake must have been forced to create some sort of false identity for himself to keep Randall Lenz off the scent. Now that I thought about it, Jake had used cash when we went out to eat in Riverton, and also to buy gas. At the time, I hadn't paid much attention, since we had far more important matters to contend with, but I realized he must have been using cash to avoid leaving any kind of electronic trail that could be traced.

Not for the first time, I thought of all the havoc I'd caused in his life, all the measures he'd had to take to keep me and the rest of his family safe. Not that anyone could say it was my fault—I was more than happy to lay the blame at Randall Lenz's feet—but still….

"Okay," Jake said. "I'll text Bethany and see what she can do. It's no big deal."

"And I can get some cash for you," I broke in, thinking of all the money Connor had set up for me from an inheritance I hadn't even known about until a few weeks earlier. Then I paused and sent Jeremy a worried glance. "Or…can I?

Connor set up some accounts for me under 'Adara Wilcox,' but…."

"They know about those," Jeremy told me. "So, that's really not a good idea."

"It's fine," Connor said. Unlike the rest of us, he didn't appear too worried by the situation. "The bulk of the money hasn't even been transferred yet. Tomorrow morning, I'll go to the bank and withdraw a chunk of cash. You'll need to keep it at the house, since obviously, it won't do you any good to put it in your own accounts, but at least that way, you'll have something to work with."

"That sounds good," Jake said. His posture appeared a lot more relaxed after Connor made the offer, and he looked over at me briefly and gave me a reassuring smile. "I have a safe for important papers, so we'll just keep it in there."

I wanted to smile back at him, but once again, pangs of guilt assailed me. They were all acting as if this was just a temporary inconvenience and nothing more, but what if it wasn't? What if he was forced to keep hiding from Randall Lenz for months…for years? What if Jake would have to end up legally changing his name in order to keep Lenz and the SED off his trail?

What if I would be compelled to do the very same thing?

They're just names, I told myself. *They're not…us.*

Which was true, and yet I didn't much relish the idea of having to spend the rest of my life in the witchy equivalent of the witness protection program. But the alternative was far, far worse, and I knew I'd suck it up and do whatever was necessary to ensure a safe and happy life with Jake in Flagstaff.

"This is all temporary," he said then, and reached under the table to give my hand a quick squeeze. "We just have to be careful for a while until all this gets sorted out."

That time, I forced a smile. Since I couldn't see myself, I had no idea whether it looked as manufactured to everyone else as it felt to me.

"It's going to be fine," Lucas said. He and Margot had been silent up until that point, probably because they didn't have a lot to contribute, but apparently, he'd decided that I needed further reassurance. "Maybe all we really need to do is have a sit-down with this Agent Lenz and tell him a few home truths about himself."

Laurel stared at her cousin as if he'd just lost his mind. "You're joking, right? That guy is dangerous."

I was inclined to agree with her. At the same time, she hadn't been present when we'd discussed the possibility of Randall Lenz being a warlock, and I guessed it was time to bring her up to speed. "Lucas thinks Agent Lenz might be one of us," I said.

Her dark, arched brows lifted in shock, and she gazed at him blankly. "You think he's a *Wilcox?*"

"No," Lucas said calmly. "I think he's a warlock. I definitely got a ping off him when he confronted us at the SED facility last night. Everyone else thinks I'm nuts, but…." The words trailed off there, and he gave an eloquent shrug as he lifted his glass of iced tea and took a sip.

Jeremy also looked sort of gobsmacked, which made me think no one had thought to discuss that particular tidbit with him. Voice flat, he said, "So, what…you want to sit him down and tell him he's a warlock, and hope that'll be enough to get him to give up the whole thing and come sing 'Kumbaya' with us?"

Put that way, the whole thing did sound sort of ludicrous. And honestly, I didn't know what to think. Lucas had no reason to be lying about whatever it was that he'd felt from Randall Lenz… and neither did Genoveva Castillo, who claimed to have experienced basically the same thing.

But they didn't know the man in question. Maybe I didn't, either. Not really. I'd had far more face-to-face time with him than anyone else present, however, and even if we somehow managed to concoct a plan that would allow me —or Connor, or Angela—to approach him and explain that he might be a bit more than an ordinary human, I had no reason to think he'd believe a single word of it. No, he'd be much more likely to dismiss any of our arguments as some kind of crazy strategy to get him to back off from me and the Wilcox clan in general.

"I think we should do whatever we can to stay as far away from him as possible," I said. "Even if what you felt is true, Lucas, he's never going to believe it. Not for a second."

Margot tilted her elegant dark head. Once again, I was struck by the contrast between her and the easygoing, "what, me worry?" Lucas, and I had to wonder how two opposites like them had ever ended up together. I didn't have time to puzzle through that conundrum, however, because she remarked, "You seem very sure of that, Addie. While I know you have your own reasons for never wanting to deal with him, do you really think it's fair to deprive Agent Lenz of something that might very well be his birthright?"

Anger flared within me, even as I told myself that Margot was asking a fair enough question. She could look at the situation coolly because she didn't have any personal involvement. If Randall Lenz actually was a warlock, was it right to withhold that information from him, allow him to continue his life thinking he was no different from the rest of the normal population?

I didn't have an answer to that question. The anger I felt for him told me one thing, but my brain was thinking something very different.

"And I'm not sure it's fair for you to ask Addie that question," Jake broke in, his tone abrupt. Obviously, he was all too willing to go to the mat for me when I didn't know whether or not I should try to defend myself. "The guy killed her mother."

Margot's eyes flashed dark fire. "I'm well aware of the situation. He did a terrible thing…probably lots of terrible things. I'm not disputing any of that. I'm only asking whether we're all okay with allowing someone who might be witch-kind to remain ignorant of that knowledge. I think it's something we might want to consider before we make any other decisions."

An uncomfortable silence fell. Laurel's face was full of righteous anger on my behalf, and I didn't have to guess what her opinion on the matter might be. Connor and Angela were a bit harder to read; although I thought I saw sympathy in their expressions, if the faint frown that pulled my brother's brows together and the way his wife's mouth pursed slightly were any indication, they seemed to be having a difficult time seeing the problem in purely black and white terms.

It was Connor who spoke at last. Maybe Angela knew it was his call, just because the Wilcoxes were his clan and he'd have to make the final decision. "A big part of me would like to let Agent Lenz just rot," he said. "But…." A breath escaped my brother's lips, and he went on, sounding very tired, "But the whole reason you came up with Trident Enterprises, Jake, was so we could reach out to witches and warlocks who didn't know anything about who they were or where they came from. If we don't do the same for Randall Lenz, then aren't we being just a little hypocritical?"

Jake still held my hand under the table, out of sight. He let go then, placing his hands on the tabletop. "I don't think so. We're just being careful. Like Addie said, the guy isn't going to believe a word of it anyway."

"Why not?" Margot asked. Her cool dark gaze met Jake's. "After all, the man clearly is ready to believe in the fantastical, or he wouldn't be heading up a program that specifically seeks out people with extraordinary abilities."

"Because he thinks he's dealing with some sort of extra-sensory stuff," I told her, since Jake's mouth tightened, and he appeared unsure as to the best way to respond to her comment. "They want to measure those abilities and test them, teach people how to control them. He doesn't believe that any of it is magic. He thinks it all comes from untapped abilities in our brains."

"Still," she argued, "he has to have a fairly open mind, or he wouldn't be working in that field at all. There are many civilians who are so close-minded about the whole thing that they'll deny the evidence of their own eyes if it better fits their worldview."

As much as I wished I could poke holes in her assertion, I knew she was right. Randall Lenz wanted to believe on some level, or he would have pursued a different line of work. For all I knew, maybe he'd detected traces of his own power over the years, and that was what had made him focus on seeking out others with gifts far beyond what was considered normal.

If our hypothesis was true and it turned out that somehow my lightning attack had awakened Randall Lenz's magical talent, then he must be wrestling with the same problem that had tormented me for more than ten years, of having a strange and unruly gift with no way to control it. As much as I hated him for what he'd done to my mother, could I live with myself if I condemned him to a lifetime of fighting something he couldn't see and didn't understand?

As soon as I asked that question of myself, I knew the answer. It wasn't one I wanted to acknowledge, and yet I understood that I had to face it, no matter what happened.

Jake must have detected some shift in my posture or expression, because he sent me a worried look. "You don't owe Randall Lenz a damn thing," he said, his tone fierce.

Maybe I didn't. And yet...and yet, I knew I owed this to myself.

"We have to help him," I said softly, then glanced around at everyone else gathered at the table. "Now we just have to figure out how."

15

HE STARED DOWN AT THE SKETCHES HE'D composed when he got home from work that evening. At any other time, he might have stayed late to see if Dawson could come up with anything helpful about their hacker or the trio of strangers who'd abducted Adara Grant, but he knew he was tired...and possibly a little more rattled by his confrontation with Wallace Bryant than he wanted to admit.

Now a glass of single-malt scotch sat on the table next to the sketches, a half-eaten sandwich from his favorite deli resting on a plate a little farther away. Randall Lenz reached for the scotch, took a swallow, and set the glass back down.

He didn't know why those faces haunted him so. Somewhere deep within, he seemed to recognize that they held greater significance than simply being Adara Grant's kidnappers, but his tired brain didn't seem able to grasp the pattern.

Probably, the scotch wasn't helping, either, but one glass certainly wasn't enough to cause any detectable impairment. And he needed the spurious sense of well-being it provided.

What was it about the people in those sketches, especially the younger man and the woman? They'd both been wearing wedding bands, he was almost certain. Husband and wife?

A possibility, but he couldn't be sure. They hadn't engaged in any public displays of affection, but then, why would they, when it was clear they were intent on rescuing Adara Grant and nothing else?

Frowning, he stared down at the portraits again. These were new sketches he'd quickly traced out after he got home from the facility, focusing on their faces. They'd been wearing nondescript clothing, jeans and T-shirts, the older of the two men in a polo shirt and khakis. Because their clothes had been so ordinary, Lenz didn't see the point in trying to analyze them. No, it was in their features that he hoped to find illumination.

Once again, he got a flash of the woman bending over him, her expression worried, possibly even a little frightened. Unconsciously, Lenz winced as he waited for the inevitable burst of pain in his head that seemed to accompany such a glimpse, but it never came. Cushioned by the scotch, possibly?

He didn't know. Rather than try to analyze why the blinding migraine held off, he instead did his best to hold on to that image of the strange woman, to commit every detail to memory. Her wavy dark hair was pulled back from her face in that glimpse, rather than falling to her shoulders the way it had been when she came to rescue Adara Grant from her room at the facility. No T-shirt, either; she'd been wearing jeans, but she had on a sleeveless top of cotton or linen, with turquoise and silver drops hanging from her ears. Minimal makeup, he thought, only mascara on the thick lashes that surrounded her brilliantly green eyes and a touch of peach-hued gloss or sheer lipstick on her full mouth.

In a way, he was startled at how much he could remember of her. And then, as if recalling those details awoke even more memories, he realized the man had been there, too—tall and dark-haired, with greenish eyes as well, although his were mixed with gray, subtler in hue but striking as well. Lenz didn't know why he was so certain of the fact, but he somehow knew that they were indeed husband and wife.

Connor and Angela.

The names leapt out of nowhere, and he quickly wrote them down. Where they'd come from, he had no idea. Had they addressed one another while in his presence? Had someone else spoken to them, called them out by name?

That piece of the memory didn't want to surface. However, Lenz realized there had been other people in the room: an older woman with graying dark hair, and two more.

Jake Wilcox and Adara Grant.

You don't know he's Jake Wilcox, Lenz told himself. *Dawson had only one hit on that name, and he was someone twice this man's age.*

And yet…he somehow knew he was right. No matter what the evidence was trying to tell him, the man in question was definitely Jake Wilcox. He must have done something to obfuscate his true identity. Not so far-fetched a theory, not when they already knew their servers had been breached by an unknown hacker intent on hiding as much evidence about Adara Grant as possible.

So, they'd all been there—Connor and Angela and Jake and Adara, along with the older woman. Eleanor? That felt halfway right, although he couldn't be entirely certain. Lenz realized that the memories felt so odd and distorted because he'd been drifting in and out of consciousness, his body battered, aching. He'd lain on a sofa, although his first recollections of the scene seemed to have been from a vantage point lower down, as if he'd started out on the floor and then gotten moved to the couch later on.

Yes. He'd confronted Adara, and she'd summoned a lightning bolt to strike him down. The pain had been searing, intense, far worse than anything he'd suffered in his life, including the time a car had struck him in a crosswalk when he was just in high school and broke both his legs and fractured his collarbone. No wonder he'd been such a mess for the past few weeks. While people could be struck by lightning and survive, there were often serious side effects that lingered for months or even years afterward.

He couldn't even be angry with her for what she'd done. In the same situation, he probably would also have used his native abilities to mount some kind of defense. Actually, he was more puzzled by the memory than anything else. All the data seemed to suggest that she didn't have much control over her abilities, but it seemed clear enough to him that she'd been able to use lightning to make a single targeted strike. Now her success on the training field with Dr. Woodrow made a great deal more sense. His team had been pleased to see her progressing so quickly, but it seemed to him now that she'd been playing them for fools all along.

He wanted to be irritated with her for her

duplicity. Instead, he couldn't quite hold back an unexpected surge of admiration.

Another swallow of scotch, and Lenz stared down at the sketches again. What was the connection between all these people? Why had Jake sought out Adara in the first place? Memory had begun to return, but it wasn't filling in all the details.

Except he was now almost completely convinced that Connor and Adara must be siblings. How, he didn't know.

Was Connor also a Wilcox? Were he and Jake related in some way? They didn't resemble one another all that much, except for the superficial similarities of being tall and dark-haired and well-built, but that theory made more sense than anything else he could come up with.

Maybe…maybe they'd just discovered that Connor and Adara were related, and Jake had gone to seek her out in Kanab to make sure. Why Connor hadn't undertaken such an errand himself, if Adara truly was his sister, Lenz didn't know. In the end, it didn't matter so much. What mattered was that she was clearly important to them, important enough that they'd undertaken a risky rescue in a secret government facility to ensure her safety.

How had they managed such a thing? Lenz knew what he'd seen with his own eyes—the four of them disappearing into thin air before he could take a single step forward to prevent their departure. Which seemed to indicate that Connor had powers of his own, powers that made Adara's seem almost insignificant.

But why the presence of the woman Lenz believed was Connor's wife, or the older man, the one who also seemed as if he must be related to Connor somehow? Did they also possess extraordinary powers? Were all of them required to be present in order to generate the teleportation power they'd used to get Adara away?

Again, he couldn't know for sure. However, he felt he was on the verge of discovering something big, something that would neatly put together all these scattered pieces and create a coherent picture to prove they truly were connected.

For the moment, he needed to follow up on one thing. It was late, and Agent Dawson would be at home as well. However, he wanted her working on this, not Agent LaRue, who took over her duties during the overnight hours and who was competent but not as thorough or as insightful.

Lenz got out his cell phone and typed a quick message. *Check on Connor Wilcox. Wife possibly named Angela. Get back to me with any information you find.*

He sent the text to Dawson's personal phone,

knowing that even though she was technically off-duty, she would follow up as soon as she received it. As far as he could tell, she didn't seem to have much of a personal life—no husband or significant other of any kind, no close family ties. Originally from Omaha, Nebraska, she seemed to exist mainly for her position at the SED and not much else. Because of this, he had no reason to believe that he wouldn't have the information he sought in the very near future.

Maybe at last he'd be able to place the final pieces in the puzzle and then decide what to do next.

Addie hadn't wanted to go out to dinner, so Jake had Door Dash deliver from Brix, another of his favorite Flagstaff restaurants, one owned by the same people who operated Criollo. They would be missing out on the ambiance of Brix, which was located in a converted Craftsman house near the northeast edge of downtown, but the food would still be good, and at least he had a fairly decent wine stash on hand, so he wouldn't have too difficult a time choosing something that complemented both their meals.

Now they sat at the dining room table, the fixture that hung above them dimmed to provide a soft romantic light, candles flickering from the metal stands placed at the center of the table. Quiet music played in the background. Everything seemed perfectly in place for an intimate meal—well, except for Taffy perched on the floor directly between the two of them, ready to beg for scraps—and yet Jake had a feeling none of this was turning out the way he'd planned.

"I can't believe you want to help the guy," he said, and Addie's lips thinned.

"Are we really going to go over this again?" she asked as she reached for her glass of zinfandel.

He could feel his jaw clench, and did his best to relax. While he didn't want to get into an argument, he also couldn't help thinking that if she would just listen to him, she'd understand why her misplaced idealism was unwarranted in this situation.

"Look," he replied, "I suppose I can understand why you all would think Randall Lenz is deserving of some sort of consideration, but I don't see the point in putting yourself out there for him when we still don't know for sure that he's even a warlock at all."

She lifted the wine glass and took a measured sip, then put it back down. However, even though the movement had been almost too precise, as if she'd done so as a way to keep a check on her emotions, Jake wanted to believe he'd detected a slight softening in her expression.

"No, we don't," she said. "And believe me—I'd much rather walk away and let him stew in his own juices. But if there's even the slightest chance that he could be one of us, then we have to do something. If nothing else, he could be a danger to himself and everyone around him if he's got some kind of power that's suddenly started to manifest and he can't control it."

It figured she'd come up with the one argument that would make him pause and re-analyze the situation. He hadn't even thought of that angle, mostly because it really wasn't a problem when kids' powers started to develop, since they always had adult witches and warlocks around to guide them. But if those powers suddenly appeared in an adult, and were therefore by extension much stronger, and the person in question didn't know what in the hell was going on…

…well, that was a recipe for disaster right there.

"Okay," he allowed. "Do you have any idea what kind of ability we're talking about here?"

That question made her frown slightly, her expression distracted. Jake had the feeling that she was mentally scanning through her more recent encounters with Randall Lenz and trying to determine if he'd done or said anything that might have provided a clue as to his supposed witchy talents.

"No," she said after a moment, expression dejected. She speared a piece of ribeye and took a bite, chewing meditatively. Once she'd swallowed, she added, "It can't be anything too flashy, because otherwise, I should have seen some sign of it. I mean, there were no flashes of thunder or objects moving around. He wasn't flinging balls of fire or reading my mind or doing anything that seemed like any of the talents I've heard of so far." Another pause, and she asked, "How many different talents *are* there, anyway?"

"I don't know for sure," he responded. "Hundreds, I guess. I mean, some are a lot more common than others—healing, working with plants, seeing the future, telekinesis. I'm not sure why, except it seems as if most of those have a survival component to them, so it makes sense that they would continue to pop up in each generation. But then you have people who can talk to ghosts, like Angela, or people who are good at making potions, or people who can find lost objects or create shields around themselves...there's just lots of them to choose from. And not all of them are that obvious. I mean, Lucas has an amazing gift that's helped him out a lot, but I'm not sure you'd be able to tell just from being around him that he was super lucky, unless you were playing cards with him or something."

At those words, Addie sat up a little straighter, her eyes widening. She set down her fork and stared at him for a moment. "Maybe that's it."

"What's it?"

"Luck," she replied. "Maybe that's Randall Lenz's talent as well. It would make sense—he said once to me that his hunches usually played out. What if those weren't hunches at all, but his talent manifesting itself? That's why my lightning bolt didn't kill him outright…and that's why he was always so close on my trail. His gift kept giving him the necessary guidance, pushing him so he'd be in the right place at the right time."

Her face had brightened as she spoke. While Jake had to admit to himself that some of what she said made sense, he still didn't know whether she was on the right track.

"If he's so lucky, then why didn't he catch you right away?" he asked. "All our maneuvering shouldn't have even worked."

"'Right away' was before he was struck by lightning," Addie pointed out. "We were able to get away from him in the beginning because his gift just wasn't strong enough. Afterward…well, I can't explain exactly why he didn't catch me in Santa Fe, or why it took him a while to find me in Riverton." She was quiet for a few seconds, fingers tapping against the base of her wine glass. "But tell me—is Lucas one hundred percent lucky in every single thing he does?"

About all Jake could do was shrug. "It's not like I hang out with him every second of every day, so I can't say for sure. Probably not. It's mostly the big stuff, the things that would change his life if his luck wasn't guiding him in the right direction. Also, sometimes it seems as if he's not particularly lucky in something—his love life was nothing to write home about until he met Margot —until you kind of step back and realize his luck was guiding him to where he was supposed to be."

"Like meeting her, even though she was a McAllister?"

"Exactly," Jake replied, a little surprised that Addie had been able to read between the lines on that one. After all, she hadn't been around long enough to know much about Lucas' history with Margot, although he supposed she must have done some quick math based on the age of Lucas and Margot's daughter Mia and the time when Connor and Angela had broken the curse that had hung over the Wilcox *primuses* for more than a hundred years. After that singular accomplishment, everything began to change in the Wilcox clan. Jake scrubbed his hand through the hair at the back of his head and gave Addie a sideways look. "So…you're saying that Randall Lenz's talent was trying to guide him to a place where he'd be most likely to figure out what he actually was?"

"Or have someone else tell him," she said. "Which is where we are now."

"Sort of. It's not as if any of us have come up with a concrete plan as to how we're supposed to let him know that he might not be your ordinary government agent next door."

Not that the guy was even close to your run-of-the-mill agent. Jake actually knew a real-life FBI agent, because the father of a friend from college had worked for the agency for more than twenty years. David Whitaker seemed like a normal guy—maybe a little strict, but not too bad —while Jake really couldn't imagine Randall Lenz relaxing at a backyard barbecue or showing up in the middle of the night to drive his drunk son home from a frat party. The guy seemed like the type who didn't have any kind of a personal life at all.

Addie let out a breath, her expression somber. Fingers still playing with the base of her wine glass, she said, "I know. I mean, I understand that Connor and Angela probably have the powers necessary to zap themselves right into Lenz's house or something—"

"They do," Jake broke in, grinning a little despite the seriousness of the topic. "I mean, they need to have a visual of where they're going, but since Jeremy dug up photos of Lenz's house online from when it was listed for sale, that would be easy enough."

Her mouth pursed in amusement. "Why does that not surprise me? Anyway," she went on without waiting for a response, "even though we have the means to get right to him if we want to, I kind of doubt he'd respond very well to that sort of an intrusion. But I know we'll figure something out."

Jake watched her for a moment, marveling at how composed she seemed. After all, they were talking about the man who'd killed her mother, even if it might have been by accident. "I'm still kind of surprised that you'd want to do anything to help the guy."

"I suppose I realized I had a choice," she said, her tone musing. Her gaze wasn't directed toward him, but apparently fixed on something beyond the windows in the dining room, now not much more than dark rectangles looking out into the night. "I try not to be a bitter person—that's something I learned from my mom. She always tried to see the best in people."

"I'm not sure Randall Lenz has a 'best,'" Jake remarked as he reached for his glass of wine.

"Everyone does. He just hasn't found his yet." A pause, and then she said, "He lost his father on 9/11. I think that really did a number on him.

Ever since then, he's been doing his best to feel as if he's working to make the country safer."

"Up to and including kidnapping people with special abilities?"

Jake had been half joking when he asked the question, but Addie appeared to take him seriously. "Yes. Because he thinks that people who have our kinds of powers can be recruited to be another line of defense against terrorists. I'm not saying what he's doing is right or that I agree with him at all, but it's also not as if he woke up one day and decided to be evil just because."

It took a few seconds for Jake to absorb all this. Honestly, he didn't like hearing those details about Lenz's father because it forced him to acknowledge that Randall Lenz was a person with a family and a past, and apparently his own share of tragedy. Much better to look at him as the embodiment of evil and go from there.

"Anyway," Addie continued, once it became clear that Jake had remained silent because he wasn't sure how to reply, "I guess I told myself that I could try to get some kind of revenge on him by leaving him to stew in his own juices…or I could try to be a better person and help him understand that he doesn't have to continue on his present course."

Jake stared at her for a long moment. Right then, she looked extraordinarily beautiful, with the candlelight shimmering on her sleek brown hair and awakening golden gleams in her gray-green eyes, but he realized he didn't love her because she was physically beautiful. He loved her because the beauty he saw in her face was reflected in her soul.

"You're an amazing person," he said at length. "You're a much better person than I am."

She let out a deprecating chuckle and shook her head. "Don't sell yourself short, Jake. You're pretty amazing yourself."

He wasn't so sure about that. But one look at the warmth in Addie's eyes, the beautiful curve of her lips as she smiled at him, was enough to let him know he shouldn't waste his energy on protests. If she wanted to think he was amazing, fine. He'd just have to do whatever was necessary to make sure her belief in him wasn't misplaced.

They were nearly done with their meal. He reached for his glass of wine and swallowed the last of the zinfandel within, then removed the napkin from his lap and set it on the tabletop next to his plate. Addie seemed to understand his intention, because she finished her wine as well and pushed her chair away from the table.

As soon as they were standing, he reached out and pulled her close, allowed himself to taste her glorious mouth. She responded at once, her body pressed against him, letting him know that she was all too ready to leave the discussion of Randall Lenz behind and focus on just the two of them.

Moving together, they ascended the stairs and went into the master bedroom. No words, just their clothing discarded piece by piece so they could fall onto the bed and lose themselves in one another and the moment.

And for the moment, it was enough.

His phone rang, and Randall Lenz picked it up immediately. He'd gone to the family room in his home after consuming a cobbled-together dinner, figuring he'd watch some television while he waited for Dawson to get back to him, but he hadn't been able to focus on much of anything. No, his thoughts had kept racing, circling back to those disjointed but vivid images —Connor and Angela Wilcox. Jake Wilcox. Adara Grant. A house that had seemed small but cozy and well-furnished. An Airbnb or other short-term rental?

Possibly. As with everything else, it seemed that every detail he latched on to only generated more questions.

Dawson's voice came in his ear. "I hope it's not too late, sir."

The display on his phone had told him it was

a little after eleven. "Not at all," he replied. "Thank you for working on this after hours."

A pause followed those words, as if she wasn't quite sure how to handle the unexpected show of gratitude. Lenz realized he rarely praised Dawson to her face for her work, although her performance reviews were always glowing and he made sure that all her pay raises were at the top of the allowed scale.

"Um…that's no problem at all, sir," she said. "I have some information for you on Connor and Angela Wilcox."

"So, they are married."

"Yes. Angela legally goes by McAllister-Wilcox. They've been married for nearly eight years."

That piece of information didn't surprise him very much. Something about the way they interacted spoke of the sort of rapport that only evolved after a good deal of time together. "What else?"

"They own residences in both Jerome, Arizona, and Flagstaff, Arizona. They—"

"Flagstaff," Lenz said, his tone flat. Suddenly, his mind was assailed by more images—sweeping vistas of ponderosa forests surrounding his car as he sped along the interstate…a small bungalow-style house with its shutters painted dark red… Adara Grant and Jake Wilcox standing on the porch of a much larger Victorian home as they shared a prolonged kiss.

All those scenes exploded into his brain at once, and he had to blink back a wave of dizziness. Why they were all so vivid, he didn't know, except that he realized they must be images of what he'd experienced in the moments leading up to Adara's attack with the lightning bolt. Was it the shock of that trauma which had caused him to lose his memories, or something else?

"Are you all right, sir?"

Dawson's voice, clearly troubled, managed to penetrate the fog in his mind. He blinked, then said, "Yes, Dawson. It's just—hearing about Flagstaff seemed to bring back some of my missing memories."

"That's excellent, sir." A pause, and she asked, "Was it in Flagstaff that you were attacked?"

"Yes. Adara Grant did hit me with a lightning bolt. I blacked out immediately afterward, but some bits and pieces are starting to come through." He thought then of the image of the young men taken from the security camera at a motel on the outskirts of Kanab, Utah. Those two men were also tall and dark-haired and well-built, seeming to indicate that they must be Wilcoxes as well. Was the whole family in on this?

It certainly seemed that way at first glance.

"Go on," he said. "What else did you find?"

"Connor and Angela Wilcox have a part-interest in a winery in the Verde Valley. The Wilcox family has been in the Flagstaff area since the late 1870s. Very prosperous. There are many of them in Flagstaff and northern Arizona in general, although I don't have exact numbers at the moment."

"That's all right," he told her. At the moment, he didn't think he needed the minutiae of all the various Wilcox family members. It was enough to know that there were a lot of them, and obviously they had the wherewithal to carry out any number of schemes.

Which made the situation much more difficult. If he had been dealing with a few loners, that was one thing. A small group of people would have been easy enough to neutralize, if it came to that. But when it seemed that his foes were members of a prominent family, then all at once, his options had become far more limited.

Still, he wasn't about to stand idly by and allow the Wilcoxes to triumph. If nothing else, they'd infiltrated a government facility and taken one of his test subjects, thereby breaking a number of federal laws. Unfortunately, he couldn't press his case in court, because doing so would only expose the Daedalus Project for what it was, and he couldn't have that.

"Give me the addresses of their two residences," he said, and Dawson dutifully reeled them off as he typed the information into the notepad program on his phone.

"What do you plan to do, sir?"

The trepidation in his assistant's voice was clear enough. It seemed obvious that she feared he was about to go tearing off to Arizona to confront the trespassers directly.

As a matter of fact, that was precisely what he wanted to do. Strike hard and fast, and not give them time to prepare. But he realized that just because Connor and Angela Wilcox had been involved in Adara Grant's rescue, that didn't mean she would be staying with them. No, it seemed far more likely that she was with Jake Wilcox, a man who'd somehow managed to erase any evidence of his existence from the official record.

Even as he frowned, however, Lenz realized he didn't need to access any of Wilcox's online data. He'd been there, parked on the street down a few doors from the big Victorian house that appeared to be his. Once, before Adara blasted him with her lightning, he'd known exactly where to find Jake Wilcox. Now his memories had begun to return, so Lenz knew the information had to be trapped in his brain somewhere, just waiting to be liberated.

"I'm not sure yet what I intend to do," he told Dawson. "Thank you for the information, though.

At least now we know who was behind Adara Grant's jailbreak."

"Yes, sir," she replied. "Is there anything else?"

"No. It's late—get some sleep."

He ended the call there and set the phone down on the coffee table in front of him. Without really seeing any of the images flashing across the screen, he stared at the television, his mind already ranging outward, far to the west, where the Wilcoxes lived.

They thought they'd gotten away with it. For the moment, they had. But he knew how easily the tide could turn, and Randall Lenz wasn't ready to admit defeat quite yet. His mind had been opened, and now he just needed that one particular memory to return to him. As soon as it did, he would be on his way.

And soon after that, Adara Grant would be back with the rest of the test subjects, as she was meant to be.

16

I WANTED TO BELIEVE THAT OUR LOVEMAKING of the night before had fixed everything between Jake and me, and yet I could still sense the tension in him, the words he wanted to say and held back because he didn't want to get in an argument. In a way, I understood his baffled anger. After everything Randall Lenz had done, why was I allowing myself to even entertain the thought of helping him?

Good question. I certainly wasn't the crusader type, had spent a good chunk of my formative years doing whatever I could to blend into the woodwork and avoid attracting notice. And I also wasn't naïve enough to think Agent Lenz would be so thrilled to hear that he was actually a warlock, he would immediately repent his evil ways and turn to a life of doing good.

No, it was more that I didn't want to spend the rest of my life harboring a grudge. My mother had never spoken a bad word about Jackson Wilcox, even though one could have argued that he'd taken advantage of her, using his age and experience and wealth to seduce an inexperienced young woman. Actually, she'd always done what she could to paint their brief tryst in a romantic light. Maybe that was only because she didn't want me thinking ill of my father—there had been many times when I'd tried to make her reach out to Jackson, arguing that I should at least get to meet him, if only once. She'd always shot me down, saying that it had been her decision to have me, and she wasn't going to hold him responsible. That assertion had always seemed a little too noble to me, but now I thought I finally understood her motivations. She hadn't wanted me to think that our lives were somehow lesser just because he hadn't been a part of them. No matter how tough things were, she'd always believed they would get better.

So, while I could see that Jake thought I was crazy for wanting to give Randall Lenz any kind of help, I knew deep down that I needed to do so because I didn't want to turn my back on someone who might be floundering through the same sorts of problems I'd had to deal with. He didn't know who or what he was, and he needed to be told.

Also, I couldn't stop thinking of all the other test subjects at the facility—Ethan and Natalie and Matthew and Lorna. They needed to be freed so they could also learn about their witch heritage, and it seemed to me the simplest way to accomplish that goal was to get Randall Lenz firmly on our side.

Easier said than done, unfortunately.

For the moment, I needed to do what I could to repair things between Jake and me. We sat at the dining room table, sharing a cup of coffee and a bagel, but we hadn't said much except to exchange a few perfunctory remarks about the weather and the possibility of a grocery run, since he didn't have all that much food in the house.

I swallowed some French roast for courage and said, "You think I'm nuts, don't you?"

At once, his dark eyes flared with shock…and possibly a twinge of guilt. "No, I don't think you're nuts." A pause as he sat there with his hands wrapped around his coffee mug. They were strong, capable hands, browned by the sun—I'd noticed that most Wilcoxes looked as though they tanned easily—and I remembered how good it had felt the night before to have them caressing me, holding me close. "I guess I'm still just trying to figure out how you could be so willing to forgive Randall Lenz for what he's done."

"I'm not sure it's exactly forgiveness," I responded.

"What, then?"

Good question. I had to dig deep inside myself for the answer, because it wasn't something that was immediately obvious to me. "More like…moving on," I said after a moment. "I could hate him and do whatever I could to make his life miserable, but what does revenge serve in the end? Hate never got anyone anywhere. I want to go on with my life…my life with you," I added, just in case Jake hadn't gotten the point. "But part of that life is making sure that the people I met in the SED facility get a chance to live their lives as well. Two of them—Ethan and Natalie—are obviously in love with each other, but they can't do anything about it because they're stuck being lab rats for Lenz and the doctors and scientists he has on staff. If we can get him on our side, then we can maybe have him help us get all of them out of there."

"So…he's a means to an end," Jake observed. His eyes were still slightly narrowed, but I could tell from the way he tilted his head to one side that he was seriously considering what I'd just said.

"That's kind of a harsh way to look at it, but yeah." I reached over and wrapped my fingers around his, was gratified to see that he immediately gave them a squeeze and didn't try to ignore me or pull away. Obviously, he didn't like this friction between the two of us any more than I did. "Like Connor said yesterday, Trident is about finding witches and warlocks who don't know who they are and helping them to connect with their clans and their gifts. We can't walk away from all those people and pretend they don't exist."

For a moment, Jake didn't say anything, only sat there with his fingers entwined in mine as he appeared to consider my words. "No," he said at last. "I guess we can't. So, do you have a plan?"

I really didn't. Even though I supposed we could infiltrate the SED facility again, I wasn't sure whether that was the best idea. For one thing, the only place in the facility I knew well enough to help Angela and Connor teleport to was the big "multipurpose unit" where the gang all gathered. Even if I put aside the very real constraint of the place being under video surveillance at all times, it would take too much valuable time to get fourteen people teleported away, since Jake had told me that both the *prima* and the *primus* could only take one person at a time.

No, it seemed the best way to handle this was to approach Agent Lenz, convince him of his inborn powers, and then have him come up with a plan to get all the test subjects out of there. How he'd manage that, I didn't know, but presumably he would have some insights to offer, since the program was his baby and he'd know of any weaknesses in its setup that could be exploited.

"I guess I thought that maybe we could approach Randall Lenz at his home," I said. "Jeremy knows where it is, right?"

"Yes, and he has photos of the interior from a real estate listing, so it wouldn't be too hard for Connor and Angela to get you and me in there." Jake hesitated, worry clear in every line of his face. "But I hate to think of you taking that kind of risk. He's already proven that he's kind of hasty about pulling a gun, which means there's a very real possibility that he'd do the same thing if we confronted him in his own house."

Right. I supposed I should have thought of that. Then again, if we went there in the middle of the night, while he was asleep—I assumed even Randall Lenz had to sleep sometime—then he wouldn't have much opportunity to whip out his service pistol.

Well, unless he slept with the gun under his pillow.

"I know," I said, trying my best to push that disturbing mental image away. "But I still think it's the better option, just because there are way too many cameras and other people at the facility. If we went while he was sleeping or something, we'd get the drop on him. And it wouldn't even have to be all that late, thanks to the time difference between here and Virginia."

Jake lifted his free hand to scratch at the stubble on his chin. While I liked him a little scruffy, he'd let it go for days at that point, and I wondered if it would be totally out of line to ask him to shave.

Then I wanted to shake my head at myself. Considering all the things we were up against, a bit of stubble should have been way down my list of priorities.

"Maybe," he allowed, although I could tell he didn't want to seem much more approving than that. "I still think we could be letting ourselves in for a world of hurt."

"We could be doing that by sitting here and doing nothing," I pointed out, and he gave me a reluctant smile.

"I know. I just wish I knew what he was up to —every minute we're sitting here, I keep waiting for the hammer to drop."

I knew the feeling. I also hated not knowing what was going on back in Virginia, whether Randall Lenz had figured out where we'd gone and the only reason why we hadn't been nabbed yet was because he was still coordinating teams of paratroopers to swoop down on us, or whether he simply had no leads and was currently frustrated, stymied.

While I would have preferred the latter, I knew I couldn't take anything for granted.

"Which is why it would be better for us to go on the attack," I said. "I mean, not a real attack, but meet him on his home ground."

"If Connor and Angela go for it."

His expression was dubious, and I could see why. It was one thing for them to take the risk of going into the SED facility to rescue me, and quite another to pop into Randall Lenz's house so I could try to convince him that he really was a warlock.

If he was. Lucas had seemed pretty convinced, though, and while I obviously didn't know the man well—or hardly at all—I still could tell he wasn't the type to go around telling casual lies. He said he'd felt something, which meant he probably had. And apparently Genoveva Castillo had experienced much the same thing. My brief meeting with her was also enough to convince me she wasn't the type given to wild fancies or whimsical impressions. If she'd felt something, then she had.

"Connor seemed pretty emphatic at our meeting yesterday," I said. "I mean, he was the first one to point out that we wouldn't be following Trident's mission statement if we didn't try to bring Randall Lenz into the fold, so to speak."

From the way Jake appeared to deflate at my

remark, it seemed obvious enough to me that he'd conveniently forgotten that part of the discussion. But he didn't try to argue with me. "You're right. But he might not be quite so idealistic when faced with the reality of having to confront Lenz on his home ground."

"Maybe not," I allowed. After all, Jake had been around Connor his entire life, and obviously knew my half-brother a lot better than I did. But I'd seen the steady resolve in Connor's eyes, the way his gaze had shifted to Angela for just a second as he'd spoken during their meeting, as if they'd already come to an agreement that they'd reach out a hand to Randall Lenz, no matter how problematic doing such a thing might be to them personally. "I still think we need to let him know what we're thinking."

"Okay." Jake picked up his mug of coffee and took a large swallow, then broke off a piece of his bagel and smeared some cream cheese on it. It was the second bagel of the morning for him, and so I had the feeling he was occupying himself with his food so he wouldn't have to say anything else until he'd gathered his thoughts. A bit of silence while he chewed, and then he said, his expression a little brighter, "Do you know where Lenz is from? I mean, there isn't any chance he's a Wilcox, is there?"

Those questions made me realize why Jake

suddenly looked a little cheerier. Yes, we'd have to deal with Randall Lenz in the interim, but there probably wasn't much chance of us having him in our lives in the long term, not if his family turned out to be a witch clan on the East Coast. "He made it sound as if he grew up somewhere in New York," I said. "I don't know the clans at all, so I have no idea what family that would be."

"The Van Horns, I think," Jake replied. "I'd have to check with Jeremy to be sure. Actually, I only know that much because the original Wilcoxes hung in New York for a while before they headed out to Arizona." *

"Couldn't hurt to ask," I said. "But yeah, I'm pretty sure Randall Lenz is an East Coast guy. I don't think you have much to worry about."

Jake seemed to relax at those words, and lifted his coffee mug to drink down the last couple of swallows it contained. I took that as a signal to finish my own meal, so I picked up the remnants of my bagel and took a bite. At the same time, some of the tension in my shoulders began to ease. We might not have resolved everything, but I could tell that at least we'd gotten the beginnings of a plan formulated, and we could go from there.

Maybe I was being crazy. And yet…

…and yet I was still so new to knowing I was a witch, was part of a clan full of people just like me, that I knew all too well what it was like to feel like I was a freak, someone who could never fit in. Maybe Randall Lenz didn't deserve the sort of acceptance I'd met among the Wilcoxes, but I realized I didn't want to be his judge and jury. Better to give him the opportunity to learn what he really was. What happened after that was up to him.

It didn't seem like the sort of conversation we should have over the phone, so Jake got in touch with Connor and asked if we could come over and discuss the Randall Lenz problem in person. To my relief, Connor said it would be fine for us to drop in, so we headed down to the house where he lived with his family when they were spending their half of the year in Flagstaff.

I supposed I was expecting something similar to the house he and Angela shared in Jerome, but their place in Forest Highlands was much newer, a sprawling two-story home with a big stone fireplace and soaring ceilings and enormous windows that provided amazing views of the woodlands that surrounded the property. Almost as soon as Jake and I entered, we were pounced on by the kids, who wanted to know where the "little dog" was and why we hadn't brought her along. Jake and I gave each other a helpless glance—we hadn't even thought about bringing Taffy with us, since this was going to be a quick visit—but luckily, Angela came to our rescue and said we needed to have a grown-up talk, and maybe the dog could come along next time. She ended by ushering the children outside to play in the yard, showing the patience and skill of long practice at doing that sort of thing. Eventually, though, she joined Connor and Jake and me in the living room.

"They're playing hide and seek, so with any luck, that'll keep them occupied for a while," she said, settling down on one of the sofas next to my brother. "Of course, Miranda sometimes has trouble keeping up, but the other two try not to take too much advantage."

I wondered why there was such a big gap in their ages—the twins looked like they were about four years older than their little sister—but I had a feeling that wasn't the time to ask. Instead, I smiled awkwardly and reached for the glass of ice water Connor had fetched for me. "Sorry to barge in like this—" I began, but Angela only shook her head.

"You didn't 'barge in,'" she said. "You called and checked to make sure it was all right if you came over. That's completely different."

"And we wouldn't have done that if it wasn't important," Jake said. "But we had an idea about how to deal with Randall Lenz."

At once, the pleasant smile Angela had been wearing vanished, and she glanced over at Connor. His expression had also sobered at the mention of Lenz's name, but all he said was, "Go on."

"Well, since it seems as if everyone's on the same page about letting him know he's a warlock, Addie and I thought the best thing to do was be proactive." Jake ran his hands over the knees of his jeans, as if they might have been damp with nervous perspiration. A breath, and he continued. "We thought you should take us to his house in the middle of the night when he won't be expecting us. And we figured we might as well do it tonight before he gets too far with any investigations he might be conducting into who was behind Addie's rescue."

Connor settled against the back of the sofa, expression dubious. "I'm not sure if that's the best idea. I mean, I know we need to do something about him, but aren't we just asking for trouble if we show up on his home turf?"

"Better than him showing up on ours," I replied. "I mean, we think we're protected here, but we don't know that for sure. Like Jake said, I think it's better to be proactive. Once we've gotten through to him, then he can work to shut down anything on his end that might lead them to Flagstaff and the Wilcoxes."

"*If* we get through to him," Angela said. "That is, I know both Lucas and Genoveva Castillo claim that he set off their witchy senses, but we still don't have any idea what his power might be."

"We do," Jake told her. "Or at least, Addie and I have a feeling that his talent is the same as Lucas's."

"Luck?" Connor inquired, left eyebrow lifting slightly. "What makes you say that?"

"Just a combination of things," I said. "He told me he had hunches, which makes me think his magical intuition was doing its best to guide him even before my lightning bolt really activated his talent, so to speak. And there's the simple fact that he survived getting hit by lightning, which isn't exactly guaranteed. We're just making educated guesses, but it's what Jake and I think."

Silence for a moment as Connor and Angela exchanged another one of those glances. What they were thinking, I couldn't begin to guess. For all I knew, they both thought that Jake and I had gone completely off the deep end. After all, we'd only made a series of educated guesses. We couldn't know for sure that luck was guiding Randall Lenz. His talent could be something else entirely, and we just hadn't been able to figure out what it was because we hadn't been around him enough to truly see it in action.

"If that turns out to be the case," Connor said,

his voice musing as he spoke. "Then it's going to be even harder to get him to prove his talent is real. It's not like he can summon a storm or move something with his mind or…or create an illusion, or whatever other talents can be clearly manifested."

Right. I supposed I should have thought of that, but I was still new to all this witchy stuff. Worried, I glanced over at Jake, but he didn't seem put off by the monkey wrench Connor had just thrown into the middle of the situation.

"It's still not that big a deal," Jake said. "We can get him to conjure a flame or unlock a door or something. Those are little talents that every witch and warlock has, but which I doubt he's ever used. I had to show Addie how to do it, mostly because she'd never had any reason to believe she possessed those sorts of skills. But it should be enough to prove to Randall Lenz that he isn't exactly the guy next door."

Angela's striking green eyes lit up at Jake's suggestion. "That's a great idea. Because you're right no ordinary person can make a candle light just by looking at it, but if we can get him to do that, then he'll know we're not making things up just to get him off our tail."

"Well, we *hope* he'll understand that," Connor put in, still not looking entirely convinced. "I mean, the guy doesn't seem like the type to abandon years of work just because a candle flame appeared out of nowhere. More likely, he'll suspect that one of us did it."

Damn. I hadn't even thought of that, and, judging by the way Jake's mouth tightened, neither had he. But he looked back at Connor and said, his tone level, "Maybe. I think we could probably sit here and come up with arguments all day as to why none of this will work. And if that's the case, then maybe we should give up and just wait around until he shows up again to make our lives miserable. Your call."

I could tell my brother didn't like that comment very much, because his posture stiffened and his eyes narrowed ever so slightly. However, he didn't take the bait, only sat there in silence for a few seconds before he replied, "I'm not saying we shouldn't do this. I'm just saying we need to think about any complications we might face so we're prepared."

"We are thinking," I said. "But in the end, it comes down to whether or not we're willing to make the leap. And it sounds like you're okay with our plan."

Connor rubbed the scruff on his chin and didn't respond for a moment. Then he said, "I'm not sure if 'okay' is the right word. It's more that I hate not knowing what the guy is up to. At least by going to face him tonight, we're getting it over with."

"I'm not sure if 'getting it over with' is the best criteria to be using for something like this," Angela put in. Then she let out a breath and knotted her fingers together over one jean-clad knee. "On the other hand, I kind of feel the same way. So…let's do this. I can send the kids to stay with Lucas and Margot again."

"I doubt we even have to get that elaborate," Connor told her. "Let's just have someone over to watch them—this is going to be a quick trip, and I don't want to impose on Margot and Lucas so soon after they had the kids overnight. I can call Tory."

I didn't know who Tory was—yet another in an endless supply of Wilcox cousins, most likely —but if she was willing to come hang out at Connor and Angela's house while we did a light-ning raid on Randall Lenz's place in Virginia, then that was one problem solved without too much muss or fuss. "What time?" I asked.

"Um…ten?" Angela suggested, not sounding too sure of herself. "That would be one in the morning on the East Coast, right?"

"Right," Jake said. "Lenz should be asleep. I suppose there's always the off chance that he isn't, but that's a risk we'd be taking no matter what time we went."

A nod, and Connor said, "Ten it is. You can come over a little before then, just so we get all our ducks in a row. The kids will be fast asleep by that hour, and I'll come up with some sort of explanation for Tory as to why you're showing up so late."

His comment seemed to put a cap on things, and Jake and I left soon afterward, promising again that we'd be at the house a little before ten. He maneuvered his new Jeep Wrangler out of the upscale subdivision where Connor and Angela's house was located, and headed north on the highway.

For a few minutes, neither of us spoke. I could tell Jake was keyed up, and I didn't know what to say to ease the tension that was so thick, I almost sensed it as a tangible thing hovering in the air between us.

But since he didn't seem inclined to say anything, I figured I'd better do what I could. "I know this is hard," I said. "But we're doing the right thing."

His gaze remained fixed on the road ahead of us, even though there weren't many people around. "I hope so."

"I know so," I told him, although deep down, I couldn't help experiencing a flicker of doubt. Maybe we were rushing headlong into a confrontation we honestly didn't need to face. For all I knew, Randall Lenz had reached a complete dead end when it came to discovering how I'd been stolen out of my room at the SED facility, and we were all going to a lot of unnecessary trouble.

Not unnecessary, I told myself. *He needs to know what he is.*

If he really was a warlock at all. Damn it, my brain kept going in the same annoying circles.

"And I love you, Jake," I went on. "I love that you're doing this, even though you're not convinced that Lenz deserves this kind of consideration."

Something in the taut lines of his jaw relaxed slightly, and Jake let go of the steering wheel with his right hand so he could reach over and give my fingers a gentle squeeze. "You think he does, and that's enough for me, even if I still don't completely understand why." A pause before he added, "I love you, too, Addie. I want—I want everything to work out for us. I want to get past this so we can just be together with nothing getting in our way."

God, that was exactly what I wanted as well. Pretty much the entire time I'd been with Jake, I'd had to be looking over my shoulder or making plans I knew would never pan out, thanks to the specter of Randall Lenz looming over everything we did. I supposed I thought in my heart of hearts that if we could just get him settled, could make him understand that he was just the same as we were, then he'd be forced to change his ways, and Jake and I could get on with our lives.

Was it really so much to ask, after all? To be together, to enjoy our future without worrying about having it torn from us at someone else's whim?

Maybe. My experience had taught me that there weren't a whole lot of happy endings in the world, although they seemed to abound in the Wilcox clan. My own brother and the woman he loved had beaten a curse that lasted for more than a hundred years. What was one overly dedicated federal agent compared to that sort of accomplishment?

That thought helped to reassure me a little as Jake guided the Jeep along Route 66 before turning off into the neighborhood I was already starting to think of as home. Tall green trees, lovingly restored houses, and cheerful flowerbeds surrounded us on all sides, and I could feel myself begin to relax. It was going to be okay. Jake and I would go with Connor and Angela, and working together, we'd be able to convince Randall Lenz of his inborn powers. He'd go off to live with his own witch clan—the Van Horns, or whoever they turned out to be—and Jake and I could come back to this lovely place and concentrate on our shared future.

It was going to be fine.

"We are going to get past this," I said, and gently let go of his fingers so he'd have both hands to maneuver the Jeep into the driveway. "We're Wilcoxes, right?"

As I'd hoped, that comment made him flash a quick grin, the expression lighting up his dark eyes and banishing the shadows of worry from his face. We parked in the garage and got out of the car, and I waited to one side as he pushed the button to close the garage door. Afterward, we walked hand in hand to the back porch and mounted the steps.

A moment later, we were inside. By reflex, I looked down, expecting to see Taffy trotting over to us, tail wagging, even though it was nowhere near any of her mealtimes. However, I didn't see any sign of the dog, and I glanced over at Jake.

He seemed to interpret my confusion correctly, saying, "Usually, Taffy is underfoot as soon as I walk in the door, but not always, if she's conked out in the house somewhere. I'm sure she'll perk up as soon as we go out into the living room—she tends to crash in there because she likes the rug."

That seemed like a plausible enough explanation. I nodded, and we headed toward the living room.

Only to stop short at the sight of Randall Lenz sitting in one of the armchairs, a short, snub-nosed pistol lying casually against one thigh.

"Hello, Adara," he said. "I've been waiting for you."

* That story is related in *Bad Blood* (The Witches of Cleopatra Hill: Book 12).

17

RANDALL LENZ HAD EVENTUALLY GONE TO sleep after his phone call with Agent Dawson ended, mostly because he'd realized that it didn't matter how long he sat there and beat on his recalcitrant brain—the information about Jake Wilcox's residence would surface when it wanted to and not a moment sooner. He might as well get some rest while waiting for that all-important piece of data to emerge from his gray matter.

"Rest" was a relative term, unfortunately, as he'd tossed and turned for most of the night, sleeping in fits and starts, twenty minutes here, a half hour there. When his eyelids flared awake in the pale gray light of pre-dawn and he saw it was barely five-thirty in the morning, he knew there was no point in continuing the charade any further.

He got out of bed and showered and dressed, then made himself a pot of strong coffee. By that point in his existence, he was used to getting by on only three or four hours of sleep, even if he wished he could have gotten a bit more. Maybe then the fog in his brain wouldn't feel so thick.

Eggs and toast and fruit, just because his body needed the fuel a decent breakfast would provide, since sleep had been denied him. As he ate, he reflected on the silence of the house, broken only by the humming of the refrigerator and the occasional *whoosh* of an early car passing by on the street outside. Not for the first time, he found himself wondering if he should get a dog. His family's retriever Charlie had been a mainstay for a big chunk of his life, and when Charlie passed away a year after Graham Lenz died in the North Tower of the World Trade Center, Lenz had vowed to himself that he would never have another pet. Those two losses so close together had—at the time, at least—felt like too much to bear.

But time softened all wounds, and now he thought it might be nice to have a companion in the house. Or not; his hours were so irregular, and he was gone so often, that he wouldn't be much in the way of company for a dog. There were pet sitters and dog walkers, of course, but he'd never seen the point in having an animal if you weren't going to care for it personally.

Maybe it was simply that the house felt so empty and quiet. He didn't like the sensation of being able to feel himself think...especially when his thoughts were less than pleasant.

Why did his brain delight in torturing him, letting him see some of the events of his recent past but not others? Logically, he knew there was no actual torture involved; memory could be a tricky thing, and just because you wanted to recall something didn't mean you'd be able to perform such a feat on demand.

Still, he was annoyed that he could see Jake Wilcox's house clearly in his mind and yet not remember the address. Somewhere in Flagstaff, obviously. The house was old...old enough to be registered with the local historical society?

That prospect seemed like a distinct possibility. Since he was almost ready to leave anyway, Lenz decided to put off his search until he was back at the facility. Traffic at that hour was light— well, light for the greater D.C. area, at any rate— and he was in his office and seated at his desk in less than twenty minutes.

To his relief, the Flagstaff Historical Society had an excellent and up-to-date website, one that gave a brief history of the town and called out its various points of interest. Also included on the site was a list of houses that had been designated as landmarks, with each entry on the list hyper-linked to a gallery of photos for the particular home in question.

He dutifully clicked on each one, thinking it would have been more logical to have one photo for each house that served as the hyperlink, since he couldn't tell from the street addresses which home might be the subject of his search. Midway down was an entry for 52 West Birch Street.

And there it was—an imposing green-painted Victorian house with a turret in front and stained glass bordering the front-facing windows. The photo had been taken in the autumn, and so the grass out front had been yellowed by frost, and the sycamore tree planted in the yard blazed in gold and orange hues, but it was definitely the same house where Lenz had seen Jake Wilcox and Adara Grant standing on the front porch and sharing an embrace.

The address seemed familiar, too, as if now that he'd been able to make the connection between the visuals in his mind and the concrete evidence of the street number attached to the place, his mind had finally decided to recognize they were one and the same. He wanted to shake his head at himself but didn't see the point in wasting the energy. The important thing was that he knew exactly where to find his quarry.

He'd arrived at the facility early enough that Dawson was just settling down at her workstation, covered mug of tea set carefully away from the computer, as he approached. However, her manner was brisk enough when she turned toward him and said, "Good morning, sir."

"Morning, Dawson," he replied. "I think I know where to find them. Can you pull up records for 52 West Birch Street, Flagstaff, Arizona?"

A nod. "Of course, sir. Just give me a moment."

He waited off to one side as she allowed herself a sip of tea before focusing her attention on the screen before her. Some rapid typing, and then a page from the Coconino County Recorder's website appeared. Dawson frowned slightly as she gazed at it.

"This says the property has been owned by someone named Tyler Greene since 2016."

Who the hell was Tyler Greene? Was that Jake Wilcox's real name?

No. Lenz couldn't say precisely how he knew, but something in his bones told him that Jake Wilcox was the real name, and Tyler Greene the alias. In a way, that made sense. If Wilcox had been doing his best to cover up his identity, then erasing his name from the property records for his residence would have been a necessary step. And if he was working with the same hacker who'd been causing so much trouble for Lenz and his team over the past several weeks, then it probably would have been easy enough for him to accomplish such a feat.

"Before that?" he asked.

A pause as she scrolled through the record. "Someone named Joseph Garnett. He owned the property for forty years. Before that…Thomas Wilcox." Dawson glanced up at him. "The same Wilcoxes we've been talking about?"

"Most likely," Lenz replied. "They've been in the area for a long time. No doubt they did what they could to keep important pieces of real estate like that in the family." That also answered the question as to how someone as young as Jake Wilcox could have afforded such an obviously expensive house. Lenz figured the man had been given a sweetheart deal by a relative who wanted to move to a smaller place with less upkeep. After seeing his parents spend vast sums of money to keep their brownstone on Manhattan's Upper West Side in tiptop shape, he knew all too well that Victorian-era homes could often be money pits behind their charming exteriors.

"And Tyler Greene…?" Dawson asked, although, judging by the way her brows drew together, Lenz thought she'd already drawn her own conclusions.

"An alias. Jake Wilcox doing his best to throw us off the scent."

She nodded. "And you think Wilcox has Adara Grant with him?"

"I'm almost positive of it. I'll need you to order the jet."

"Your team?"

"Just Tolliver and Ives. This needs to be quick and fast—because the Wilcoxes are such a prominent family in the area, we don't want to attract too much attention."

"Of course, sir." Dawson went to work, using the text interface on her computer to send the necessary messages to his team, asking them to assemble at Hyde Field. "You'll be able to leave in one hour."

Not perfect, but he reminded himself that it was still very early in Arizona, and he should have no problem catching up with the two fugitives before they headed out for the day. "Thank you, Dawson," he said. "While I'm gone, keep digging through the Wilcox family history. I still can't see the connection between Adara Grant and this man, but that's only because we haven't found the right piece of evidence yet."

"Yes, sir." Her expression was already somewhat distracted, telling Lenz that his assistant's agile mind had begun to pick at the problem in an attempt to determine whether they'd overlooked any important pieces of evidence, anything that might illuminate the reason behind Jake Wilcox's connection to Adara Grant.

"Stay in touch," he said—an unnecessary admonition, since he knew Dawson would reach out immediately the moment she found anything of value. Still, those words served well enough as a goodbye, and so he left her workstation and returned to his office so he could retrieve the duffle he always left packed there in case of urgent business that necessitated a speedy departure.

However, all that speed seemed to be for naught. When he arrived at the airport, Ives, who functioned as both pilot and backup muscle when necessary, informed Lenz that there was a problem with one of the jet's fuel pumps and that they'd have to wait while a mechanic made the necessary repairs.

"I could try to order another jet," Ives said, "but we'd probably have to wait just as long for another one to be available, and it would involve a lot of paperwork."

Neither of those options was at all desirable, and so Lenz said they'd wait, which seemed to be the lesser of two evils. If he hadn't just suffered the indignity of trying to defend himself and the program to Wallace Bryant in the aftermath of Adara Grant's disappearance, he might have opted for chartering another jet, and the hell with the extra expense. But the last thing he wanted was anyone looking too closely at his expenditures, and so prudence seemed to be the order of the day.

They ended up leaving two hours behind schedule, which, while not optimal, wasn't the end of the world, either. Lenz was fairly certain that neither Jake Wilcox nor Adara could have any idea that he'd figured out where they'd gone to ground. After all, Jake had expended a good deal of effort to make sure he would be extremely hard to find. He couldn't know that Lenz's memories had come flooding back, providing enough information for him to track them all the way to Flagstaff.

Because they'd done this drill multiple times before, once they were in the air, Lenz pulled out his laptop, sent a short message to Dawson letting her know he was en route to Flagstaff, and then opened up a report from Dr. Richards about her plans to parallel-test some of the subjects.

We've thoroughly explored their individual abilities, Richards wrote, *and so now it is time to study whether their gifts affect one another, creating a so-called "stacking" effect, or whether those abilities exist in isolation and can't be altered in any way.*

Her report made no mention of Adara Grant's disappearance, for which Lenz was grateful. If

Adara had remained at the facility, Dr. Richards and Dr. Woodrow probably would have spent another week or so on further preliminary tests with her. As matters stood, they had no option but to move on to the next phase of testing. Lenz would not allow himself to be annoyed by the subtext to Michelle Richards' words. After all, she'd been planning this next step for some time, and if Adara had never been brought to the facility at all, her absence wouldn't have even been a factor.

He made a few quick notes on the report, sent a reply to Dr. Richards, and glanced up from his laptop. As he'd expected, Tolliver was power-napping in his seat across the aisle. The man's ability to sleep anywhere and at any time, no matter what the circumstances, was still somewhat boggling to Lenz, who viewed slumber as an uneasy ally at best, but at least he knew the other man would be rested and ready to face any contingency once they reached Flagstaff.

Not that he was expecting any huge confrontations. Jake Wilcox couldn't possibly be expecting him to show up on his doorstep, and so Lenz's plan was to keep Tolliver and Ives close enough where they could come to his aid if neces-sary, but also far enough away that they wouldn't be able to overhear any of what might pass between Lenz and his quarry once they came face to face. The two men only knew that Project Daedalus involved acquiring subjects for testing and nothing more; they had no idea the people involved possessed talents that the more credulous might call supernatural.

But they weren't supernatural. No, it was only that they'd somehow managed to tap into portions of the mind that most ordinary people didn't even know existed. Dr. Richards and her team had managed to isolate subtle differences in EEG readings in the test subjects' brain waves from those of regular people, but they still hadn't been able to adequately explain why those slight differences in their EEG patterns translated to the ability to move objects with their mind, or alter their appearance.

Or make the wind and the weather obey their commands.

However, he had every reason to believe that —hopefully, sooner rather than later—the doctor and her team would find that elusive connection. Once they'd established that baseline, then they should also be able to determine whether those gifts slept in every individual, and all that was required to awaken a person's extrasensory talents was a subtle manipulation of their brain waves to achieve the desired result.

At least, that was Dr. Richards' hypothesis, and the main reason why she'd been brought on board as the head of research with Project Daedalus. It was one thing to seek out gifted individuals and bring them into the fold; that work was useful, but also haphazard and unreliable. No, the really important work would involve awakening latent gifts in those who already possessed the training and knowledge to make them an invaluable tool in homeland defense.

Midway through the flight, Dawson messaged him.

Still no clear connection between Jake Wilcox and Adara Grant, she wrote. *Discovered some records indicating that Lyssa Grant spent a few days in Flagstaff in mid-December 1995 for a skiing trip that was cut short when her friend was injured. Will send more info as I find it.*

Interesting. So, it seemed there was one small connection between Adara Grant and Flagstaff, tenuous as it seemed at first look.

However....

Adara Grant's birthday was in mid-September. Her mother's ill-fated skiing trip had taken place exactly nine months earlier.

Coincidence?

Not likely. While the spaces for the father's information on Adara's birth certificate had been left conspicuously blank, Lenz was finding it more and more likely that the man in question probably belonged to the Wilcox family.

Was, in fact, Connor Wilcox's father.

Of course. That was why Adara's eyes had haunted him…why he'd seen those same eyes staring at him from Connor's face. No wonder Connor had wanted to find her, although Lenz still couldn't speculate as to why he'd enlisted Jake Wilcox to search for her rather than taking on that task himself.

He typed a quick message back to Dawson. *Research Connor Wilcox's father. I think he's the connection.*

Immediately, he got a response.

Working, was all Dawson said, but that was enough.

And he was gratified to see a follow-up message appear less than ten minutes later.

Jackson Samuel Wilcox, his assistant wrote. *Deceased March 10, 1999. Survived by his son Connor; another son, Damon, died eight years ago. Estate valued at approximately five million dollars at the time of his death.*

Interesting. Lenz already knew the Wilcoxes were prosperous, but for some reason, he hadn't expected them to be millionaires. *Any other immediate family?* he wrote back in response.

No, Dawson responded. *Jackson was an only child. Wife passed away more than thirty years ago. No children other than Connor and Damon.*

So, Connor was an orphan…just like Adara

herself. No wonder the man had wanted to locate his long-lost sibling. How had he learned about her? Deathbed confession from his father?

Probably not. Otherwise, Adara would have been found much earlier. Lenz decided it was probably better not to speculate as to the "whys" behind the events that had been so recently set in motion. What mattered was that they'd all been inadvertently put on a collision course, one they couldn't seem to escape.

Which was fine by him. While Randall Lenz wasn't the sort of person to believe in fate, he also understood that sometimes you couldn't escape the circumstances you found yourself in. No, you could only go along for the ride and plan for the best possible outcome.

In this case, that meant confronting Jake Wilcox and Adara Grant, and returning her to the program. If it turned out that Jake possessed peculiar talents of his own, then he would also be added to the Daedalus Project as its newest test subject. In addition to the service pistol in its shoulder holster, Lenz carried with him a gun loaded with the same tranquilizer he'd used to knock out Adara in her rented home in Riverton, Wyoming.

They'd be coming with him…like it or not.

18

BESIDE ME, JAKE STIFFENED. BEFORE I COULD even blink, he raised his hand in a jerky, reflexive motion, and the gun Randall Lenz held went flying. It hit the polished wooden floor and skidded to a stop against the far wall.

Wow. Apparently, Jake could perform all sorts of feats with his telekinetic powers, and I murmured a thank-you under my breath to the universe for his quick thinking.

However, my gratitude evaporated in the next second, because, without missing a beat, Agent Lenz pulled another gun from his pocket and aimed it right at Jake. Even as a terrified denial burst from my lips, he pulled the trigger.

Not the explosive *bang* I was expecting. No, instead, the projectile that shot from the gun's muzzle emerged with a strange, evil hiss, and a small red dart buried itself in Jake's neck. For a single, horrifying second, his eyes met mine, wide with shock, and then he slumped to the ground.

"No worries," Lenz said, coming toward me, gun pointed at my throat. "A simple tranquilizer. I can do the same to you, Ms. Grant…or you can come with me willingly. I think you must remember that the drug does have a few side effects, even if they wear off quickly."

Oh, yes, I remembered the headache that had pulsed behind my temples when I awoke the last time he'd drugged me. I would have preferred to avoid revisiting that sensation if at all possible.

And although I knew I wasn't entirely defenseless, that I could have summoned a bolt of lightning to strike him a second time, I had the uneasy realization that I wasn't sure I could do so before he pulled the trigger and the tranquilizer dart took me out of commission anyway.

My entire body ached with thwarted fury, but I forced myself to put up my hands. "I'm not willing," I said slowly, "but I'll come with you."

"Very good," he said. Someone else might have sent me a gloating smile at that point, but his expression remained brisk and almost businesslike. With his free hand, he reached into his pocket and drew out a compact walkie-talkie. "I have them. Meet me here for pickup and extraction."

I didn't know who he was talking to. Probably the same goons who'd knocked out the men Carson Archuleta had left guarding my house in Riverton. Only this time, Jake and I didn't have anyone protecting us. We'd thought we would be safe, that we could just come back here and wait until it was time to visit Randall Lenz at his house and try to talk some sense into him.

Irony could be a real bitch.

"You're making a big mistake," I said desperately. "You need to listen to me—"

"No, I don't," he said, cutting me off without a blink. "Or at least, while at some point in the near future I would like to hear everything about your association with Jake Wilcox, now isn't the time."

I wondered what interrogation methods he'd use to pry that information out of me. Nothing pleasant, I was sure.

If the universe had been at all kind, that would've been the time for Connor and Angela to show up, swooping in to Jake's and my rescue. Unfortunately, the universe wasn't that friendly. Jake had mentioned that Connor didn't have the ability that some *primas* did when it came to detecting interlopers in their territory, and it appeared that the rest of the Wilcoxes were asleep at the switch as well.

Or maybe it didn't matter what any of us did,

because now Randall Lenz had a supercharged gift of luck in his arsenal, thwarting all our efforts. He wanted me back in his goddamn program, and it appeared he would have me…with the side bonus of bringing Jake along for the ride.

Did he suspect that Jake possessed special abilities as well?

I had the uneasy feeling I would find out soon enough.

Two big men entered the room, coming in from the kitchen, where I assumed they'd entered through the back door. A nod from Lenz, and they went and picked up Jake's unconscious form, carrying him off like a side of beef. I hated to see him like that, face slack, arms hanging limply at his sides, even though I did my best to tell myself he would be okay, that although it wasn't fun to wake up from Randall Lenz's knock-out drug, it was certainly survivable.

"Come along," he said. He hadn't gestured with the tranquilizer gun; he didn't need to.

Hating myself for not possessing the requisite skills to take all of them out—or at least to put up some sort of bat signal to let Connor and Angela know we were in trouble—I followed the two men through the kitchen, Agent Lenz right at my heels. We headed out the back door and followed the path to the driveway, where a white van with the logo of a plumbing company painted on the side was parked.

The two men opened the back doors and dumped Jake in the cargo area, then went up front to get in the driver and passenger seats. Agent Lenz and I climbed into the back seats and put on our safety belts. The whole time, he kept the gun trained on me, although the fight had pretty much gone out of me by that point. Calling down the lightning to strike a van that had both Jake and me inside was out of the question, and I didn't have anything else in my arsenal of tricks that seemed like a viable option right then.

Instead, I sat quietly in my seat and did my best to avoid making eye contact with Randall Lenz. The van didn't have any windows in the rear seat area, so I couldn't see what was going on in the world outside. About ten minutes after they'd backed out of the driveway of Jake's house, we came to a stop.

Lenz looked over at me, eyes cool, assessing, as if he was reading my expression to see whether I planned to make a break for it as soon as the doors opened. "We're going to get out and walk over to an airplane," he said. "Don't try anything."

I nodded. Maybe if I'd been a real superhero instead of a witch who possessed only one dubious skill, then I could have figured out a way to incapacitate all three men, grab Jake and throw him over my shoulder, and get the hell out of there.

Unfortunately, witches weren't superheroes… or at least, this one sure as hell wasn't. I waited while Lenz opened the door, and tried not to blink as bright sunshine flooded in. Just outside was a low building I guessed must be a hangar of some sort, and a bit beyond it was a sleek private jet, probably big enough to seat as many as twenty people, although I'd be the first to admit that what I knew about private jets could fit in a thimble.

They'd parked the van so the bulk of the jet blocked it from the view of any casual observers, and the hangar did a pretty good job of hiding both vehicles. I didn't know anything about the airport in Flagstaff, but I guessed it probably wasn't all that large, and that there wasn't much chance of anyone glancing our way to see the two burly men pick up a still-unconscious Jake from the back of the van and bundle him up a set of rolling stairs into the plane. At a nod from Agent Lenz, I followed, and climbed inside in enough time to see them lay Jake down across a bank of seats that looked more like a sofa than anything else. It was fancy in there, with a flat-screen TV mounted to one wall and thick carpet underfoot.

"Up here," Lenz said, nodding toward an

unoccupied row of seats that faced a gleaming coffee table mounted to the floor.

I opened my mouth to protest—I wanted to be next to Jake, even if I knew he wasn't in any shape to offer any help at the moment—but then shut it when I realized that Agent Lenz certainly wasn't going to appreciate such a request. Instead, I sat down at the far end of the sectional-style seat he'd indicated and buckled myself in.

He did the same, and a few minutes later, we were nose up and heading eastward, away from the sun. How long did a flight to the East Coast take, anyway? I had no idea, since I'd never been on a plane in my life, or even planned a plane trip. Still, I guess it must be several hours at the very least, and grimaced inwardly. On top of my worry about Jake and what exactly Randall Lenz had planned for the two of us, I couldn't think of anything more awkward than being stuck in a private jet with him for hours and hours.

Now that he'd accomplished his goal of getting me back in his clutches, he didn't seem too concerned about what I was doing. He sat down at the other end of the sectional-style seat I occupied, opened a laptop, and began typing quickly. The screen was angled in such a way that I couldn't see what he was writing, and I doubted he would appreciate it if I leaned over and tried to take a look.

Instead, I made myself settle against the back of the seat and force in a breath, doing my best to remain calm. Inwardly, I was annoyed with the seating setup, which had my back up against the window so I couldn't see the landscape passing by far below us, but I wouldn't give Randall Lenz the satisfaction of seeing me wriggle around in my seat like some antsy kid on a long road trip.

I sat there, and wondered what the hell I was supposed to do next.

Nearly five hours later, we landed at a small airfield that I assumed must be located close by the SED facility. Jake was still out cold; the two men who'd accompanied us—neither of whom had said a single word to me—carried him down the stairs to a waiting ambulance, which whisked him away as I watched in horror.

"I thought you said he would be okay," I said, rounding on Agent Lenz, who regarded me with cool blue eyes.

"He's fine," he replied, unperturbed. "He's being taken to the facility so the medical doctor on staff can take a look at him. Afterward, he'll be placed in a suite similar to yours. Speaking of which, that's where you'll be going now."

Those reassurances failed to comfort me. But

since it seemed better to cooperate for the moment—at least Jake and I were going to more or less the same place, which meant I'd have a better chance of busting him out later—I gave a small nod and then followed Lenz to a black Suburban parked a few yards away on the tarmac. The same man who'd flown the jet got behind the wheel, while once again Lenz and I rode in the back seat.

At least I could see out the windows, although by that hour, the sun had nearly set and I was only able to make out what looked like a semi-industrial area dotted by warehouses and office parks. A few minutes later, we passed through a gate in a chain-link fence and followed a narrow road that led to the semi-familiar bulk of the building that housed the SED.

No one was around; I didn't know whether that was because of the hour or simply because Randall Lenz wanted to make sure there weren't any observers as he led me out of the Suburban and inside the building to a bank of elevators. We rode down a number of floors, and emerged in a hallway that also looked familiar.

"Here you are," he said as he stopped in front of one of the doors and paused to let the biometric locking mechanism scan his retina. "I'll have some food sent to you shortly—you must be hungry."

Food was the last thing on my mind in that particular moment. My gaze slid past him to take in the blandly attractive interior of the suite where I'd stayed only a few short days earlier. Just seeing it once more was enough to make panic rise in me.

I couldn't get trapped in there again. I just couldn't.

Without thinking, I reached out and grabbed Randall Lenz by the arm, his muscles like granite under my desperate fingertips. "No, wait," I gasped. "You have to listen to me!"

A single jerk, and his arm slid from my grasp. "Ms. Grant, you are perfectly safe here," he said. "None of this should be a surprise to you."

"No, *listen!*" I said to him, my voice shrill in my ears. "You don't know what you're doing!"

"I assure you, I do," he replied. "You are distraught. You need to go in and sit down, and collect yourself."

"I'm not distraught!" I shot back. "You— you're wrong about *all* of this! Wrong about the people you've trapped here, wrong about me… wrong about yourself!"

That last comment made him lift an eyebrow. "And what exactly am I wrong about, Ms. Grant?"

"You think we're all freaks that you can poke and prod and use as you like, but this whole time, you've been just the same as the rest of us!"

A frown pulled at his brows for just a moment, but then his expression relaxed slightly, and I thought I detected a faint lift at the corner of his thin lips. "Oh, no…I don't have any special powers. I'm just an ordinary man."

I'd known he would probably respond that way, so his words didn't deter me. Besides, I'd already set myself on this course, and now I needed to finish what I'd started. Maybe this wasn't the confrontation we'd envisioned when Jake and I cooked up our plan to go directly to Randall Lenz and tell him who and what he truly was, but I'd do my best to convince him of the truth.

"No, you're not," I said. I tried to speak calmly, because I could tell he thought I was on the brink of hysteria. The only way to get through to him was to be as cold and measured as he was. "It took us a while to figure it out, because your gift is a more subtle one. But you're a warlock, just like I'm a witch. That's where our powers come from. We were born to long lines of witches and warlocks, and carry those powers in our blood."

For the longest moment, he stared at me, expression so blank that I couldn't begin to guess what might be going through his mind. Then he laughed, a derisive chuckle that might as well have been fingernails down a chalkboard. "'Witches'?"

he repeated, his lip curling. "'Warlocks'? That's your story?"

"It's not a story," I said. "It's the truth."

His jaw tightened. "The government doesn't fund research on witches and warlocks, Ms. Grant."

"That's because none of you know what you're really dealing with," I told him. "You think our powers are something that can be measured and quantified, but they can't, not really." He didn't respond, only continued to stare down at me with eyes that were like chips of glacier ice. His expression was positively forbidding, but since he remained silent, I took that as license to go on. "Did you ever figure out why everyone's powers first emerged at around the same time? Everyone in your program told you they were around ten or eleven, right?"

Not even a blink. "Dr. Richards and her team have theorized that the connection is hormonal in nature. Since we don't have any test subjects that age, we have yet to prove that theory."

Maybe it was hormonal…I hadn't asked Jake about that, and I figured there was a good chance he didn't know, either. I supposed it made sense—children's bodies started waking up around then, preparing for their shift into puberty, and so I thought it entirely possible that another shift occurred at the same time, rousing the strange abilities that had come to them from their witch and warlock parents.

"That's when *all* witches and warlocks have their powers start to show," I said. "The same way it's been happening for hundreds or even thousands of years. And the reason why everyone in your program here was either adopted or brought up in the foster care system is that one of their biological parents was either a witch or a warlock, and for whatever reason, they decided they weren't in a position to raise a child on their own. That's why no one here—not Ethan or Natalie or Matthew or anyone else—knows anything about their witch blood. They were left to fend on their own."

Those words seemed to strike a nerve; for the first time, I saw a flicker in Randall Lenz's cold eyes. What that flicker precisely meant, I wasn't sure, but did I dare hope that I might be getting through to him?

All hope died with his next words, though.

"That's quite a fairy tale you've spun for yourself, Ms. Grant," he said. "I suppose I can understand why you would want to believe you're connected to a greater world of witches and warlocks, rather than believe you're simply someone whose genetic makeup isn't quite the same as everyone else's."

"It's not a fairy tale," I retorted.

"Of course not." One brow lifted slightly as he added, "So, of your parents, who was the one with the witch blood? Your mother, or Jackson Wilcox?"

My eyes flared wide with shock, and inwardly I cursed myself for reacting in such an obvious way. But the damage was done.

"Yes," Lenz said, "I was able to do a bit more digging recently. It wasn't so difficult to piece together, once I realized that your mother spent a few days in Flagstaff twenty-five years ago. That was where she met Jackson Wilcox, wasn't it?"

I could try to deny it, could tell him he didn't know what he was talking about. Unfortunately, Randall Lenz would ignore my protests. He already had the data in hand. How he'd guessed, I didn't know. Maybe it didn't matter so much.

What mattered was what he would do with that knowledge.

"Yes," I said, and left it at that. He might have been able to dig up the truth, but that didn't mean I intended to volunteer all the details of my mother's fling with the Wilcox *primus.*

"I assume you believe Jackson Wilcox was a warlock," Lenz went on. "His son does appear to possess some remarkable talents. I'd like to have him in the program here, along with his wife."

Good luck with that, I thought. I still didn't truly understand the limits of my brother's powers

—especially when he was working with Angela—but I'd seen enough to guess that Randall Lenz would find himself in a world of hurt if he ever tried to confront them directly.

"Why is it so hard for you to believe our gifts might be magical?" I asked then. "Is it any crazier than thinking some weird twist of genetics is responsible for all this? What about your own talent?"

The corners of his mouth quirked slightly. "Yes, this 'talent' you apparently think I possess. What exactly is it? Because I can assure you that I've never experienced anything that might lead me to believe I have gifts remotely like yours, or those of anyone else in the program."

"You wouldn't," I said. "Like I said, yours is a subtle talent. If you weren't looking for it, you wouldn't know it even existed."

"Then enlighten me."

"It's luck," I told him, then hurried on, knowing how crazy that must have sounded. "Having things work out easily for you, having things go right even when maybe they shouldn't. Up until recently, it probably would have been even more subtle, just because we think getting struck by lightning woke it up, made it a lot more powerful than it had been before that point."

Through this recitation, he stood there,

unmoving, appearing to absorb what I'd said. His expression never changed, though, and so I had no idea what he thought of such an explanation.

But then he smiled, a cold, wintry smile that never reached his eyes. "At least you admit now that you used your power to attack me."

"I didn't have any other choice," I said. "I didn't want to."

"Very noble of you. And so your bolt of lightning somehow awakened a gift that up until that moment had been quite weak, and suddenly made me prone to good luck. If that's the case, I suppose I should go buy a lottery ticket."

Anger boiled in me at his flip tone, but I only shot him a sunny smile and said, "Maybe you should. I think you might be surprised."

"I'll take it under advisement," he replied. "In the meantime, you can remain here. I have other matters to attend to."

"Like Jake?" I asked, doing my best to keep the worry from my voice. As much as I tried to tell myself that he would be fine, that I'd survived getting dosed with that same tranquilizer and come out of it with not much more than a headache, I still hated to think of him waking up alone in a room somewhere else in this facility, not knowing where he was or what had happened to me.

"Dr. Richards' team is taking care of your

friend," Lenz said, not really answering my question. "As for the rest...well, that's something else I'll have to take into consideration. Go on."

He inclined his head toward the suite where he wanted me to stay. I hated the idea of going in there, since doing so felt like an admission of defeat. Unfortunately, I knew I didn't have much choice. Even if I dug in my heels, he'd probably just pick me up and carry me inside. After feeling the hard, taut muscle in his arms, I knew he was fully capable of such a feat.

"You're making a mistake," I said desperately, but he only shook his head.

"I don't think so. Have a good evening, Ms. Grant."

Any further protests would only serve to irritate him that much more. Right then, I thought it was probably better to accept my losses and try to regroup later.

"I doubt it," I said tartly, but I went inside the suite anyway.

Of course, Randall Lenz didn't respond. He closed the door, leaving me alone in the place I'd desperately hoped I would never have to see again.

There didn't seem to be anything I could do except stumble over to the sofa and sink down on it. I wanted to bury my head in my hands and cry, except I knew the whole place was under video surveillance, and I wasn't going to give Dr.

Richards or whoever else might be watching the feed the satisfaction of knowing they'd gotten to me.

No, I sat there, eyes dry and burning, stomach knotted with an uncomfortable mixture of despair and dread. I'd tried my best, and it hadn't worked.

I had no idea what to do next.

19

JAKE AWOKE TO A DULL THROBBING IN HIS head. His eyes opened, and he found himself staring up at an unfamiliar ceiling, smooth and painted a pale tan color. He shifted, thinking he could put his hands down on the bed where he lay —yes, that was definitely a bed—and push himself up to a sitting position.

Unfortunately, the restraints that kept him strapped to the bed had a different idea.

What the—?

"I'm sorry about those," came an unfamiliar female voice. Jake turned his head and saw a woman in her early forties standing a foot or so away. She wore a white lab coat and had dark blonde hair cut into a smooth bob. "But because of your particular talent, we thought it best to keep you restrained for a bit."

"Who the hell are you?" he asked. His voice came out as a scratchy growl, forcing its way past a dry throat. At another time, he might have worried about sounding rude. Right then, with his fear for Addie compounding the numerous aches and pains in his body, he couldn't have cared less.

Ignoring his brusque tone, the woman smiled and said, "I'm Dr. Richards. I'm in charge of this program."

"Oh, you're the sadist who kidnaps people and forces them to undergo your little 'tests'?"

Her smile slipped a little, and she replied in a brisk voice, "I'm sorry you view our work that way, Jake. I don't know what Addie told you, but I can assure you that we don't force anyone to do anything. All our guests are happy to assist us in our work."

There was a load of bull. However, he didn't see the point in trying to convince the doctor that her view of the world—and her work—was just a little skewed. He had far more important things to expend his energy on.

"Where is Addie?"

"She's here, and she's safe," the doctor said. "I can tell from your expression that you don't believe me, but we don't mean her—or you—any harm. It's best for everyone involved that you're here with us and participating in our studies.

Really, it was only a matter of time before your talents got out of control, and you ended up hurting yourself or someone else."

Those words made Jake want to laugh out loud in derision, but he kept quiet. Obviously, Dr. Richards had no experience with someone like him, a warlock who'd known how to work with his magic almost from the time it awakened. The poor souls she had trapped here had come into their powers on their own, with no guidance, and so she'd wrongly assumed it must be like that for everyone with special talents.

"I want to see Addie," he said.

"And you will," the doctor told him. "For now, though, you need to rest. How are you feeling?"

"I'm fine," he said shortly. No way would he tell her about the headache that currently pounded behind his temples. The last thing he wanted was for her to try shoving some kind of weird meds down his throat. He could cope very well until the pain subsided on its own.

"Hungry? Thirsty?"

Of course he was thirsty. His throat felt like twenty-grit sandpaper. However, he wasn't sure whether he wanted to admit such a weakness. Then again, while he could go quite a while without food, water was going to be a problem a lot sooner.

"I'd like some water."

Something in her expression shifted. Was she pleased that he'd asked for something from her? Maybe it had been a mistake, but he couldn't take the words back.

Besides, he *was* thirsty.

"Just a minute," she said.

The doctor left the room, presumably to fetch the water he'd requested. Jake couldn't see much, thanks to being strapped down on the bed, but he caught a glimpse of the space beyond the bedroom where he lay, something that looked like the back of a couch, maybe a floor lamp placed in one corner. Even those few details told him that he'd probably been placed in a suite similar to the one Addie had described from her stay at the SED facility. He didn't know whether he should be relieved by the relative comfort of his location— yes, he was strapped to the bed, but at least he wasn't in a jail cell—or worried that they'd put him here because they intended to treat him as just another test subject.

No way in hell would he allow that.

Dr. Richards returned with a glass of ice water in one hand. The glass also contained a bendable straw, but even with the straw, Jake wasn't sure whether he'd be able to drink anything without it dribbling down his chin.

"I can undo your restraints," she said. "But

you need to promise me that you won't try anything. If you do…." The words trailed off as she pulled a hypodermic from the pocket of her lab coat. "A second dose could have some serious side effects."

"I get it," he said wearily. Right then, he felt so brain-fogged that he wasn't sure whether he'd even be able to summon his gift to attack the doctor. Anyway, thanks to what Addie had told him about the facility, he knew there were hidden cameras all over the place, and that the door was secured with a biometric lock he wouldn't be able to open. Even if he managed to overpower the doctor without getting zapped by that stupid hypodermic needle, he still wouldn't get any farther than the living room before he came up against that locked door.

Another tight-lipped smile. "I'm glad we understand one another."

She set the glass down on the bedside table and then efficiently undid the buckles of the restraints. As soon as she was finished, she stepped back, as if she wasn't quite sure whether she trusted him to behave himself, despite his promises to the contrary.

Jake allowed himself an inner smile, even as he painfully pushed himself up to a sitting position. Every vertebra in his back felt as if it was cracking in succession as he straightened, and the pounding in his head intensified. Still, it wasn't so bad that he couldn't reach for the glass of ice water Dr. Richards had brought him and take a long pull through the straw.

The cold water pulsing down his throat tasted better than anything he'd ever drunk. He swallowed some more, feeling how it soothed the rawness of the muscles there. After draining half the glass, he put it down on the bedside table. His head still hurt, but he thought he might be starting to feel halfway human.

All right, maybe a quarter.

Dr. Richards had stood silently near the bed while he drank, waiting for him to finish. Jake looked down at himself, glad that he still wore the T-shirt and jeans he'd had on when he and Addie returned from their trip to Connor and Angela's house, although someone had taken off his shoes.

Since the doctor seemed to be waiting for him to speak, he said, "What now?"

"For now, you rest," she replied. "Someone will bring you your dinner in a short while. Tomorrow…tomorrow we'd like to start exploring your abilities."

A nice, polite way of saying that they planned to turn him into a lab rat. He fought back a scowl and said, "Not until I see Addie and know she's safe."

One of Dr. Richards' perfectly plucked

eyebrows lifted. "I don't think you realize that you're not in a position to be making demands, Jake. However, I can understand that you're concerned about her, so I'll see if I can set up a teleconference for you sometime tomorrow morning."

A teleconference that they'd be recording and scrutinizing. However, he realized that pretty much any conversation he had with Addie would be surveilled, so that wasn't reason enough to tell the doctor a teleconference wasn't satisfactory. Jake wanted to be able to take Addie in his arms, hold her and tell her everything was going to be all right—even if that particular reassurance might be an outright lie—but being able to see her and hear her voice was better than nothing.

"Thanks," he said, although he wasn't really all that thankful for the minimal amount of largesse the doctor seemed willing to extend to him.

Still, he knew he had to play along for now. He supposed he should have allowed the possibility of Agent Lenz somehow managing to track them back to Flagstaff, but how? The man's memories had been erased, and Jeremy had destroyed all the documentation relating to Lenz's pursuit of them from Kanab to Las Vegas and beyond. Hell, "Jake Wilcox" hardly existed anymore, thanks to the fake identity Jeremy had set up for him.

And yet, all that hadn't been enough. If he survived this, he sure as hell was going to ask Jeremy where his supposed countermeasures had failed them.

In the meantime, Jake had to do his best to make his captors believe he was being cooperative. As soon as he and Addie didn't turn up at Connor and Angela's house for their planned assault on Agent Lenz, they'd know something had gone horribly wrong. He had to assume they'd figure out the situation quickly enough, but what then? Would they mount a rescue?

Of course, they will, he told himself. *They're not going to leave Addie and me to rot here.*

The question was, how? If they brought Lucas along to ensure the rescue's success, like they had when they broke Addie out the first time, then they'd only be able to rescue one of them at a time, since neither Connor nor Angela was quite strong enough to carry two people while teleporting. They could travel in the blink of an eye…but an eye blink might be all it took for Lenz's people to realize a jailbreak was happening and to move the person left behind to a location Connor and Angela couldn't reach.

"Well, then," Dr. Richards said, her tone brisk, as if she'd realized that he wasn't going to offer any further protests.

Because he'd been beaten.

"I'll see what I can do to get the teleconference set up," she went on. "In the meantime, the bathroom is through that door, and there's a TV in the living room with access to pretty much any show you'd want to watch. Just be careful standing up the first time—you may feel a little lightheaded."

"Then I might as well do it now," he told her, then slowly swung his legs over the edge of the bed. Even that movement was enough to make his head start throbbing again, but he ignored the ache and pushed himself up to a standing position.

The room wobbled around him. He gritted his teeth and forced himself to remain where he was until the spinning stopped. Dr. Richards looked up at him coolly, although something in her expression seemed a little tight. Maybe she didn't care for the way he loomed over her, since she wasn't overly tall.

"How do you feel?" she asked.

"Okay," he replied. "I think I'll go out to the living room."

After picking up his water glass, he slowly walked past her and out into the main area of the suite. As advertised, it had a large TV mounted to one wall, with a sofa, coffee table, and armchair placed in front of it. Off to one side was a dinette set with a round table and four chairs. The furniture was upholstered in soft shades of beige and gray, and the whole place looked like a hotel suite.

Again, just about what Addie had described, although the theme of the prints on the walls appeared to be mountain scenes, rather than the beachscapes she'd mentioned.

He sat on the couch, a little surprised at how comfortable it was, and put his water glass down on the coffee table, deliberately ignoring the coasters provided. Watching this, Dr. Richards wore a pained expression, but she didn't call him out, only said, "It looks like you're doing very well. Any dietary restrictions I should let the kitchen know about?"

"No," he replied, after briefly considering telling her he was vegan and gluten-free, just to be difficult. However, that sort of lie would only result in him getting a meal he really wouldn't want to eat, and so he let it go.

"Great. The food should be here shortly. Have a good evening."

She smiled brightly and went over to the door, pausing briefly to have it scan her right eye so she could exit the suite. Then she headed out, and the door closed behind her with a soft *click* that sounded all too final.

At once, he got up from the sofa and went over to the door. It was a long shot, but…

…witches and wizards did have a facility with locked doors.

He paused six inches away from the biometric scanner and let it scan his right eye, at the same time visualizing the door opening.

Nothing happened.

Well, shit.

Another try, with the same result. Abandoning the scanner, Jake put his fingers on the door handle, willing it to press down at his touch.

Again, nothing.

Apparently, that particular witchy gift only worked on regular door locks with tumblers. Maybe if Jeremy had been here, his own talent would have allowed him to circumvent the biometric lock. Or maybe not; his power worked wonders on anything that had a microprocessor, but even he might have met his match in this particular security setup.

Deflated, Jake went back to the sofa and sat down again. He hated the thought of sitting on his ass when Addie was being held somewhere else in this same facility, but unfortunately, there didn't seem to be a whole hell of a lot he could do about it. Impotent rage boiled within him, and his thoughts began to circle to a dark place.

What if they couldn't get out of there? What if Connor and Angela and Jeremy couldn't come up with a plan that didn't involve risking their lives as well? Yes, Connor had said that the Wilcoxes took care of their own, but in the end, the *primus* and his *prima* wife were a hell of a lot more important than Jake and Addie, since they had the members of two entire clans depending on them. They might decide in the end that it wasn't a gamble worth taking.

They won't do that. They won't.

Jake just wished his inner voice was a little more confident.

Randall Lenz sat in his office, brooding over everything Adara Grant had just told him. It was late and he should have gone home, and yet he'd realized he didn't want to sit in that empty house and listen to the silence there. Much better to be here in the office, where, although he was alone, he had only to walk down the hall to be in a room with analysts and other agents, a place where the quiet buzz of activity served to reassure him that everything was humming along like the well-oiled machine he'd built the Daedalus Project to be.

But even though he sat in familiar surroundings, in a place he'd designed to be soothing and allow him to think clearly, his thoughts were anything but clear at the moment. He wanted to laugh at what Adara had said, wanted to tell himself that she'd obviously been grasping at straws, doing her best to hand him the sort of story she thought might help to extricate herself from her current situation.

Your talent is luck, she'd said.

Ridiculous.

Only…was it?

If asked, he would never have come out and said that he was a lucky person. He'd never won the lottery, never had fame or fortune dropped in his lap. He would have pointed out the loss of his father when he was barely twenty years old. How could anyone believe that having a parent die in such a horrific and tragic way was anything but an example of the very worst luck of all?

But then he realized that his own luck most likely only protected him, not necessarily those around him. Lenz had actually had plans to meet his father for lunch at the World Trade Center that fateful day in September, but he'd woken up that morning with a scratchy throat and had called his father's secretary to pass on the news and to let him know they'd have to reschedule. Less than fifteen minutes after he'd hung up, the plane had hit the North Tower.

Odd how he hadn't even thought about that incident for years. For a while, he'd wrestled with his own form of survivor's guilt, even though he'd done his best to rationalize his way through the situation, telling himself that even if he hadn't canceled the lunch date, the tower would have collapsed hours before he was supposed to meet his father there.

His luck at work, making sure he wouldn't go near the place even though he might not have been terribly at risk?

Maybe.

There were far more instances than that, however…like the way he got his first posting at Homeland Security, thanks to the sub-director of the Sciences Division being an old college friend of his father's. Again, it could have been simply serendipity or coincidence—or the plain fact that Princeton grads tended to stick together, and Leo Schumacher had wanted to do what he could to help the son of a man who'd lost his life in a national tragedy.

Or how Lenz had achieved his current position as director of the Daedalus Project when the previous director was found to be embezzling funds and quickly dismissed. Yes, he'd been next in line for the job, but no one had thought he would achieve the position so soon. His former boss was a man only ten years older, someone who should have remained as director for years and years…until he bought a cabin in Vermont to go along with his beach house in Florida, and investigators discovered exactly how much of the project's budget had been funneled into his personal accounts following his appointment to the position.

Lenz rubbed his forehead and frowned. None of this was solid enough evidence to hold up in a court of law, and yet his instincts were telling him that the pattern really couldn't be ignored. One incident meant nothing. Two…much the same. But when he sorted through his personal history and thought of all the instances when he might have been in the wrong place at the wrong time if circumstances hadn't conspired to prevent him from doing so, and when he mentally calculated all the times his career had gotten an unexpected boost through matters that were none if his doing, it became much more difficult for him to try to deny this was all natural and nothing more.

And then there was the matter of him being conveniently already in southern Colorado when Dawson unearthed the information that sent him to find Adara Grant in Wyoming. Yes, some might argue that if his talent was really that strong, it would have guided him directly to Riverton, but he wasn't so sure about that. The timing allowed him to go and collect her when she was safely asleep, rather than trying to pluck her from her job as a bar server at the local casino. At any rate, the operation had been seamless. His luck had still held.

He wanted to believe this was all madness. He wanted to tell himself that witches and warlocks didn't exist. The Daedalus Project had been created based on the theory that a certain subset of the population possessed special gifts and that those people were somehow able to tap into the hidden reserves of the human mind. Nothing there about witches or warlocks, or magic. Just harnessing the power of the portions of the brain that usually slept.

Only...what if that power could more correctly be called magic?

If that was the case, then everything Adara Grant had told him was the truth. But how could she prove such a thing?

Lenz got up from his desk and left his office. Because it was late and the evening team was on duty, Dawson had already gone home for the night. Too bad, because he might have wanted her as a witness to what he intended to do next. Or maybe not; did he really want his assistant to know that her boss wasn't quite what he seemed, was in fact a warlock?

The word itself was absurd. He was a man of science, a government agent, not someone who sounded as though he should be draped in robes, dressed like something out of a Harry Potter novel.

Down the six floors to the suite where Adara

Grant was staying, and then a brief pause at the entrance to her rooms so he could push the intercom button on the security panel mounted next to the door. Before doing so, however, he entered the code that turned down the level of the recording devices in the living room section of her suite. He would still do his best to be circumspect when he spoke, but at least that way, he wouldn't have to worry about any of his colleagues listening to a conversation that would most likely be problematic on a variety of levels. Turning them off altogether, unfortunately, was not an option, as doing so would send an alert to whomever was currently monitoring the surveillance devices.

"Ms. Grant? I'd like to speak to you for a moment."

A long pause, but then her voice came through the speaker, sounding guarded. "About what?"

"About what you told me earlier."

An uncomfortable few seconds passed, and she said, "Okay."

He found himself oddly relieved. Yes, he supposed he could have gone into her suite without asking her permission, but he guessed she would be more receptive when she had at least the illusion of being somewhat in control.

The scanner assessed his retinal patterns, and the door opened to let him in. Adara sat on the sofa, a tray with several empty plates resting on the coffee table in front of her. As soon as the door shut, she rose from her seat and faced him, her arms crossed.

Her expression was anything but welcoming, although he supposed he should have been expecting that. Not that it mattered; this wasn't a social call.

Now that the time had come, though, he found it harder than he'd thought to ask the question. Possibly, the challenging, angry light in Adara's eyes was the reason. However, he certainly wasn't going to back down now.

"You told me something strange earlier," he said, avoiding the word "warlock" and keeping his phrasing vague so the hidden cameras and microphones, even turned down as they were, couldn't pick up anything incriminating. "You know how implausible it must have sounded."

Her shoulders lifted slightly. "I know it sounds crazy," she replied. "But it doesn't change the truth of the matter."

"I'm afraid I need more evidence than that."

"With your kind of talent, that's not so easy." A pause as she frowned, clearly pondering the problem—if it was a problem at all. He supposed it was entirely possible that she'd made up the entire story to sow doubt in his mind…although he was fairly certain that wasn't the case. While he and Ms. Grant had been at odds nearly from the first moment they met, he didn't believe she would be that duplicitous.

But then she smiled and nodded to herself, as if she'd just thought of something.

"I'll need a candle," she said, and he frowned at her, wondering if he'd heard her correctly.

"A candle?"

"Yes. A real one, not one of those battery-powered kinds."

"Why?"

She smiled, the first genuine smile he'd seen from her. "Because it's the easiest way to prove you're really what I said you are."

20

FOR THE LONGEST MOMENT, I WORRIED THAT Agent Lenz wasn't going to go for it. After all—if the dubious expression on his face was any indication—he could have seen my request as a simple stalling tactic and nothing more. It wasn't, though. I'd realized as he'd stared at me, challenging me to come up with some way to offer real proof for my claims, that the door-unlocking trick Jake had shown me wasn't going to work here. It was one thing to move a few tumblers with your mind or your witchy powers or whatever you wanted to call them, and quite another to mess with a state-of-the-art biometric lock.

But then I'd remembered how Jake and Connor had talked about getting Agent Lenz to conjure a flame, and I guessed that would do just as well. Jake had told me how witches and warlocks could summon fire, could light candles by doing nothing more than thinking about it. I hadn't yet gotten the opportunity to test that particular power, but I figured it couldn't be too difficult.

So, I asked Agent Lenz to get a candle, and although he gave me some side-eye, he said he'd see what he could do and disappeared, presumably in search of the candle in question. I wouldn't let myself relax, even though I was glad to have him out of my presence, if only for a few moments. Although he hadn't done anything threatening, my teeth seemed to set themselves on edge whenever he was around.

While he was gone, I made myself sit back down on the sofa in the living room area of my suite and wait quietly for him to return, even though I wanted to pace back and forth to work off some of my nervous energy. This had to work. It wasn't just my freedom on the line—it was Jake's freedom, and the freedom of all the other test subjects currently being held at the facility. Anxiety knotted my gut, and I reached for the half-drunk glass of water that sat on the coffee table and managed a few large swallows. I didn't know if it really helped all that much, but at least my mouth felt a little less dry.

About fifteen minutes passed before Randall Lenz's voice came through the speaker unit next to the door. "I have the candle," he said.

"Come in," I replied, glad I sounded so steady.

He entered the room. In one hand he held a jar candle in a soft pink shade. It looked so incongruous against his severe black suit that I wanted to laugh.

Expression somewhat pained, he said, "Candles are in short supply in a facility like this. However, I was able to locate this one on one of the admins' desks. Against regulations, but it doesn't look as though she ever lit it." A very small shrug, and he went over to the dinette set and put it down on the table there. "I don't have a lighter, however."

"That's fine," I said. I got up from the sofa and walked over to the table, then paused a few feet away from it. "You won't need one. You see, you're going to light this candle with your mind."

Lenz stared at me as if I'd just told him he was going to strap on a pair of wings and jump off the roof of the building. "Excuse me?"

"It's something all witches and warlocks can do," I explained. "We all have this small talent— this, and being able to unlock doors...well, as long as they have regular locks, I guess. All you have to do is focus on the candle and will it to light."

His arms crossed. "What does lighting candles and unlocking doors have to with supposedly being lucky…or, for that matter, summoning storms?"

"Nothing!" I flared at him, then made myself take a breath. While he had a knack for plucking my last nerve, this definitely wasn't the time or place to lose my temper. And, on the surface, I thought I understood what he was asking. It didn't seem to make much sense that witches and warlocks had all these disparate talents, and yet they still shared those two small gifts in common. Maybe it was a quirk of evolution and nothing more. I didn't know, because I was still new to all this and was woefully short of any in-depth knowledge of the witch world and the laws that governed it. "I mean," I went on in more measured tones, "I honestly can't tell you why all witches and warlocks can light a candle just by thinking about it. All I know is that it works. Just try, okay?"

A long pause. He watched me with those icy eyes of his, and I swallowed nervously. What if he told me this was ridiculous and walked out? I couldn't make him do anything, after all, not buried hundreds of feet below ground in a place where my weather talents couldn't help me a single bit.

Then again….

I couldn't summon a storm, but I could do the one thing I was asking him to do.

"Like this," I said, and looked over at the pink candle. Even unlit, it had a fresh, bright scent. Pink grapefruit, maybe.

The wick flared to life as I gazed at it, a small steady flame surrounding the virgin unburned cord. Randall Lenz took a step backward, then paused, eyes narrowing.

"How did you do that?" he demanded.

"I'm a witch," I said simply. Strange how easy it was to utter those three words, when only a few weeks earlier, I hadn't even thought witches were real. But being a witch was just part of me, like the color of my eyes or the way I couldn't fall asleep unless I lay on my side. "Just like you're a warlock, Agent Lenz. Try it."

He glanced at the candle and then back at me, his posture oddly irresolute. In all my dealings with him, I'd never seen him look hesitant, and yet that was how he seemed to me in that moment. Unsure of himself, wondering if he was about to take a deep dive into a place from which he could never return.

Well, I knew what it felt like to fall into that

particular rabbit hole…but I also knew I'd never want to go back to who I was before, to the world I'd lived in before. Everything had changed, and for the better. That didn't mean I wasn't still mourning the loss of my mother, and yet I wouldn't allow her loss to taint the very real sense of wonder I held within me, now that I knew magic was real.

"It's all right," I said, hoping to encourage him.

"No, it's not. It's one thing for you to have done this…." He stopped there, and his gaze flickered up to an indeterminate point in the ceiling before returning to me.

For a second or two, I couldn't figure out what he was hinting at. Then I remembered that the entire suite was under video surveillance. He'd said it was "one thing for me to have done this." By that comment, I assumed he meant that whoever was watching the video would only have seen someone they'd already known had special powers use one they hadn't seen before, and while unusual, it might not rouse too many suspicions. If he did the same thing, however, he'd have a hell of a lot of explaining to do.

I supposed I should have realized they'd catch my little performance with the candle on camera. There wasn't anything I could do about that, unfortunately, but I understood his reticence. The last thing he probably wanted was for his own people to realize he had a little something more going on in his brain than he'd previously revealed.

Then he inclined his head ever so slightly in the direction of the bedroom. Again, I had to puzzle out his meaning, but a second later, it hit me. Yes, the bedroom had its own hidden cameras…but the bathroom didn't.

I nodded but didn't say anything, only bent down and blew out the candle, then picked it up and headed toward the bathroom. Lenz followed close behind, and once we were inside, he shut the door behind us even as he flicked on the light fixture mounted on the wall above the mirror.

Being with him in such close quarters wasn't exactly comfortable, but I told myself it was in a good cause. Still without speaking—just in case there were hidden microphones, even if they'd shown their test subjects the barest consideration by not having cameras in such a private place—I pointed at the candle. Agent Lenz stared at it for a moment, and then his jaw tightened.

Go ahead, I mouthed. Not that he hadn't known what I wanted him to do. But I had to hope the extra encouragement would be enough for him to take the necessary mental leap.

He shoved his hands in the pockets of his trousers, as if he wanted to make sure he couldn't affect the candle in any way except with his thoughts. The straight dark brows pulled together, and his eyes shut for the briefest moment.

And the candle came to life again, the flame bright and steady. A hiss of breath escaped his lips.

"That's not possible," he whispered. His eyes fastened on me, hard, glinting…suspicious. "Did you do that?"

"No," I said, annoyed that he'd even think I would pull such a maneuver. Then again, Connor had said Randall Lenz might suspect me of trying to trick him into believing he had powers similar to mine. Lowering my voice, I added, "Can they hear us in here?"

He shook his head, but at the same time, he reached over and turned on the bathroom's exhaust fan. It hummed away, making a good white noise generator. "There isn't any surveillance equipment in the bathroom," he told me, confirming what I had already guessed. "However, the microphones in the bedroom are sensitive enough that they might pick up our conversation. Hence, that." He pointed up at the plastic grate that covered the fan.

"Good," I said. "Anyway, no, I didn't light that candle. You did that all on your own."

His lips pressed together, and then he asked, "It's not a trick?"

I reflected that it must not be a lot of fun going through life distrusting everything and everyone around you. "No trick," I replied. "Do it again."

Without answering, he bent and blew out the candle. A long pause—I had a feeling he was testing me, waiting to concentrate on lighting the thing to see if I would intervene—and then the wick glowed with flame once more. This time, he appeared more convinced that he'd actually managed to do the impossible, because he reached up, as if to run an astounded hand through his hair. Then he stopped at the last moment, probably telling himself he shouldn't betray that kind of weakness to an audience, especially an audience that consisted of one of his test subjects.

In a way, I wished he had ruffled his hair. Doing so would have made him seem more human.

But I told myself it was enough that he hadn't protested this time, hadn't accused me of making the candle's wick glow with sudden flame. Grinning, I said, "Yer a wizard, Harry."

To my surprise, Lenz didn't ask me what the hell I was talking about. No, he only smiled slightly and said in ironic tones, "You don't look much like Hagrid."

"Thank God for that." I hesitated, then said, "So…you believe me now?"

A very long pause. For the first time, I noticed the lines around his eyes, the faintest traces of gray at his temples. He appeared tired to me then, shoulders slumped, mouth turned down at the corners. "It looks like I'll have to."

Well, at least we wouldn't have to waste more precious time arguing over whether or not he was a warlock. Through everything else that had been going on, I'd never forgotten about Jake, languishing elsewhere in the facility. Yes, it was nighttime, and I guessed that Dr. Richards and her team wouldn't start in with the experiments until the following day, but we still needed to get him out of there as fast as we could.

Actually, I realized as my gaze shifted from Agent Lenz to the room beyond the one where we stood, we needed to get *all* of them out of there.

To my surprise, Lenz seemed to guess the direction my thoughts were running, because his tone turned wry as he went on, "You have the look of a woman plotting a jail break."

Supposedly, his talent was luck, but right then, I couldn't help but wonder if he was the teeniest bit psychic as well. Or maybe part of his gift involved instincts that were far more developed than those of most people. "Was I that obvious?" I asked, trying to smile.

A lifted eyebrow was his only answer. "Whatever you're thinking," he said, "it won't be easy. As you know, all of the test subjects' suites are monitored 24/7. I might have the authority to move them from one place in the facility to another, but even I don't have free rein to do whatever I like. If I start shuttling them out of the building, people are going to start asking questions, even if Dr. Richards and her team might not be on duty at the moment."

"Well, we'll have to come up with some sort of a diversion," I replied. I stopped there and gave him a considering look. He'd spoken simply, without any accusation in his voice, no hint at any subtext, but I had to wonder whether I could really trust him. "You're not going to give me a speech about how all these test subjects are vital to Homeland Security and it's treason for me to even be thinking about getting them out of here?"

Several uncomfortable seconds passed as he stood there, gaze fixed not on me, but on something that seemed to be located far beyond the walls of the underground facility where we stood. The set of his shoulders and neck was so tense, he looked as if he would snap in two if I reached out and touched him.

Not that I had any intention of doing so.

When he spoke, his voice was quiet enough that I had to strain to hear him over the hum of the ceiling fan. "How many witches and warlocks are there?"

The question felt as though it had come straight out of left field, but I still thought I had a notion as to why he'd asked it. "I don't know," I said, which was only the truth. "But Jake told me there are hundreds of Wilcoxes, and there are witch families in almost every state in the Union —and also around the world. You do the math."

"Tens of thousands."

"Probably."

He went silent again, although a muscle in his cheek worked, as though he clenched his jaw while he processed that information. "If all those witches and warlocks have managed to keep their identities hidden for this long, then I wouldn't be doing them a very great service by exposing them, would I? Especially since I seem to be one of them as well."

There was such brooding speculation in his expression that I had to ask, "Which of your parents…?"

"Neither," he said quickly. "My *adoptive* parents," he added, the emphasis clear on the one word, "were very successful people, but there's nothing supernatural about either one of them. Someone left me in a basket on the front step of Fire Station 226 in Brooklyn, and I was adopted a few months later. But obviously, I don't know a single thing about my biological parents. I tried to find out, but there was nothing to find."

If someone had told me a few weeks earlier that I might end up actually feeling sorry for

Randall Lenz, I would have told them to put down the crack pipe. However, as I stared into his face and saw the toll decades of unanswered questions had taken on him, I couldn't quite hold back a rush of pity. Yes, up until a few weeks earlier, I hadn't known anything about my biological father except his name and the barest few details about him, but at least I'd had something. I'd known he was rich and handsome, and had two sons. Agent Lenz didn't have even that much to hold on to. Had he spent his life wondering as he passed strangers on the street whether any of those people were his father, his mother?

Wisely, I held back any words of sympathy, since I doubted he would appreciate them. Instead, I said, "Jake thought your witch parent—or parents—might be from the Van Horn family. I guess they're the witch clan in New York."

"The Van Horns?" Lenz replied, looking almost startled.

"That's what he said. You've heard of them?"

"Anyone who lives in New York has heard of them," he said. "Or at least, anyone who moves in the same circles my mother does. Very old money. Philanthropists—you know, the kind of people who give millions to charity the way most of us put money in the Salvation Army pail during the holidays. I suppose if one of their daughters had gotten pregnant out of wedlock, then she would have done whatever she could to cover it up."

Did anyone say "out of wedlock" anymore? I'd honestly never even cared that my parents hadn't been married, despite getting teased a few times about not having a father by some of the nastier boys at the schools in the more conservative areas where my mother and I had lived. But if the Van Horns really were "old money" like the Rockefellers or something, I supposed I could see why getting pregnant without being safely married could be a problem.

All that was something to worry about at a later date, however.

Randall Lenz seemed to be thinking the same thing, because he said, "It's one thing to have a program where each of the test subjects is believed to be one individual out of twenty or so million, nearly unique. It's quite another to suddenly discover that there are tens of thousands of people with special abilities living among us. That would create a seismic shift in our society, one we might never recover from." He paused, and once again his cool blue eyes took on a faraway look, one that appeared to be focused on something neither of us could see. "I came to work for Homeland Security to protect this country, and right now, I believe the best way to protect it is to make sure that Dr. Richards and her team never know the truth about the witch clans. And to do that…." The words trailed off, and his shoulders squared as he gazed down at me, those eyes now piercing as laser beams.

"To do that, we'll have to end the Daedalus Project."

21

He couldn't quite believe those words had come out of his mouth. Had he really just suggested to Adara Grant that they put an end to the program which had consumed his life for the past three years?

Apparently, he had, because she was staring at him in shock, gray-green eyes wide with surprise. When she found her voice, her first words told him she wasn't sure she could trust what he'd just said.

"You want to close down the project?" she demanded. "After everything you've done to get me here?"

"You and the others," he corrected her. "Although you were a bit more difficult to acquire than any of the other test subjects." Since Adara continued to stare at him, disbelief clear in her expression, he went on, "You think I don't under-stand what I'm proposing? If I help you with this…if we're successful…then my career is over. But when the alternative is revealing the truth about witch-kind…."

The words died away, the only sound that remained the persistent buzz of the bathroom fan overhead. Adara still gazed at him as if she couldn't quite trust the evidence of her own ears. Not that he blamed her. He'd begun to wonder if he'd completely taken leave of his senses.

At the same time, deep down he understood why he had to do this. He'd taken an oath to protect the United States of America and its citi-zens, and the people of the witch clans were also those citizens. The risk of what might happen to them—to all those thousands of people just trying to live their lives—if the truth should ever come out was far too great. People's fear of the unknown was a terrible thing.

Adara was quiet, her expression troubled, although she didn't argue with him, only stood there, apparently wrestling with her own thoughts. At last she said, "Okay. But if this is another trick—"

"No tricks," he cut in. Paradoxically, he felt much better now that he'd made a decision and only had to come up with an actionable plan. Some people might have called him crazy for throwing away nearly two decades of work with Homeland Security, but he knew he was doing the right thing. When he came out the other side of this—*if* he did—then he could decide what to do with the rest of his life. For the moment, however, the main problem at hand was how to free Jake Wilcox and the rest of the test subjects being held at the facility. Lenz knew he might not have a better opportunity than now, if only because it was the middle of the night and there weren't nearly as many people around as there were during the day. "I told you I would help. You may not believe this about me, Ms. Grant, but when I say I'm going to do something, I do it."

"'Addie,'" she corrected him. Although she wasn't precisely smiling, her expression had lightened a bit. "I mean," she went on, "if we're going to be allies in this, we might as well be on a first-name basis. Do you prefer Randall or Randy?"

"Randall," he said at once, trying not to grimace. His mother had called him Randy up until the time he was around nine, at which point he'd solemnly informed her that he didn't like the nickname and wanted her to use his proper name.

Adara's mouth twitched. "Good. You really didn't seem like a Randy to me. So, do you have a plan?"

He didn't—not yet, anyway. All of the project's test subjects were housed on either the floor where he and Addie stood or the one below it, but those suites were closely monitored by the facility's security system. While he might have been able to usher one or two of the "guests" out of their rooms and off to a waiting vehicle, there was no way he'd be able to get all fourteen—well, fifteen, if you counted Jake Wilcox—away before someone noticed what was going on.

If they were all together, however....

He nodded to himself, and Addie tilted her head at him. "What is it?"

"Our protocols call for all the test subjects to gather in the multipurpose unit in case of an emergency. Once they're at the unit, they'll be moved to a waiting van to be housed off-site."

She nodded, clearly grasping what he was suggesting. "And then you hijack the van."

"For lack of a better term, yes." He didn't like the idea very much—he could already think of at least a dozen scenarios where things could go very wrong—but he also knew it was probably the best chance they had.

"And you want me to manufacture an emergency," she said.

His thoughts had run precisely along those lines, but once again, he was surprised by how quickly she'd been able to grasp the situation. "Could you?"

A shrug. Her expression was almost studiously

casual, and yet he detected a tension in her slender form, as though she feared she might not be up to this particular task after all. "Well, lightning can be pretty destructive," she said. Her face brightened a bit as she added, "Are you on the regular power grid, or do you have your own power plant here?"

"We're an independent facility," he told her. "So no, we're not on the grid. The power generating plant is located on the property to the west of the main building."

"A direct strike would knock you out for how long?"

"I don't know whether it would knock us out at all," he said. "We have redundancies built in to avoid that sort of situation."

Strangely, Addie didn't look too dismayed by that particular piece of information. In fact, she smiled slightly. "Could those redundancies keep up with multiple lightning strikes in a short period of time?"

Good question. While he knew the building had been designed to withstand hurricanes and even low-level tornadoes, he somehow doubted the engineers who'd built its self-contained power grid had ever imagined the system being struck repeatedly by lightning. "It's never been tested in that sort of scenario. Educated guess...probably not."

"Well, then, I know what I need to do." She paused and glanced up at the ceiling. "But you'll need to get me out of this suite. I can't do much stuck ten floors underground."

"Eight," he corrected her, although he knew the exact number didn't matter that much. "And getting you out isn't a problem. No one is going to question me as to why I'm taking you up to the ground level."

"Being the boss has its perks, I guess."

Yes, it did. Not that he had the ultimate authority at the SED—that rested with Under-Secretary Bryant—but Lenz doubted anyone was going to ask questions about him guiding one test subject to the courtyard. And while he knew his authority to move freely about the facility would be short-lived once it was found out what he was up to, he figured he might as well exploit it while he could.

"So, you'll short out the power grid with coordinated lightning strikes," he said. "As soon as the power plant fails, the facility will switch to generator power, and the guards on the two dormitory levels will take everyone to the multipurpose unit to keep them safely in one place. Emergency texts will be sent to Dr. Richards and her team, but with any luck, they won't be able to reach the facility before I've gotten everyone out of the building."

"And into the van."

"Yes."

Herding the test subjects would be the trickiest part of the plan, since the task of moving all their "guests" was supposed to fall on any guards who were on duty at the time. However, Lenz didn't think they would have too much trouble with him wanting to manage that task himself; it made sense that the director would oversee the evacuation of the test subjects in the event he was present during such an emergency.

"And after that?" Addie asked.

To Hyde Field, he supposed. He had the codes that would get him into the hangar where his jet was stored. True, while he had a pilot's license, he'd only trained on Cessnas and Pipers and had never actually flown a jet, but he supposed that was where they'd get to see how strong the rumored "luck" gift that Addie claimed he possessed actually was.

"I'll fly us out of here," he said. "Luckily, the jet seats eighteen, or we'd be in trouble."

"Even more trouble than we already are, you mean," she said, mouth twitching slightly.

Was she not taking this seriously? Lenz wanted to frown, but a closer look at Addie's face told him she was probably just trying to make the best of a bad situation, while at the same time steeling herself for the tasks that lay ahead.

"I suppose so." He glanced down at his watch. Five minutes past midnight. A new set of guards would have just come on duty. That might not be a good thing, because they'd be fresh and alert, rather than tired at the end of a shift and wanting to go home. On the other hand, they might not have settled down into their routine quite yet, and might be more likely to make mistakes.

And he could go back and forth with himself all night if he didn't stop now. While he'd always thought of himself as a decisive person, he knew precisely what lay ahead for him if he continued on this course of action. Disgrace, the loss of his job, the loss of any hope of a future working for Homeland Security...or the government at all. It might not be too late to turn back.

But he looked down at Addie, at the way she was watching him quietly, determination clear in the set of her jaw and her slender shoulders. She meant to do this thing, and he realized then that he couldn't leave her hanging. He'd destroyed the life she once had, which meant it was his destiny to do what he could to ensure a happy future for her.

If he destroyed his own life in the process, so be it. He couldn't deny that he deserved such a fate after what he'd done to her...and to the rest of the people in the program.

Her expression was also just the slightest bit

speculative, as if she still wasn't quite sure whether he was truly going to follow through with his plans. Could he blame her for her distrust?

He'd done a great deal to earn it, after all.

Well, he'd have to do his best to make her believe he had her best interests at heart…starting now.

"Let's go," he said, and reached over to turn off the bathroom fan.

It took exactly forty-four steps to cross the living room of his luxurious prison cell. Jake knew that because he'd already paced back and forth across the space at least ten times. His head pounded and his legs felt wobbly despite the food he'd been provided—a surprisingly decent slab of well-seasoned roast chicken breast accompanied by mashed potatoes and steamed green beans. He'd eaten because he knew he'd probably regret it if he didn't, although the dinner didn't seem to have done much to improve his condition.

Most likely, he should be sleeping, but he knew trying to get any rest would be a futile endeavor. How could he sleep while his thoughts raced, urgent with worry for Addie? As much as he tried to tell himself that she would be okay, that she'd already been held in this same facility for several days and had lived to tell the tale, he didn't know if he truly believed that. After they'd caused him so much trouble, Randall Lenz might be out for revenge.

Never in his life had Jake felt so helpless… except maybe after he learned of Sarah's death, had realized that if he'd gone along on that ill-fated kayaking trip, he might have been able to save her. If something happened to Addie while he sat here on his ass, he'd never forgive himself.

Maybe that was why he kept pacing. If nothing else, it made him feel as if he was doing something.

A small popping sound, followed by another, and suddenly, Connor and Angela were standing in the room, blocking Jake's progress. Their appearance was so unexpected that for a second he could only stare at them, wondering if he'd finally lost his mind.

"Hi, Jake," Connor said.

"What—?"

"It's okay," Angela said gently. She glanced up at her husband before adding, "You didn't think we were going to just leave you here, did you?"

"I—" Jake closed his mouth, then shook his head. "How did you find me?"

"How do you think?" Connor said. "Jeremy still has access to the surveillance system here. When you and Addie didn't show up at ten like you were supposed to, we knew something had to have gone wrong. Angela and I went over to your place and found Taffy locked up in the downstairs bathroom and the two of you missing, and we guessed what must have happened."

"Taffy's okay?" Jake asked, inwardly berating himself for not even thinking about his poor dog. She'd been nowhere in evidence when he and Addie had come home, and he realized Agent Lenz must have locked her up to keep her out of the way.

"She's fine," Angela replied. "She had a bowl of water and some food. Mostly, she was just annoyed at being trapped in there."

"Anyway," Connor said. "It didn't take us too long to figure out what must have happened. I called Jeremy and asked him to take a look at the facility's security feed and see if he could find any trace of you. Which he did, and once we had a good visual, Angela and I teleported here to bust you out."

While Jake was relieved to hear that Taffy hadn't suffered too much during her ordeal, he couldn't help noticing that neither Connor nor Angela had said anything about Addie. "And Addie?"

The *prima* and *primus* looked at each other, and Angela's shoulders lifted slightly. "We don't know," she said. "Jeremy was able to tap into the feed in her room, but she wasn't there."

Which meant Lenz must have taken her somewhere else. Jake hated the thought of her trapped someplace with the man, unable to get away. "We've got to find her!"

"And we will," Connor said. "But first, we need to get you out of here. Jeremy's working his magic on the security cameras, so no one will be able to discover that we infiltrated the facility a second time, but we still shouldn't be hanging around for too long."

Under other circumstances, Jake would have been all too glad to get out of there as quickly as possible. At the moment, though, he refused to leave until he knew Addie was safe as well. "If Jeremy's messing with the surveillance system, then we have time. I'm not going anywhere until I know Addie is all right."

Connor's jaw set, and his eyes glittered. For just a second, he looked uncomfortably like his brother Damon. "We'll find her, Jake. But digging in your heels isn't helping the situation."

"Wanting to make sure she's okay isn't 'digging in my heels,'" he argued.

An exasperated gust of breath escaped Angela's lips. "We all want her to be okay, Jake. And Jeremy's conducting the search from his end. He can probably do a lot more good than any of us can.

Once he finds her, Connor and I can jump right back in and grab her, no matter where she is."

"Even if she's with Lenz?"

"Even then," Connor said. "Lenz is no match for Angela and me working together. You know that. For now, it's better to just get the hell out of here."

Jake stood his ground, irresolute. What they were saying made sense, and yet every fiber of his being protested leaving Addie behind.

As they stood there, the floor shook under their feet, and then again…and again. Abruptly, the lights in the room blinked and went dead. Angela gasped in alarm, but almost immediately, dim orange emergency fixtures turned on from opposite corners near the ceiling, illuminating their pale, worried faces.

Connor gave a wild glance around the room. "What the hell?"

Incongruously, Jake's lips curved in a smile. He had no idea where the thought had come from, but as soon as it passed through his mind, he knew it to be nothing more than the truth.

"It's Addie," he said, his smile broadening into a grin. "She warned Lenz she would bring down the thunder. Well, now she has."

"She knocked out the power?" Connor asked. His expression was incredulous…but then, he'd never really seen Addie in action.

"Hitting them where it hurts," Jake said. "We need to go find her."

"Well, if she brought a storm, she's got to be up there somewhere, right?" Angela pointed toward the ceiling.

"I think so," he replied. "She told me she couldn't use her gift when she was so far below ground, so she has to be outside the facility somewhere."

"Only one way to find out," Connor said. He wore a grim expression, as if steeling himself for whatever confrontation might await them out in the wind and the weather. Extending a hand to Jake, he added, "Let's go."

Jake stepped toward his cousin, let Connor grasp him firmly by both hands. No words, only a swirl of darkness, and they were gone.

22

As Randall Lenz had promised, no one had tried to stop us from walking out the front door of the facility. I'd kept my head down and tried to look cowed, like a prisoner being escorted from one jail cell to another. As far as I could tell, the guards on duty had bought the act. Probably, they couldn't wrap their heads around the possibility that the man in charge of the whole place had decided to turn traitor.

Honestly, I was still having a hard time wrapping my head around the concept, too. I kept waiting for the other shoe to drop, kept thinking that this had to be an elaborate ruse on his part, some kind of subtle psychological torture designed to see how far he could lead me along a high wire before he pushed me off.

Or at least, that was what I thought, right up

until the moment when we stopped fifty yards or so from the enclosure that surrounded the SED facility's dedicated power plant. Lights picked out the outline of the blocky buildings inside the chain-link fence, but I couldn't see any sign of movement.

"Go ahead," he murmured. "This is a dead spot in the surveillance camera coverage. No one's going to know we were here."

Those words reassured me somewhat. Then again, I didn't know whether being reassured was my best bet right then. I needed to be upset in order to bring the storms and the lightning buried within them.

No, you don't, I reminded myself. *You control the weather. It doesn't control you.*

Breathe.

The night was warm and humid, and mostly clear. But a few clouds hugged the coastline, not so very far away, and I reached out to them. They swirled at my mind's touch, flowing toward the facility and the spot where Randall Lenz and I stood. The wind picked up, turning chilly, awakening goosebumps on my exposed arms. With the wind came the scent of rain, and inside the clouds I'd called, lightning pulsed and grew.

And stabbed downward in a thick jagged bolt, striking the largest building inside the enclosure.

The lights that outlined its silhouette flickered, then held.

"Again," Lenz murmured, paying no attention to the wave of rain that had accompanied the cloud, dampening his short-cropped hair and shining wetly on the shoulders of his dark suit.

Let go, I thought, and lightning flared again, crackling through the night, searing my nostrils with the sharp scent of ozone. This time, the bolt struck the ground next to the building, sending the lights flickering once again.

But they didn't go out, and I held back a curse. Goddamn—Lenz hadn't been lying when he'd said the place had been built to withstand hurricanes and tornadoes.

Despite that, I doubted it would be able to hold up to Hurricane Adara.

A third bolt, bigger and brighter than the previous two, shattered the heavens. Even though I'd known it was coming, I winced as it hit the building dead center. The ground under my feet shook, and I staggered backward.

The night went black, the only light the uneasy pulsing of the unspent energy within the clouds I'd summoned. A few seconds later, emergency lights turned on inside the enclosure and in the main building as well, their pale orange looking wan and tired in the black night.

"That did it," Lenz said. "Quick—we need to get inside."

I turned to follow him…only to see a trio of dark figures materialize from nowhere and stand directly between us and the entrance to the facility.

Alarm sang along all my nerve endings—until I realized those figures were Connor and Angela and Jake. He seemed to recognize me in almost the same moment, and he ran toward us.

Not to embrace me, as I'd thought, but to deliver a roundhouse punch to Randall Lenz's jaw. The blow knocked the agent backward onto the wet grass, and he stared up in shock at Jake even as he pushed against the ground to maneuver himself into an upright position.

"Jake!" I cried, then grabbed him by the arm as he advanced on Lenz, clearly ready to deliver however many punches were required to knock the man out cold. "Stop it!"

His jaw clenched. "I'm only giving him a little of his own back."

"No!" I held on to Jake's arm with both hands, grinding my feet into the muddy turf. "You don't understand! He's helping us!"

"What?" Connor said, looking from me and Jake over to Lenz, who by that point had managed to climb to his feet. Even in the unsteady illumination from the emergency lights on the power plant, the angry-looking splotch on his jaw where Jake had punched him was growing darker and darker. "What do you mean, he's helping us?"

"Whatever he told you, it's a trick," Jake growled. Under my desperate fingers, his arm felt like a rock, unyielding, merciless.

Lenz approached us then. Ignoring the darkening bruise on his jaw, he said, "No trick. I'm not crazy enough to let someone destroy millions of dollars' worth of government property just to prove a point."

"We have to go," I said. "Knocking out the power made them put emergency measures in place. All the test subjects are being gathered in one room so they can bus them out of here to another secure facility. We've got to go get them now, or we'll lose our chance."

Jake shook his head, eyes still shooting daggers at Lenz, but Connor frowned as he faced the man. "Is this true?"

"Yes."

"Why are you helping her?"

Lenz's cool gaze flicked to me for a second before returning to Connor. "Because I'm not just helping her. I'm helping *us*. Witches and warlocks."

Angela stared at him, eyes wide. "She told you?"

"Yes…and after a few demonstrations, I actually believed her." Randall Lenz paused, his mouth tightening. "But we don't have a lot of time. I need to get down to the multipurpose unit to direct the evacuation, or we'll lose our chance."

"No worries," Connor said. "I'd offer to take you there directly, but since I don't know where I'm going, my power can't help."

"Interesting limitation," Lenz observed.

"But we've got some backup if you need any surveillance directed elsewhere," Connor added, apparently deciding to ignore the other man's remark.

Randall Lenz didn't appear to miss the significance of that offer. "Your hacker?"

"Yes," Connor said, then tilted his head toward Jake. "His brother."

Jake's mouth was a flat, angry line. It was obvious enough to me—and probably everyone else there—that he didn't much like the idea of having to treat Randall Lenz as an ally. While I understood how Jake felt, I knew we didn't have much choice. Without Lenz's assistance, we'd have a hell of a time getting all those people safely away from the facility.

But Jake didn't waste time with any more accusations or attacks. His eyes narrowed, but he sounded calm enough as he said, "Just tell me what Jeremy needs to do."

"He's in the system?"

"Yes, he has access."

"Tell him to grab the feed from the multipurpose unit starting now. The test subjects should already have started gathering there. If he can get enough footage to create a five-minute loop, we can use that to replace the live feed. That way, no one will be able to see us interacting with the group. And if he can shut down all the cameras in the corridors, that will provide additional cover. Ten minutes should do it."

A nod as Jake absorbed those instructions. Then he reached into the pocket of his jeans, only to pause, scowling. "Your people took my phone."

Of course, they did. My new iPhone was still safely at Jake's house, since I'd set down my purse on the kitchen counter as we came in. Probably it was silly to be relieved by that realization, except I would have hated the thought of Lenz's team confiscating the thing when I'd only had it for a couple of weeks.

Connor pulled out his phone and handed it over. "Use mine."

Jake took it and began entering a rapid-fire text, then sent it off. A few seconds later, a faint *bing* from the phone appeared to indicate that Jeremy had replied. I was sort of surprised he'd be so quick to respond, but I realized it wasn't all that late back in Arizona, and Jeremy probably had

388 | CHRISTINE POPE

been camped on his phone anyway, what with everything that had been happening.

"He's on it," Jake said. "Now what?"

"Now we go," Lenz replied. He didn't wait to see whether any of us were following him, only turned and began walking swiftly toward the building—not toward the entrance he and I had used earlier, but one at the rear, where it backed up to open land.

Naturally, we all went with him, sticking close. It wasn't full dark, because even though the SED campus didn't have any close neighbors, enough ambient light from Alexandria's suburbs made its way there to keep the night from being pitch black.

Jake's hand stole into mine. "You okay?" he murmured as he jogged along at my side.

"Fine," I said.

"I can't believe we're trusting this guy."

Unspoken was the intimation that he couldn't figure out why I'd allowed myself to believe Lenz would truly want to help us. While I could understand why Jake felt that way, I knew it would be impossible to explain everything that had happened in the past half hour, not when we were hurrying along in the near dark, doing our best to get under cover before someone came out to investigate the outage at the power plant.

"It's okay," I assured him. "He wants the same thing we do."

My comment only elicited a raised eyebrow. However, by that point, we'd reached the rear entrance to the building, clearly a service access point, since it had only a plain metal door and no biometric lock, just a keypad.

To my relief, Lenz entered the code without hesitation, and soon enough, we were all inside, the door shut firmly behind us. At once, he began to walk quickly down the narrow corridor where we found ourselves—also dimly lit by the emergency lights—only to stop at another door.

"The elevators are shut down," he said. "These stairs should be safe enough, since the security team will be using the main stairwell closer to the test subjects' quarters. We'll come in from behind." A pause as he scanned all of us, eyes narrowing slightly. "Are any of your powers good in a fight?"

"I've got telekinesis," Jake said shortly, and left it there. Since it seemed that Randall Lenz's memories had returned to him, he should have remembered well enough the way Jake had aimed a few well-placed flowerpots at his head.

Was that a slight wince I detected, as if the recollection pained him? Maybe; Lenz nodded and said, "Right. Anything else?"

"We've got a whole lot of 'anything else,'" Angela told him. "It won't be a problem."

For a second or two, he watched her narrowly. Maybe he was sizing up her slim frame and wondering if her words were pure bravado, or whether there was a whole lot more to her and Connor than met the eye. But apparently, he decided to go with it, because he inclined his head slightly and said, "Okay. Let's go."

We all entered the stairwell and hurried down flight after flight of stairs. Although we moved quickly, I couldn't help feeling the pressure of time, wondering if we were going to be fast enough. It felt like forever since I'd used my power to direct those lightning bolts at the power plant, but I knew only about five minutes or so had passed.

Still, a lot could happen in five minutes.

I also hated the thought of all the hidden cameras embedded in the walls and ceiling. Yes, Jeremy was probably handling all that—and honestly, with how dim the corridor was, thanks to the emergency lights that barely illuminated our way, I doubted anyone watching the surveillance feed could make out many details—but still, I felt horribly exposed as we all jogged along after Randall Lenz, following him to the multipurpose unit.

An awful thought slipped into my mind.

What if Jake was right? What if this was all an elaborate act on Randall Lenz's part to deliver some new and highly valuable test subjects to Dr. Richards and her team?

I told myself that was ridiculous. While I could understand why Jake would want to think the worst of Agent Lenz, he hadn't been there when Lenz first learned he possessed powers he'd never dreamed of. He hadn't seen the understanding come alive in his face, the realization that everything he'd believed about himself was a lie.

Distrust was understandable in this case…but also very misplaced.

Or so I tried to tell myself.

I didn't have time for any more disturbing thoughts, however, because we emerged from the access corridor we'd been using and into the open space I recognized as the reception area outside the multipurpose unit.

Unfortunately, we weren't the only ones there. Three guards stood just outside the doors, which were open, allowing me to see inside. With the lighting as bad as it was, I couldn't be completely sure, but it looked as though the entire group had been gathered there. They stood in the middle of the space, murmuring to one another in confusion…understandable, I supposed, considering they'd all been roused from their beds and made to assemble in one place.

Then my heart sank, because I thought I recognized Dr. Richards standing inside, with Dr. Woodrow and another man I didn't know but who was probably Dr. Keegan huddled in conversation. From the way Randall Lenz paused briefly before resuming his stride, I guessed that he spotted them, too, but then he continued toward the guards as if he had nothing on his mind beyond the safety of the program's test subjects.

"Is everyone inside?" he asked briskly as he approached the security guard closest to us, a hard-faced man with a square jaw and his light brown hair in a bristly buzz cut.

"Yes, sir," the guard replied. "The doctors are with them. Do you know what happened to the power?"

"Not yet. The tech team is assessing. We need to move the test subjects now. Is the van ready?"

"Yes, sir." The man's gaze flicked past Lenz to settle on the rest of our little group, waiting uncertainly near the entrance to the service hallway. "Who are these people?"

"Consultants," he said briefly.

"Consultants…during an emergency?"

To my surprise, Angela stepped forward and smiled brightly at the guard. "Yes, we're emergency consultants," she said. "And this is definitely an emergency."

I couldn't even detect exactly what she did—

maybe lifted her hand just a fraction of an inch in a small, dismissive gesture—but the next second, the security guard slumped to the ground, snoring slightly.

His companions startled, no doubt shocked by one of their own keeling over out of the blue like that. However, their training seemed to kick in then, because their expressions grew guarded, and they both began to reach for their guns.

Jake lifted a hand, and one of the guards' service pistols flew out of its holster and landed in his outstretched fingers. At the same time, the other guard let out a yelp of pain and dropped his own gun, which appeared to be glowing from within, as if it had become super-heated in the span of a few seconds.

Before either of them could call out the alarm, Connor and Angela both did the same hand-waving thing she'd done on her own to the first guard, and they dropped to the ground next to him in a dead faint.

Lenz stared at the *prima* and *primus* in amazement.

"I told you it wouldn't be a problem," Angela said, still smiling.

He shook his head and looked as though he was about to reply, but then Dr. Richards approached, brows drawn together as she stared down at the comatose security guards and then at

Agent Lenz. Her gaze traveled to Angela, then me and Jake, and finally to Connor.

"Agent Lenz, do you want to tell me what's going on?"

"Not really," he said. To my surprise, he was smiling. "Even if I did, I doubt you would believe me."

Jake and I moved forward, even as Connor went to stand by his wife. Dr. Richards' frown only deepened as she appeared to take in our presence. "What are these two doing out of their rooms? The guards went to fetch them to evacuate them with the others, but they weren't there—"

"Because they were with me," Randall Lenz cut in.

"What—?" she began, then stopped there, mouth open as if frozen in place.

Actually, that's exactly what she was…frozen. I blinked, realizing that either Angela or Connor— or maybe the two of them working together—had put some kind of whammy on her. Was there anything they couldn't do?

"I figured you didn't want to waste time on chitchat," Connor said, then sent a quick glance toward the group assembled in the multipurpose unit. Dr. Woodrow and Dr. Keegan had begun to move forward, and the test subjects were following, obviously drawn to see what was going on in the reception area just outside the room.

"Can you neutralize the other two doctors?" Lenz asked. "The two men in front."

At once, they came to a dead halt. Matthew was immediately behind Dr. Woodrow and bumped into him. Under normal circumstances, Woodrow probably would have stumbled forward, but because he was magically held in place, it was Matthew who staggered backward like someone who'd just walked into a wall.

"What the hell?" he exclaimed.

Lenz smiled thinly. "It's a good thing we're both on the same side now," he said to my brother and his wife. "Or I would very much have liked to have you two in the program."

"No, thanks," Connor replied, while Angela's mouth curled slightly in amusement.

I looked over at Randall Lenz, glad that Jake still held my hand—and that he didn't seem inclined at the moment to instigate any more violence. Actually, Jake's expression was almost thoughtful, as if he was still trying to figure out what Lenz's end game might be.

To tell the truth, I was wondering the same thing. Yes, I'd been there to see the wonder awaken in his face as he realized he'd made that candle come to life with nothing more than the power of his mind…but I'd also spent the past few weeks doing my best to evade his pursuit. I still couldn't quite believe he was willing to walk away from the work that had consumed his life for the past few years.

"Everyone," Lenz said, raising his voice slightly, "I'm going to take you to the van now. You're being moved to a secure location."

"That's what Dr. Richards told us," Ethan said as he and Natalie approached, everyone else grouped uneasily behind them. His gaze strayed to the doctor, still frozen unnaturally in place, mouth open to utter a word she'd never finish. "Do we want to know what's going on?"

"I'll explain later," Agent Lenz replied. "For the moment, the important thing is to get you out of here."

"Where are you taking us?" Natalie asked. I noticed how she held Ethan's hand, hanging on to him in much the same way that I clung to Jake.

For a second or two, Lenz was silent. He looked over at Connor, brows slightly lifted, and Connor gave him a nod, as if confirming that he would be able to provide sanctuary for the fugitives.

"Someplace safe," Agent Lenz said at length. "Someplace where you can start over."

Dead silence. Matthew pushed his way forward, expression almost belligerent. "You're letting us go?"

"In a manner of speaking," Lenz said. "I'm afraid you can't go back to your lives, but…."

Connor spoke then. "But you can start a new one with us…with other people like you."

Ethan and Natalie looked at each other. Voice wondering, he said, "Other people like us? How many are there?"

"More than you ever knew," I told him, a smile of my own touching my lips. How generous of Connor to offer to take them all in—but I understood then that he would never turn away a witch or warlock in need. Maybe in time, we'd be able to figure out whose clans all of the Daedalus Project test subjects belonged to, but in the meantime, they'd be able to make a home in Flagstaff.

Just as Jake and I would.

The dawning wonder in their faces awoke a cautious joy in my heart. Yes, we would take them away from here, and give them back the lives that Dr. Richards and her team had stolen.

As for Randall Lenz…well, he would have to figure out for himself where to go from here. He hadn't just burned this particular bridge; he'd blown it up with a few pounds of C4.

But I somehow knew that he, just like the rest of these orphaned witches, would always have a home with the Wilcoxes…if he wanted it.

My fingers tightened on Jake's, even as I smiled at the group of people who would soon be our neighbors.

"Let's go home," I said.

EPILOGUE

W‍HEN SOMETHING LIKE THE D‍AEDALUS Project fell apart, it was with little fanfare. A program so terribly secret needed to be kept secret, even if it might have flamed out like a test rocket entering the atmosphere at the wrong angle.

Having allies such as Connor and Angela Wilcox had proved to be very handy. Not only had they facilitated the removal of all the test subjects to Flagstaff and its environs, putting them up in various properties owned by Wilcox witches and warlocks in the area, but a little judicious meddling with the memories of Dr. Richards and her team had made it so they remembered absolutely nothing of the events of the night in question. And since Jake Wilcox's brother Jeremy had doctored all the security footage so there was absolutely no record of the events which had transpired that evening, not even the best forensic analysts could find the smoking gun to prove gross negligence had been involved.

It was as though all those test subjects had disappeared into thin air.

There had been multiple inquiries, of course. But because everyone on the team's stories were so full of holes, or contradicted one another completely, the investigative body overseeing the probe came to the conclusion that the entire thing had been a ridiculous boondoggle that involved the waste of many millions of taxpayer dollars. Dr. Richards and her immediate team were dismissed, and the other analysts and agents and guards reassigned to other postings.

Randall Lenz wished he could have put in a good word for Dawson, but since he was now a pariah, he knew doing so would have hurt her situation more than it helped. No, better to let her skills speak for themselves, and when he heard she'd been sent to work in the Homeland Security office in New York, he felt reassured that she'd landed on her feet.

As for himself....

Property in Alexandria was always at a premium, and he sold his home for nearly thirty thousand over the asking price. He had few connections there, and so he didn't have to worry about severing too many personal ties, although his mother was clearly worried about the sudden collapse of his career and his subsequent decision to leave the area.

"But what are you going to do?" she asked during their last phone call, just the night before he planned to leave. It was a question she'd asked multiple times, and his answer hadn't changed.

"Travel," he said vaguely. "Reassess. I'll keep in touch."

Which he would, even though he knew he wouldn't be able to tell her anything substantive. Still, phone calls and emails to his mother would let her know he was alive and healthy, which had to count for something. After all, if he made a promise, he kept it.

What he absolutely couldn't do was tell her he would be heading west to Flagstaff. Connor had offered him sanctuary there, and Lenz had decided to take the man up on his offer. Maybe at some point he'd decide to seek out his own witch clan—the Van Horns or whoever else they might be—but for the moment, he wanted to come to terms with this new and unexpected side of himself. No worries about anyone in the government tracing him there, thanks to Jeremy Wilcox and the efficient way he'd made sure that every mention of Flagstaff and the Wilcoxes had been thoroughly erased from the agency's servers.

Now Randall Lenz stood in the driveway of the house that was no longer his, taking it in one last time, absorbing the significance of the "sold" banner that had been placed over the "for sale" sign out front. To be honest, it had never truly felt like home. But it had been a good investment; he certainly had a decent cushion to rest on while he decided what to do with the rest of his life.

In the meantime, he'd do what so many other Americans had done throughout the nation's history.

He would head west.

Spreading trees shielded us from the worst of the late July heat. I wore a wide-brimmed straw hat and dark sunglasses, but their true purpose was to conceal my face, rather than protect me from the blazing desert sun.

Jake waited a few feet off as I took the bouquet of yellow roses—my mother's favorite—and went to lay them on her grave. The headstone the people of Kanab had put up to mark the gravesite was simple, just a plain rectangle of smooth granite inscribed with that dates of her birth and death—and mine, too, since everyone believed I'd perished in the gas explosion at our house as well—but I thought my mother wouldn't have wanted anything ornate. She never had been much into fuss.

Tears pricked my eyes, but I breathed in and forced them back. Maybe it would have been all right to let them flow, there of all places, and yet I didn't want to attract any attention to myself. The cemetery was nearly empty, thanks to the oppressive heat, but I didn't see the need to take any chances.

"I'm sorry," I murmured, although right then, I didn't quite know what I was sorry for. That my mother's life had been cut short…that she wasn't there to see me find the match of my soul, to know everything had turned out all right in the end.

That I'd somehow found forgiveness in my heart for the man who had taken her from me.

Probably a little of all of those things, and more.

I lingered at the grave for a long moment, staring down at the cheery yellow of the flowers against the cool grayish tones of the granite and the deep green of the grass under my feet. I gave myself time to hold that picture in my mind and engrave it in my memory, since I had a feeling I would never come back there. Randall Lenz had assured Connor that there was no way I or any of the other test subjects could ever be traced to

Flagstaff, but I still didn't see the point in taking unnecessary risks.

Just in case.

Besides, from that point on, I wanted to look forward to a bright future, not back to a painful past.

Even with the shade the trees provided, the heat was getting to be too much. I murmured, "Goodbye," then made myself turn away from the grave and walk back over to Jake.

His fingers twined themselves with mine, strong, reassuring…welcome. "Are you okay?" he asked, his voice gentle, concerned.

"I'm fine," I told him.

Because it was Jake, he didn't press me. Hand in hand, we walked back to his white Wrangler, which we'd left parked on the street. After we'd gotten back to Flagstaff, I'd urged him to buy another Gladiator, but he only shook his head and told me he didn't think that was a good idea. The vehicle was just too distinctive.

Like me, he was being cautious these days.

We got in the Wrangler, and he cranked the A/C to maximum. A rush of cool, welcome air flowed over me, and I leaned against the back of the seat as he pulled away from the curb, pointing us back to Highway 89 and the route home.

Silence for a few moments. Then he asked again, "You okay?"

I pulled in a breath. The desert landscape flashed by the car windows, and off in the distance, thunderheads reared in the east, gaining strength with the growing heat of the day. They might cross our path during the journey home, but I knew I had nothing to fear from them, even though those clouds could release rain so intense, we wouldn't be able to see more than a few yards ahead.

If that time came, I'd urge the clouds to move on so we could pass into the sunshine, into the light.

I reached over and touched Jake's hand, and marveled again at the strength in his fingers, how just his lightest touch could make me want him with an intensity I could never have imagined just a few short months earlier.

We were going home, together. In the end, that was all that mattered.

"Yes, Jake," I said. "I'm okay."

The End

∽

The Witches of Wheeler Park series continues with Jeremy's story in *Mind Games*.

(Paranormal Romance)

Sympathy for the Devil

Charmed, I'm Sure

A Wing and a Prayer

THE WITCHES OF CANYON ROAD*

(Paranormal Romance)

Hidden Gifts

Darker Paths

Mysterious Ways

A Canyon Road Christmas

Demon Born

An Ill Wind

Higher Ground

Haunted Hearts

THE WITCHES OF CLEOPATRA HILL*

(Paranormal Romance)

Darkangel

Darknight

Darkmoon

Sympathetic Magic

Protector

Spellbound

A Cleopatra Hill Christmas

Impractical Magic

Strange Magic

The Arrangement

Defender

Bad Blood

Deep Magic

Darktide

THE DJINN WARS*

(Paranormal Romance)

Chosen

Taken

Fallen

Broken

Forsaken

Forbidden

Awoken

Illuminated

Stolen

Forgotten

Driven

Unspoken

THE WATCHERS TRILOGY*

(Paranormal Romance)

Falling Dark

Dead of Night

Rising Dawn

THE SEDONA FILES*

(Paranormal Romance)

Bad Vibrations

Desert Hearts

Angel Fire

Star Crossed

Falling Angels

Enemy Mine

~

STANDALONE TITLES

Hearts on Fire

Taking Dictation

Night Music

Golden Heart

* Indicates a completed series

ABOUT THE AUTHOR

USA Today bestselling author Christine Pope has been writing stories ever since she commandeered her family's Smith-Corona typewriter back in grade school. Her work includes paranormal romance, fantasy romance, and science fiction/space opera romance. She makes her home in Arizona's beautiful Verde Valley.

Christine Pope on the Web:
www.christinepope.com

facebook.com/ChristinePopeAuthor

twitter.com/ChristineJPope

pinterest.com/ChristineJPope